DEEP
COVER

DEEP COVER

STEVE ROOS

Bookcraft
Salt Lake City, Utah

Library of Congress Catalog Card Number: 95-79004
ISBN 0-88494-1-57008-181-6

First Printing, 1995

Printed in the United States of America

To Jeremy—"The right thing no matter what."

Prologue

Jeff Foster steadied his elbows on the dash of the patrol car and pressed the binoculars to his eyes. The runway beacon dispersed just enough light to make out the van.

Brian spoke through a mouth full of Ritz crackers. "If the sergeant catches us this far off our beat, we're going to be in deep distress."

Jeff brushed cracker crumbs off his arm. "Didn't your mother teach you manners?"

"I was raised by wolves." Brian burped once and tore open another package. "I figured Mormons would prefer crackers to cigarettes."

"I do. Thanks."

"So what if the sergeant catches us?"

"Eating crackers?"

Brian rolled his eyes. "Off our beat."

"Don't worry about it." Jeff tried to hide his own apprehension. The bars in Idaho Falls had long since closed, and most of the domestic beefs would be over. If they did get a hot call they could punch it to Grandview, across Anderson, down Holmes, and still arrive before the sergeant.

"That's easy for you to say. You passed probation months ago. They don't even need a reason to fire me."

Jeff kept his eyes glued to the binoculars. "Relax. I'll take the heat."

"As if it matters. If I don't lose ten more pounds, I'll never pass the agility test." Brian rubbed his nose and popped another cracker into his mouth.

Jeff glanced at the box of crackers, then at Brian.

"Hey, I'm working on it. A starvation diet isn't going to keep the weight off." He crunched down on another cracker. "What are we watching for anyway?"

"We'll know when we see it."

"If we make a bust, what are we supposed to tell the sarge?"

"How about the truth?"

"Oh, great! We got bored, so instead of covering our beat we decided to take a cruise to the west side?"

Jeff shrugged. "No guts, no glory."

"I hate that saying."

The dome light in the van flashed on and sent jets of acid through Jeff's stomach. "He's staying inside. White male, long hair, beard, white T-shirt. You getting all this?"

Brian scribbled notes in the dark. "Yeah."

Jeff tried to fine-tune the focus. His teeth gripped his bottom lip. "Not close enough."

"You want me to get the telephoto?"

"No time." Jeff opened the door. "Take the car in dark, but give me a couple minutes first. If I make contact, check us out and move in fast."

Brian shoved the crackers under the seat and slid over. "Got it."

Jeff gently pressed the door shut. He adjusted the volume on his portable and circled through an undeveloped field.

A burst of light from an approaching vehicle lit the area. Jeff hugged the ground and glanced back at the patrol car. It was well hidden.

He inhaled deeply as he stood up, and traversed two hundred feet. He covered the shiny badge pinned on his

2

chest with the palm of his hand and slowed his pace. The approaching truck, a new four-wheel drive Ford, parked on the wrong side of the road, facing the van. Dropping to his hands and knees, Jeff crawled the remaining fifty feet to the rear of the van.

A young man wearing a denim jacket, jeans, and five-hundred-dollar cowboy boots stepped off the running board of the truck and ambled to the side of the van.

Jeff matched the jacket to the warm June night. *Bad sign.* He touched the Smith & Wesson 40 pouched on his own hip.

The driver of the van opened the door and nodded at the cowboy. He tugged at the extra-large white T-shirt that covered the top half of his belly and flipped his hair behind his shoulders.

"Nice truck, dude."

Cowboy's smile faded for a moment and returned. "You been waitin' long?"

"Long enough. Where's Margo?"

Jeff strained to hear the fading conversation. He watched as Cowboy pulled a large Ziploc bag from inside his jacket. He couldn't tell for sure, but he could guess the contents. Without waiting any longer, Jeff depressed the mike and whispered into the radio. "8B27, we need assistance on International Way west of Skyline."

The female voice squawked over the radio, "Last unit, 10-9?"

Jeff repeated his location as he watched Cowboy hand T-shirt something. A moment later, the sergeant's voice came over the radio. "27, 10-9 your location?"

Cowboy started walking back to his truck. Jeff searched the darkness but could see no sign of Brian. He swallowed. *Now or never.* He ignored the radio and rose from the sagebrush.

Jeff slid the gun from his holster and yelled, "Police! Don't move!"

Cowboy hesitated by the truck door. In a microsecond,

Jeff read the expression on his face. *He's thinking about it.*

Jeff's eyes darted to T-shirt. *Not good.*

T-shirt took a step toward Jeff. His lips parted, showing an ugly space between his teeth. "Put that thing away or I'm going to shove—"

Jeff didn't wait for the end of the sentence. With lightning speed, he slipped the gun to his left hand and brachial-slapped T-shirt under his left ear.

T-shirt's eyes rolled back and his legs buckled.

Cowboy saw his chance and dove for the truck. Not taking time to shut the door behind him, he threw the gears in reverse and hit the gas. Tires smoked as Jeff lunged for the still-open door. His arm caught the mirror. Cowboy jammed his foot on the emergency brake, spinning the truck 180 degrees.

Centrifugal force shut the door and threw Jeff against the truck bed. Acting on reflexes, he quickly hooked one leg over the edge of the bed while gripping the mirror to keep from spinning off onto the pavement.

Police sirens pierced the air. Jeff screamed, "Stop it now or I'll blow your head off!"

Cowboy glanced through the side window at Jeff and slammed on the brakes. Jeff's feet tore loose and bounced off the pavement. He grappled onto the running board just as the truck sped forward again. He wanted to let go. Just get away. But he couldn't figure how to do it without getting run over.

Blue lights flashed in front of the truck as it veered to the left, pushing him against the door. With the split-second advantage, Jeff drew his weapon with his free hand and smashed the window.

Rage took over. "Stop now. You're gonna die! Get ready to die! Die, you maggot head!"

Cowboy threw his hands over his face and raised his foot off the gas. "Please no! Don't shoot!"

"Die, you maggot head!"

"I'm stopping—don't shoot!"

"Die, you maggot head!"

"I'm stopping, I'm stopping!"

The truck coasted into a curb, bounced once, and stopped. Jeff yanked the door open. He grabbed Cowboy in an arm lock, threw him to the ground, and slapped handcuffs on his wrists.

Jeff withdrew a 357 Colt Python from Cowboy's shoulder holster and a thick wad of hundred-dollar bills from the jacket pocket. He gasped for air. "You have the right to remain silent. Anything you say—"

"I want an attorney."

"I haven't got to that part yet."

"I know my rights. I want an attorney."

Two police cars screeched to a stop behind the truck, followed by a red Camaro. Jeff recognized the Camaro as an undercover car. Brian piled out of a patrol car. "You okay?"

Jeff nodded. "What about the other one?"

"Rick has him. He was packing."

Jeff fingered the Python and tipped his head toward Cowboy. "So was he. What about the evidence?"

Brian licked his lips. "I saw it. There must have been over two pounds of crack."

"Where is it?"

Brian whispered, "The narcs got it. I guess they were watching the whole thing."

Another uniform showed up. It wore sergeant stripes. More stomach acid.

"Foster, I hope you have a good explanation for being off your beat."

Brian kicked at a rock. Jeff scanned his imagination for believable lies. *Following a drunk? No—too far away. En route for a break at Weston's? Yeah, headed for a break when we started following a suspected burglar.*

The shift lieutenant joined the sergeant. The sergeant acknowledged the lieutenant and flashed a bulldog smile. "Well, Foster?" He turned back to the lieutenant, proud of his catch, and then to Jeff again. "Got a good explanation for being off your beat, Foster?"

Jeff remembered his answer to Brian. *The truth.* "We were bored."

Brian turned ashen. His eyes closed.

Disbelief covered the sergeant's face. "Bored? That's supposed to explain why you're on the opposite side of town? Bored?"

"At least he's honest." The lieutenant shook his head, then smiled. "Nice work, Foster. I like to see initiative."

The sergeant again glanced at the lieutenant and then back to Jeff. With the savvy of an experienced politician, he slapped Jeff on the back. "Yeah. Good work, Foster. We could use more go-getters like you."

Sergeant followed dutifully as the lieutenant strolled back to his car. Brian escorted Cowboy to the patrol car.

Jeff's eyes caught the image of a barrel-chested man leaning against the Camaro. He recognized him as Detective Gary Jenkins, a narcotics officer.

Gary wandered over to Jeff and spoke flatly, "That was a stupid stunt."

"The truck—you saw what happened?"

"I saw the whole thing."

"I didn't plan it that way."

"Why'd ya hang on?"

Jeff studied Gary's eyes. He liked what he saw. "I was afraid to let go."

The corners on Gary's mouth turned up. "But you adapted."

"I hope I didn't foul up your case."

Gary surveyed the scene as if filling his lungs with fresh air. "Bad guys in jail, we got the dope, nobody got hurt."

"Then it turned out okay?"

Gary neither smiled nor frowned. "Nobody got hurt."

Chapter One

Jeff peered out the two-story window into the darkness. The tingling in his stomach developed into a knot.

"You okay?" Gary asked from the other room. "Look, don't worry. I'll hear the whole deal over the wire."

"It's cool," Jeff said.

Gary tugged at a roll of tape. "Just for the record, I think the captain's off center."

"What do you mean?"

Gary shook his head. "You don't have to get drunk and chase women to work dope."

"You don't?"

Gary laughed. "I do have a wife and kids. But I'm afraid the captain's right on that one. Divorce is high."

"You and Sue seem okay."

"Yeah, and divorce won't be a problem for you either. You'll be single forever."

"Not if my mother has anything to do with it."

Gary shook his head. "You Mormons are all alike. You think you have to run out, get married, and populate the earth."

Jeff wiped his face sober. "It's a dirty job, but someone has to do it."

"Right." Gary tossed him the body wire. It was jet black and smaller than a deck of cards, with thirty inches of skinny wire leading to a tiny microphone. "Strip down to your waist and I'll show you how to put it on."

Jeff's well-defined muscles tightened. They weren't massive, resembling more those of a finely conditioned gymnast. His black hair and strong-bridged nose hinted at Italian ancestry. He looked at the wire. "So you'll be able to hear everything, right?"

Gary eyed Jeff and cuffed him on the shoulder. "Just remember, kid, they can kill you, but they can't eat you."

"Thanks, I feel better. Is that supposed to be some deep philosophical statement only narcs can understand?"

"Yeah—like they can't get your soul." Gary grabbed a spool of first-aid tape and taped over the bug on the front of Jeff's waist, then ran the thin wire up the side of his chest, underneath his left arm, and across the clavicle to his throat.

Jeff tugged on his shirt. Opposite the bug, he tucked his Glock model 23 into the small of his back.

"So that's the gun that won you all those contests?"

Jeff's face flushed red. "Most of them."

His razor blade and handcuff key were zipped in a compartment inside his belt, a trick he'd learned from his training officer.

"Okay," Gary said. "Let's cover the bases. All we know is the chick's first name, Heather. She works as a waitress at the West Bank and supposedly sells coke by the gram. She has short blonde hair. My source claims she'll sell to anybody. I'll be outside parked by the river with the receiver." He paused. "I wish we had more intelligence on her, but this is a small deal anyway. It'll be good practice for you."

"So what if she recognizes me?"

"How's she going to recognize you?"

"I don't know. Maybe I wrote her a ticket when I was in patrol. Idaho Falls isn't that big."

Gary folded his bulky arms. "I've only been burned once in five years."

"What happened?"

"I was in the Ritz bar. Lots of pukes hang out there and one of them recognized me from a bust."

"What'd you do?"

"I left."

"Didn't everybody tell who you are?"

Gary snatched a driver's license from his pocket and stuck it in Jeff's face. Like the one provided to Jeff, it showed the right picture but used an assumed name.

"But they would tell everyone what you look like."

"Describe me."

A mischievous smile grew across Jeff's face. "Let's see. Five three, two hundred and fifty pounds—"

"Be nice."

"Okay. You're about five nine, thick chested, sandy hair." Jeff fingered his chin. "Blue eyes, early thirties . . ."

"How many people in Idaho Falls fit that description?"

"I see your point."

Gary pointed out the window. "Working a small city can be a rush. A guy doesn't have to wade through as much paperwork, and there's more flexibility."

"Because we don't have the big-time dealers?"

Gary shook his head. "Don't kid yourself. CBS did a story on a coke deal in Vegas. They traced it from Vegas to Salt Lake to Idaho Falls to Driggs, and from Driggs to Colombia."

"Driggs, Idaho?"

"Small airport with very little law enforcement." Gary stood up. "You ready?"

It only took a few minutes to drive from the office. The temperature was on the cool side for a mid-June night. They parked in sight of the front doors, but several hundred feet down the road. Jeff ambled alone down the river side of the sidewalk and crossed the road toward the West Bank Hotel. He noticed a candy-red Ferrari just thirty feet up the street with personalized license plates, DMARGO.

Something felt familiar about the name. The dull pain

returned to the pit of his stomach as he walked through the front doors of the coffee shop. He could visualize *cop* written in red letters across his forehead.

Most of the tables were empty. Jeff took a seat on a bar stool next to the counter. An impatient female voice called out, "Heather, you have one waiting."

A young woman with short blonde hair walked through the kitchen doors toward Jeff. At first she looked like an eighteen-year-old, perhaps attractive. As she moved closer, he could detect a face with experience and pushed her age toward thirty.

Heather smiled politely. "May I help you?"

Jeff's brain tuned out. After a moment that seemed way too long, he blurted out, "I'd like a Big Mac, fries, and milk."

Heather gave him a puzzled look.

"Uh, I mean a hamburger and, uh, mashed potatoes, and a tall glass of milk."

"Would you like anything else?"

"No, nothing else. That will be fine, that's all."

Heather turned and walked back into the kitchen.

Jeff bit the inside of his cheek for punishment. *Milk! I'll bet that impressed her.*

He glanced down at his watch. He straightened his shoulders and wiped his palms over his thighs.

A few minutes later, Heather strolled behind the counter, supporting a large tray.

"So what's there to do in this town?" Jeff asked.

Heather stopped and looked at him. She wore a white uniform dress with a light blue apron. Red eyes matched her hollow cheeks and skinny wrists.

"Depends," she said. "What are you into?"

"I like to party, but I'm new to the area."

Heather wet her lips, studying his fresh beard. "There's places to go dancing, or you can just listen to the tunes and get wasted—if that's what you're into."

"I like the part about getting wasted." Jeff's mind

flashed back to the time when he had promised his Primary teacher he'd never break the Word of Wisdom.

Heather responded with a throaty laugh. For a few minutes their conversation centered around the lack of entertainment in Idaho Falls.

"So what are you into?" Jeff asked innocently.

"I'm with you. I'm not into the bar scene, but I do enjoy a little cola now and then."

"Cool." Jeff smiled. "I could use some of that about now." Then he turned his lips down. "Too bad I'm out."

"Poor baby," she teased. "Maybe I can help."

"You'll share your connect?"

"I can do better than that. I'll share what I have, but I need money to pay the bills."

"No problem." Jeff pulled out a wad of twenties.

Heather eyed the cash like a hungry wolf. "So what's your preference?"

"I like smoke, but I'd prefer a little cola."

Suddenly all business, Heather responded, "I can do a gram for a hundred bucks."

"You're kidding. I never have to pay more than eighty."

"Look, I don't know where you're from, but prices are higher here. Besides, I personally guarantee the quality, and they're heavy. I weighed them myself."

"Okay," Jeff smiled, "I'll take it." Then he let his smile fade. "But it better be good."

"Trust me."

Right, like I'm going to believe some dope-selling coke-head who says "Trust me."

"Meet me out front in ten minutes," she added. Without waiting for a response, Heather turned and hurried into the kitchen.

Jeff took a slow breath to quiet the pounding of his heart. He forced down the plate of potatoes, gulped down the last of his milk, and turned to pay his bill.

As Jeff left the West Bank, he could hear the roar of

the Snake River as it tumbled over the twenty-foot concrete embankment and continued on its way toward the
Broadway bridge. Maple trees lined most of the streets
around the river, with occasional patches of willows closer
to the water. A circular drive surrounded by evergreens lay
in front of the hotel lobby.

Jeff glanced to ensure that Gary was watching, then
wandered across the street to the greenbelt next to the
river. The faint odor of decaying minnows briefly reminded
him of fishing with his father before the accident. He tried
to think about something else.

Looking above the water, he could see the statue of
Moroni poised atop the Mormon temple. Jeff marveled at
the contrast. The white walls of the temple and the purity
it represented, only a stone's throw from a seedy neighbor-
hood that wallowed in drugs and violence.

Twenty minutes later, Heather bustled out the front
door with a brown purse slung over her shoulder. He
moved out in the open, and she walked briskly across the
street to meet him. They slid into a shadow behind one of
the evergreens.

Her eyes darted from side to side. Seeing no one, she
pulled out a snow seal the size of a shortened stick of gum.
In light blue print, the envelope boasted the portrait of a
seal balancing a snowflake on its nose.

"You got the money?"

Jeff wiped the sweat from his hands and reached into
his pocket. "Of course." His voice cracked as he choked out
the words. He added a baritone "Yeah" to prove he wasn't
entering adolescence and counted out five twenty-dollar
bills.

"If you want more, you know where to find me."
Heather turned and walked back into the coffee shop.

A minute later, Jeff was in the car with Gary.

"Good job!" Gary said. "You had me worried though."

"Why's that?"

"A tall glass of milk? I mean, come on. I know you're Mr. Mormon, but milk?"

Jeff felt his face burn. "What can I say? A man's got to keep up his strength."

Gary pointed to the West Bank. "Did you see Dennis Margo while you were in there?"

"Margo." Jeff repeated the name. His mind flashed back to the red Ferrari with DMARGO on the license plates.

"He's one of the major dealers in town," Gary said with a you-should-already-know-this look on his face. "He owns Eagle Aviation."

"Eagle Aviation? Isn't that where we drove by and saw the Cessna 310?"

Gary laughed. "Get your head out of the clouds and think about something other than flying. I don't know why you ever gave up flying commercial to be a cop."

Jeff ignored Gary's statement. "What do we have on him?"

"His name has come up a few times, but we've never been able to make a case on him."

"Too careful?"

Gary shook his head. "I don't think he's invincible. I just haven't spent the time yet."

The memory of Cowboy and T-shirt flashed in his mind. T-shirt had used Margo's name.

"Does he deal in crack?"

"Mostly coke. In spite of the media hype, crack isn't all that popular, except in some inner-city areas."

"Has anyone ever got close to him?"

"Once. I had an informant working off a possession charge—a couple ounces of coke. Said his source was Margo. I was going to wire him up and have him make a buy. But Margo wouldn't sell. Probably heard about him getting busted after I got the feds involved." Gary shook his head. "Nope, I think the way to make a case on him will be surveillance."

"Margo refused the sale?"

"Well, not exactly. Word on the street has it that Margo set him up with a woman and a houseboat in the Seattle area. He's never been seen since."

"So he's on some tropical beach enjoying a back rub and a martini."

"I doubt it. I don't think Margo would spend that kind of money and still risk him talking. He's probably pushing daisies with Jimmy Hoffa."

Jeff stared into the darkness. Silence.

The red interior of the Camaro soaked up the afternoon sun in spite of the dark tinted windows. When the light turned green, Jeff punched the accelerator. Gary monitored the wire from the Ford.

This time it would be a buy-bust. Heather had agreed to sell him an eight ball for $280. They were to meet at the Circle K on West Broadway at 3:00 P.M.

"I'm crossing the river." Jeff spoke as if Gary sat next to him. The wire still felt awkward but reassuring. They had decided the takedown signal would be "I wish my cousin was here."

Besides monitoring the wire, Gary's main job was to watch for countersurveillance. Jeff hoped that if Heather had backup to protect her from a rip-off, Gary would see it.

Jeff turned into Circle K at 2:57, knowing that dopers were notorious for being late. He parked near the rear of the building and decided he would wait fifteen minutes, secretly hoping Heather wouldn't show up at all.

At 3:15, a decrepit Chevy pulled in and stopped next to him. Jeff's heart began to race as he recognized the figure inside. He stepped out of his car.

Heather waited several seconds before she opened the car door. She looked around and forced a smile.

"You're late." Jeff regretted the comment as soon as it came out.

Heather ignored the criticism. "So, uh, you got the money?"

"Yeah, sure." Jeff retrieved two hundred-dollar bills and four twenties. He stuck one thumb into his pocket and tapped on the cash with the other.

Heather glanced around and withdrew a plastic baggy from her purse. The crystal white powder sparkled in the bright sunlight.

Jeff glanced over his shoulder. "I sure wish my cousin was here. He loves to party."

"Look, you can see rocks in it."

Right now Jeff could care less about the quality of the drug. He looked around for Gary. "I bet my cousin would like to see this stuff." *Maybe the wire is dead. Gary is probably watching right now.*

"Does your cousin live around here?"

"No, but I wish my *cousin* was *here.*"

No sign of Gary. Jeff decided that Gary couldn't hear the conversation. Was he waiting for Jeff to make the first move?

Heather gave Jeff a perplexed look. "Well, if you or your cousin want some more, just give me a call."

"I guess my cousin isn't coming." Jeff took in a deeper breath of air and gritted his teeth. He hesitated and took a step toward her. "Heather, you're busted."

"Hey, don't joke about that."

Jeff smiled grimly. "I'm serious, you're under arrest."

Jeff studied her eyes. The eyes would tell. For a moment Heather's hands trembled, her face tightened, and her eyes hardened—focused on Jeff, but somehow darting from side to side like a cornered tiger. *She's thinking.*

Then she pleaded, "Let me go, please. You don't have to do this. I'll do whatever you want. I promise I'll never do it again."

Jeff stared at her blankly, his muscles primed for action. Then he watched her shoulders slump. The resignation.

Still no Gary.

Jeff's eyes darted around. *No backup. Bad move, Foster.*

Jeff remembered seeing a pay phone in front of the store. Fumbling in his pocket, he located a nickel, but no quarter. Jeff considered asking Heather if she had a quarter but immediately thought better of it.

Chiding himself for his stupidity, he remembered that he didn't need a quarter to dial 911. After looking around for Gary one final time, he hooked Heather's arm to march her around the corner of the store to the pay phone.

Heather jerked her arm away. "Where are you taking me?"

Jeff locked on to her arm, hoping she would follow. Even after two years' street experience, it bothered Jeff to use force on women.

Sensing his indecision, Heather swung her purse at his head. Jeff ducked but still caught part of the swat with his ear. Then he grabbed her purse away, threatening, "Knock it off!"

But Heather was just getting warmed up. Seeming to remember her grandmother's advice, she kicked at Jeff with all her might. Jeff turned quickly and blocked the attack with his hip. Then he grabbed her by the throat and pinned her against the cinder-block wall of the building.

"You gonna cool it, or do you want me to get violent?"

Unable to speak from the pressure on her throat, Heather nodded. Jeff clasped her skinny wrist with a come-along hold and marched her to the phone. He held the receiver with his neck and punched in the numbers with his free hand.

"Emergency 911," answered a polite voice.

"This is Foster. I need a black and white for a transport in front of the Circle K on West Broadway."

"Jenkins tried reaching you on the radio a few minutes ago. Do you want me to advise him of your location?"

"Find out his location first."

After a few seconds, the dispatcher's voice returned. "He's near the Circle K on 17th."

"Just tell him to meet me at the station."

"10-4. Johnson will respond from Riverside."

"Thanks."

Jeff backed away from the phone and waited. Except for the expressions on their faces, they looked like a typical boyfriend and girlfriend locked arm in arm.

Captain Fowler commanded respect and wasn't in the habit of repeating himself. His towering physique and deep voice backed up his General Patton demeanor. It wasn't often that the captain made a special trip to the under-cover office.

Waving aside formalities, Captain Fowler insisted that Jeff and Gary remain seated. He then sat against the corner of the desk and folded his arms.

"Gary tells me you're doing a great job."

"Thank you, sir." Jeff decided Gary hadn't told him about the Circle K mix-up. Gary winked.

"After reviewing your reports, I've decided to give you a special assignment. Starting immediately, I want you both to set aside your other cases and devote all your time to Dennis Margo. How you work him is between you two. Just keep me informed." Then he stood, signaling that the meeting had come to an end.

Leaving Gary and Jeff to work out the details, Captain Fowler paused in the doorway and added, "I want Margo, but don't do anything that will jeopardize your safety." He turned and left.

Gary swung his fist in the air. "Yes! Now we can do some serious work on the jerk. We just need to figure out how to reach him."

"You got any informants that can introduce us?"

Gary stroked his chin. "No way. They're all afraid of him. Maybe one of us could get a job at the airport and work into him that way."

Jeff's face brightened. "How about if I take flying lessons? You know he's got to be smuggling dope with his planes. Maybe I could even end up flying for him."

"Okay, that's a start. I'll have Mindi arrange for the money. Go ahead and set it up." Gary flashed a wicked grin. "I have something we can do tonight though. It's time for you to be introduced to the fine science of garbology."

"Garbology?"

Gary reached in his desk drawer, pulled out a pair of latex gloves, and tossed them at Jeff. "Ten o'clock okay?"

Chapter Two

The gravel crunched under Jeff's feet like glass popcorn. He looked down with eyebrows knitted together, willing his feet to silence.

Gary whispered in Jeff's ear, "Walk in the middle on the grass. It's quieter." Gary continued slinking down the darkened alley toward Margo's house.

As a child, Jeff had always wanted to be invisible. Now he had his chance. Dressed in jungle fatigues and face paint, he blended into the darkness.

Suddenly, Gary froze and motioned for Jeff to do likewise. The sound of young voices invaded the alley. After a moment, Gary continued, apparently satisfied.

Jeff approached the spot where Gary had been crouching. He detected the outline of two sleeping bags in a backyard a few yards from the edge of the alley. An eery chant from a young voice drifted through the air, "I am the ghost with the one black eye . . ."

Ghost stories. I could give them something to talk about. Jeff chuckled inside, guessing what their reaction would be if he were to make himself visible.

Margo's house would have been considered a mansion forty years ago. Rosebushes bordered by a rock wall ringed the backyard. "Doesn't look like anyone's home," Gary whispered. "I'll get the garbage. Cover me." He disappeared into the hedge.

The garbage was in two metal cans just inside the fence. Gary returned carrying several large trash bags. He jabbed his thumb next door. "We'll need somebody else's garbage to replace his."

"Why?" Jeff asked.

"Pickup isn't until Thursday. He might notice the missing bags."

After they finished loading the garbage into the trunk of the Camaro, they headed for a secluded area. Gary pulled into a vacant lot near a streetlight and unloaded the cargo. "I'll be back in an hour to pick you up. Remember, garbology is a fine science and requires the utmost attention to detail."

Before Jeff could respond, Gary slammed the door.

"Fine science," Jeff groaned. With a sigh of resignation, he shook open a new garbage sack, donned the latex gloves, and tore open the first bag. He pinched a plastic bag with his pinky extended and lifted it slowly to eye level. The rancid fragrance of warm beer wafted through his nostrils.

"Lovely," he mumbled.

The odor reminded him of how it felt to sit in the bar, music blasting, people laughing at crude obscenities, the numbness he felt after leaving.

That flood of senses contrasted sharply with his memory of being in church last week. He had smiled inwardly as he studied the faces around him. *If they only knew.* Inside, it felt exhilarating to work undercover. He felt proud of his job, proud of the fact that he stood between the people around him and the harsh world outside.

He remembered observing the serene smile of a mother watching her infant daughter during the sacrament. He shook his head. *She has no idea, no concept, of the real world.* The thought struck him oddly. *Maybe it's the people in the bar that have no concept of the real world.* The revelation startled him.

He peeled open a packet of aluminum foil. Brown matter, with the consistency of sour cream, oozed onto his fingers. He decided gloves were a wonderful thing and carefully placed the refuse into the empty garbage sack.

Forty minutes later, Jeff ripped open the last bag. By now, the odors and slime seemed as natural as the smell of a wet dog.

Jeff's right nostril quivered. The quiver developed into a passionate itch. Instinctively, Jeff ran his index finger across the bottom of his nose with vigor. Instantly, he realized from its new intimate proximity that the brown goo had indeed been sour cream at one time.

Jeff ripped off his right glove with the finesse of a skilled surgeon and frantically wiped off any detectable trace of the vulgar stench. "Great! This is exactly what I want to do when I grow up."

Jeff resumed his search and opened a crumpled piece of paper. "Pick up 2 key T. S. 11:30." Jeff studied the note. A glimmer of hope trickled across his face.

"2 key, hmm . . . probably 2 kilos. But who is T. S.?"

He stuffed the paper in his pocket and continued the search. An occasional empty bottle of Dom Perignon together with empty pizza boxes and bags of half-eaten take-out food from Louis' Italian Restaurant now filled his sack.

The low rumble of the Camaro signaled Gary's return.

"So is this fun or what?" Gary smirked.

"Or what."

"Did you find anything?"

"The guy can't be all bad. He likes Italian."

"And?"

Jeff reached into his pocket and pulled out the paper. "Just a note from the Cali Cartel telling us where to pick up the dope."

"Right." Gary snatched the paper. "Give me that."

He leaned forward and studied it. "T. S. I wonder who that is. No doubt the time is already past, but it might help establish a pattern."

Gary jammed the note in his pocket and opened the trunk. "Come on. Let's get this junk back to Margo."

"Why? You said the neighbor's garbage—"

"Dopers get really paranoid. I just don't want to take any chances."

"Sounds like you're the one who's paranoid."

Gary shrugged. "It's easy to get more paranoid than the dopers." Then he added with a knowing smile, "But just because you're paranoid doesn't mean they're not out to get you."

After they replaced Margo's garbage and returned the last garbage bag to the neighbor, they positioned themselves next to a clump of pine trees near the front corner of the house. From here they could see anyone coming—or going. The front had a large circular driveway with a small grove of birch trees guarding the center. It was flanked by pine trees on the left side of the house and an attached garage on the right.

"Let's see if we can hear anyone inside," Gary whispered.

Jeff pointed at a lighted bedroom. "I'll check the window."

Gary nodded and scurried to the other side of the house. Jeff crawled next to the driveway until he was directly under the bedroom window. He raised up and carefully pressed his ear against the glass. Nothing.

A flash of light jerked his head to the front of the house—car lights approaching fast. Jeff dropped to his stomach rather than risk detection. He slowly lifted his head. No Gary.

The approaching car slowed. Jeff felt his heart lurch to his throat. A white Corvette turned directly into Margo's driveway. He could feel the heat of the headlights against his cheeks. Jeff pressed his face into the grass, fighting the impulse to bolt up and run.

Stay cool, he reminded himself. *If I don't move, they won't see me.* The car door slammed and a lone male walked quickly toward the house. Jeff wondered if he had been spotted. His mind raced. *If I look up, then I risk being seen. If I don't, then I risk a bullet in my head.*

Just as he decided to face the unknown enemy head on, he heard footsteps, followed by the slam of a car door.

As soon as the Corvette pulled onto the road, Gary dropped to Jeff's side. "Come on! That was Victor Alvarez."

Gary sprinted for the Camaro with Jeff a breath away. Diving into the car, they left a streak of burning rubber.

In the distance they could see taillights turning toward 17th Street. Jeff gained a deeper appreciation of the 427 engine buried inside the Camaro as the acceleration thrust his torso back against the seat.

When Jeff became convinced they would never make the corner, Gary hit the brake hard enough to slow them, but not hard enough to throw them into a skid. As they entered the corner, he took his foot off the brake and pressed it firmly against the accelerator. They came out of the corner intact.

No taillights.

Gary blew the stop sign at 17th and turned left. Jeff spotted the Corvette two blocks ahead in mixed traffic.

As they settled into the regular traffic flow, Jeff turned to Gary. "How did you know he turned left?"

"I didn't."

"So we just got lucky?"

"Some of my best cases were solved by luck. But the harder I work, the luckier I get."

The Corvette turned left off 17th. Now Gary tried to keep more distance between them to avoid detection.

He pounded his fist against the dash. "We're going to get burned if we're not careful. Should have brought another car." He backed off the gas.

"So who's this Victor Alvarez?"

"A real half-wit," Gary said. "Used to be a small-time dealer. Lately he's been doing bigger things." Gary chuckled as he shook his head. "When I was a rookie, I saw him walking down Capital. He saw me and took off running. Naturally, I chased him."

"Naturally."

"Then he started tossing quarter-ounce baggies of pot. I'm kind of like scooping them up as I go. He looks back to see how close I am, and smack!" Gary drove his fist into his open palm as Jeff eyed the unmanned steering wheel. "Ran right into a telephone pole. Knocked him out cold."

The Corvette pulled into a driveway and stopped. If the driver saw them, he didn't show it.

Gary turned the corner and clubbed the brake, throwing Jeff against the dash. "Run back and see if he got out."

Jeff hopped out and scrambled to the first house. He peeked around the corner and spotted the Corvette parked three houses down. The car looked empty. He low-crawled through the front yards and stopped behind a motorcycle parked in the neighbor's driveway. Nothing.

He reported back to Gary. They phoned dispatch on the cellular phone and found the address was listed in city utilities to Alvarez.

"He must have moved here recently. Last I heard, he was in Shelley." Gary opened his door. "Let's go see what he's up to."

It was a small two-story house with a tall red fir tree in front. Darkness encased the house except for a second-story light in front of the tree.

Gary leaned forward. "Got any good ideas?"

Jeff sized up the tree. "I grew up with trees like this."

"Go ahead, have a look," Gary said. "Heights scare me."

"What if he comes out?"

"Pretend you're a sparrow."

Jeff raised one eyebrow.

"Look, if you don't want to, you don't have to."

"No problem. I was just wondering what to do if—"

"If you hold still, he won't see you."

"Yeah, okay," Jeff said with some hesitation.

The first branch hung eight feet above the ground. Jeff

leaped up and wrapped his hands around the limb. They were immediately followed by his legs.

Gary's head popped up. "Man! You could join the circus."

Hanging upside down, Jeff smiled. "This is a circus." In a quick twisting action, he vaulted upright. Gary executed his usual disappearing act, so Jeff continued up the tree.

He passed a large tomcat perched on a branch. It glanced at him once and looked away, unconcerned.

From Jeff's new position he could see a lone male through the window, hunched over a table. Thirty feet separated them. *Medium build, Hispanic male.* Jeff automatically cataloged the information in his mind. *Curly hair, brown leather jacket. It has to be Victor.*

Victor stood up. He walked to the window and stared in Jeff's direction. Jeff froze. His breath came in tiny puffs. Victor abruptly pivoted and walked out the door.

Jeff began calculating how long it would take him to be on the ground. His mind flashed back to his childhood days, spiraling down the tall red firs in front of his house, alternating limbs, arms moving in an exhilarating flurry until he leaped the last six feet to the ground. Coming back to reality, he decided he would be better off taking his chances in the tree.

A trail of lights popped on, ending at the front door. Victor strolled onto the front porch, accompanied by a brindle pit bull. He reached into his pocket and fumbled for a cigarette lighter.

Jeff breathed relief. He'd escaped detection—for now.

Victor finished his cigarette and returned into the house. The dog stayed outside.

Jeff waited several minutes for Victor to return to the upstairs room. When he didn't show, Jeff finally gave up and began working his way down the tree.

Ferocious snarling from the pit bull sent shock waves through his limbs. The snarling turned to barking. He instantly knew how burglars must feel when they are caught inside a store with an alarm blasting.

Jeff looked down. The dog looked up at him with his front paws planted firmly against the trunk. The lazy tom, now at eye level, gazed down once and looked away, still unruffled.

"Here, boy, it's okay," coaxed Jeff. But his words seemed to add to the dog's indignation.

Jeff clenched his teeth to try hissing like a cat, when the front door burst open. He jerked his head up in time to see Victor walking directly for the tree. Only a few branches separated him from the snarling teeth below.

Victor paused halfway across the yard and yelled, "Bruno, shut up!"

Obediently the canine sat down in silence, but continued to stare at Jeff.

Victor squinted his eyes and looked up into the tree.

With a flash of inspiration, Jeff grabbed the tom's tail and yanked it backwards off its resting place. *Sorry, buddy, it's time for you to go.* The big tom twisted as it bounced off the bottom branch and landed squarely on Victor's head. Taking advantage of his thorny claws, the cat briefly regained his footing before racing down Victor's back and up another tree.

Victor threw his arms over his head and screamed out a few sadistic curses. Then he turned to Bruno. "Mongrel! Why didn't you do something?"

Bruno cocked his head and studied Victor as if baffled why his master didn't "do something" when he had the heathen within reach. Victor muttered a few more obscenities and walked back inside.

"All right, kitty! Way to go," Jeff whispered. He looked around for Gary and stepped to a lower branch.

In an instant, Bruno sped back to the tree, bicycling off chunks of bark with his paws and sounding the alarm.

"Bad Bruno! No!" Jeff shouted as loud as he dared.

The front door flew open. Victor stomped his feet across the porch with clenched jaw. Jeff groaned inside.

Taking a two-step approach, Victor kicked Bruno halfway across the yard. A sharp yelp pierced the air. "Get back there and sit down!"

Bruno stole back to the porch with his tail tucked between his legs. Victor cursed softly and retraced his steps inside.

Bruno sat anxious on the porch and dared the intruder to move. Jeff cautiously inched his way downward.

Bruno looked toward the house and then back at Jeff. Guttural tones reverberated from his throat. He made one last glance toward the house. With an uncontrolled "woof" that surprised even Bruno, he dashed against the tree with a vengeance.

Jeff's heart sank as Victor tramped out in a blind rage. Without blinking, Victor produced a small club and rewarded his faithful guard with several cruel blows.

Refusing to run away, Bruno ducked his head and silently absorbed the flogging.

Victor scowled at the dog. He grunted in satisfaction and marched across the porch and into the house.

Mystified by his master's behavior, Bruno seemed to decide the intruder must be a guest, perhaps even a friend playing some unfamiliar game.

Jeff slid down the trunk. The stoic animal tilted his head with a look of "Why didn't you tell me this was a game? It would have saved both of us unnecessary suffering."

Chapter Three

The light from the morning sun heated the runway, creating a pleasant warmth compared to the shade-covered parking lot where Jeff Foster had just left his car. He felt rested and was ready for work—if taking flying lessons could be called work.

Though not as obvious from the ground, Jeff could see the name *Eagle Aviation* plastered on the red tin roof above the log building. He watched an approaching Cessna circle the string of corrugated metal hangars jammed between the north end of the runway and Interstate 90. It wasn't clear whether it would land here or at the longer runway belonging to the Idaho Falls Airport.

"Hello, may I help you?" The receptionist flashed an interested smile.

"Hi, I'm Jeff Spenelie. I'm here for flying lessons." His cheeks colored as he said "Spenelie." Lying to dopers was one thing, but the receptionist was a different story. He decided that she was probably a doper too and blocked it from his mind.

Captain Fowler's secretary had provided Jeff with a driver's license changing only his last name. Jeff knew it was important to alter his background as little as possible. It would make his reactions more natural.

He could still remember lying to his father about a baseball he took from the next-door neighbor.

"Where did you get the ball?" his dad had asked.

"Ricky gave it to me."

"Did Ricky say you could keep it?"

"Yeah, he didn't care."

"I'll call his parents."

Jeff remembered his panic as the lie grew bigger. "They're not home."

"I'll call them later."

"They'll be gone all week."

"When did they leave?"

"Yesterday."

"Where is Ricky staying?"

"With his grandma."

"Doesn't she live in Oregon?"

"Yeah, but she brought him back to visit his dog."

"Didn't you say his parents just left yesterday?"

"Yeah, but he was really homesick for his dog."

Jeff smiled at the memory and his father's not-so-tender lesson about honesty.

The receptionist's words jerked him back to the present. "You'll be taking your orientation flight in our Cessna 152. I think your instructor is already in the second hangar."

"What's his name?"

The receptionist flashed a strange smirk. "Evans."

Jeff pushed through the front door and committed the name to memory. *Evans, Evans, Evans . . .*

The doors to hangar two were wide open, displaying a red and white Cessna 152. Jeff had learned to fly in a Piper Tomahawk but preferred the high wing Cessna. It made landing in the bush safer.

Jeff stopped. A slender figure with a wet sponge stood between a bucket of soapy water and the plane. She pushed off her toes and reached above the fuselage where the wings met. It looked as if she were trying to scratch a hard-to-reach place on the ungrateful plane's back. From this angle, Jeff could see dark blonde hair bouncing off her shoulders.

He shifted his weight to one foot, folded his arms, and studied her features as she stooped for more water. Her picture wouldn't be found in *Redbook* or *Glamour*. But she could easily be an attractive model for Patagonia or Nike running shoes. The rich color in her face showed little makeup; unusual for a blonde, he thought.

The recipient of his careful study glanced up and caught his stare. Her slight hesitation turned to a knowing smile. "Hello!"

Embarrassed at getting caught watching, Jeff returned, "Uh, hi. I was just looking for Evans, the flight instructor. They told me he would be here."

Taking a step forward, she extended her hand. "Stephanie Evans. And you're . . ."

"Jeff Fos . . . , ner, uh, Fosner Spenelie. Jeff Fosner Spenelie. Fosner is my middle name. It's after my great-grandfather." Jeff tried to remember if his new driver's license showed a middle name.

Not wanting to be on the defensive, he charged ahead. "You're the instructor?" It sounded more incredulous than he intended. "But you're a—"

She finished the sentence for him. "A woman?"

"Yeah, I guess so, but I, I mean, it's no big deal. It's just that . . ."

Stephanie's smile became a bit strained. "You weren't expecting a female?" It was more statement than question.

"No, I guess not. Look, I'm really sorry if I offended you. It's just that you kind of caught me off guard."

The warmth returned. "That's okay. I'm used to it."

She emptied the bucket of water. "So, they tell me you've already been through ground school."

"Yeah, about four years ago in Moscow."

Stephanie's right eyebrow dropped. "Moscow, Idaho?"

"Yeah, where the University of Idaho is."

Stephanie nodded. "You must have a good memory. You scored 98 on our test."

He'd deliberately missed two questions and considered

missing more, but he hadn't wanted to risk going through ground school for three weeks. "I guess I studied."

Stephanie eyed him for a moment and scooped up a clipboard. "Before we go up, let's cover the basics. We'll start with the checklist . . ."

He tried to act as though he were hearing this for the first time, but soon he began thinking about his new identity. He scratched his beard and wondered what his mother would think. He'd already recieved the third degree from some Church members, especially last Sunday.

He mentally followed the sound of the prelude music into the chapel, where he had headed for the bench closest to the door. Brother Hensley, first counselor in the bishopric, had intercepted him. "Hello, Brother Foster. It's good to see you."

Jeff accepted his hand, still feeling that most members considered him only partially active because of his shift work. "It's good to be here."

Hensley gave Jeff's face a once-over. "You on vacation?"

"Something like that." Jeff wouldn't mind telling Brother Hensley that he was working undercover, but he didn't want the word to get out. He edged his way toward the bench.

Sister Moor, an opinionated woman who had been widowed for over twenty years, looked up and planted herself in front of Jeff. She cocked one eyebrow. "I thought policemen couldn't wear beards. My son-in-law's a policeman in California and they can't wear beards."

Jeff tried to ignore the question. "Good morning."

"You know, things in California are a lot more liberal, with all those hippies and fruit loops, but the police there can't wear beards."

Jeff hadn't heard the term *hippie* since he was a child. "Lucky I'm not in California then."

"I knew Chief Bennington before he retired, and he wouldn't have it."

Jeff vaguely recalled some of the more experienced officers talking about Chief Bennington. "Have what?"

"Beards. My mother always said that a man with a beard has something to hide."

Jeff nodded as if eager to receive the sage wisdom. "I've heard that's true."

Sister Moor snorted and moved down the aisle. Jeff breathed a sigh of relief as he slid onto an empty bench.

". . . Use a low power setting until the oil temperature and pressure increase to normal levels."

Stephanie's words jerked him back to the present. He leaned forward in his seat. "You know what the worst sound in the world is when you're flying?"

"What?"

Jeff spread his arms out like great wings. Then with straight arms, he quickly raised them high over his head, bringing his palms together with a loud smack, mimicking the sound wings would make if they broke off and collided.

Stephanie let out a groan and then feigned thoughtfulness. "Yes, I can see where that would be rather disconcerting." She tilted her head. "Okay, let's take it up and try a few maneuvers. You're in the pilot's seat."

Jeff admired her teaching style. The crusty old pilot that had taught him how to fly always said the best way to learn to fly is by flying.

Stephanie picked up the microphone. "Idaho Falls radio, Cessna one niner zero four November, for taxi to active for southeast departure."

After a burp of static, a garbled voice on the radio returned, "One niner zero four November, taxi to runway 5. Contact tower on 126.4."

"Are you familiar with radio protocol?"

"I think so."

"Good, take over."

After coaching him down the taxiway, Stephanie said, "Go ahead and get tower clearance, and I'll take us up."

"Idaho Falls tower, Cessna one niner zero four November ready for takeoff."

After the static pop the voice returned, "One niner zero four November cleared for takeoff."

Stephanie gained the necessary speed and gently pulled back on the control wheel. Gravity tugged on Jeff's inner organs as the plane lifted above the ground. A few hundred feet later, Stephanie trimmed the flaps.

"So what do you do when you're not flying?" Jeff asked.

"Actually, this is just part time. I'm a legal secretary for Bower, Combo, and Hunnington." Stephanie glanced at her watch. "I'm due there at 9:30."

"Who's your boss when you're flying?"

"A guy named Dennis Margo. He owns Eagle Aviation."

"I saw that they advertise chartering. You do any charter flights for him?"

"A few, but not too often. He usually wants them at odd hours or during the week when I'm working at the law firm."

"What do you mean, odd hours?"

"Like sometimes in the middle of the night. I guess he can't get anyone else to fly, because he usually does them himself."

"Who would want a charter in the middle of the night?"

"It's usually just a delivery."

"What does he want delivered that late at night?"

"Hey, what is this? Twenty questions?"

Jeff silently scolded himself for being too pushy. "Sorry, I guess I was just wondering what it'd be like to fly for a living."

"Well, first it takes a private pilot's license. Let's see how you do at turns."

Jeff twisted the control wheel to the right, banking the craft at a fifteen-degree angle. He deliberately over-turned the rudder.

"Easy on the rudder. Back off just a little bit—good. Okay, maintain level flight. Watch the instruments."

Somehow he couldn't picture Stephanie as a druggie. He wondered if perhaps she was just a mule, flying drugs over the border for Margo.

He decided to test the former. "So, do you like to party?"

"Excuse me?"

"Party, you know, flying while you're on the ground."

"You mean use drugs?"

From her tone, Jeff began to wonder whether this was a mistake, but decided to press on. "Sure. Don't you ever like to unwind?"

"No way! I think it's a rotten, irresponsible thing to do. I'd rather tear a wing off."

Jeff was surprised at her strong response. "So other than that, do you see any problem with getting high?"

Stephanie couldn't help but smile. "I know that sounds kind of self-righteous, but I really am adamant about it." She added, "Do you—how did you put it—like to party?"

Jeff felt trapped. "Well, I had a lot of friends that partied, and sometimes I went with them, but usually I was the, you know, designated driver."

"So, do you use drugs?"

Jeff's total life experience with drugs consisted of Tums and Tylenol. He even dodged chocolate most of the time. His mind raced with strategy. *Is she testing me? But if she thought I did use, maybe they wouldn't trust me because of the drug use.*

"No, I don't use, but I think it's okay for others to use them if they want."

"So you think drugs should be legalized?" Stephanie sounded surprised. "You don't care what they do to people?"

"It's none of my business if someone wants to mess himself up."

Stephanie's eyes darkened. "You think they're the only ones affected by their decision to use drugs? You think it's all right for an airline pilot to smoke pot before his flight? You think it's fine for a brain surgeon to snort a little coke before surgery?"

Jeff raised his hands. "Hey, take it easy, I give!"

Stephanie gave a reluctant smile. "I guess I get carried away."

"No problem." Jeff's thoughts were racing. *Either she is a convincing liar, or she has nothing to do with Margo's illegal activities. On the other hand, she skillfully avoided my question about what Margo was delivering on the late night flights.*

Stephanie changed the subject and began talking about the aerodynamics of low-speed flight. But Jeff's mind was somewhere else.

Jeff returned to the office and found Gary typing a report.

"How do you spell *Bruno?*" Gary quizzed.

"Very funny. I think we can leave that part out."

Gary briefly flexed his cheeks. "We'll do better tonight. So how did the lesson go?"

"The instructor is a gal named Stephanie Evans."

"Do you think she's dirty?"

"She works as a legal secretary during the week."

"Aha! Already a connection with organized crime."

Jeff grinned. "No, I don't think so. Not her anyway."

"So, you've already been seduced by her cunning ways," Gary teased. "Is she a looker?"

Jeff turned defensive. "No, I mean, yes, but that didn't have anything to do with it. She's just not the type."

Gary gave Jeff a boy-are-you-naive look. "And just what is the type?"

"I don't know. The way she talked about things, I just can't see her—"

Gary cut him off. "Does she do any flying for Margo?"

"Yeah, a little, but most of the time she can't because he wants them done during the week." His voice trailed off. "Or late at night."

"She said late at night?"

"Yeah."

"People or packages?"

Jeff heaved air and swallowed. "She said deliveries."

"And you don't think she would suspect a thing?"

"She seems kind of naive."

"*She* seems kind of naive? Look, you don't deliver packages in the middle of the night for someone like Margo and think everything's legit."

The muscles in Jeff's jaw tightened. "You weren't there. You don't know." Then he let his shoulders sag and let out a breath of air. "I know it sounds crazy, but I don't think she's involved." Even as Jeff said the words, he realized how foolish they sounded.

"Look, kid," Gary said in a fatherly tone, "I've been had a dozen times. Believe me, I know how you're looking at this. I've been there." He picked a piece of thread off his sleeve and flicked it into the air. "Just promise me one thing."

Jeff folded his arms. "What's that?"

"That you'll watch her carefully." Gary held up his finger for emphasis. "And don't blow your cover."

"Of course. She's just a way to get an introduction to Margo." Jeff wasn't completely convinced that Margo was the only reason he wanted to see Stephanie again, but he knew one thing for sure. He couldn't reveal his true identity to her.

Chapter Four

"Summer solstice." Jeff stared down at the street through the office window. A few of the passing cars had their headlights on.

Gary dabbed the last bit of face paint and turned from the mirror, wrinkling his nose at Jeff. "Summer what?"

"June twenty-first. It's the longest day of the year."

Gary flashed him a why-are-you-telling-me-this look. "Do you think I should warn the others?"

"It means we can start surveillance a bit earlier every night from here on out."

"Hopefully it won't take too many more nights." Gary deposited the camouflage hat on his head and examined himself in the mirror.

Jeff looked up from tying his shoes. "You need a little more on the bottom of your left ear."

Gary dabbed some dark green paint on his right ear and began rubbing it in.

"No, your other left."

Gary looked in the mirror and changed hands. "There. How's that?"

"Who said that? Gary, is that you? I can hear your voice, but I can't see you."

"Cute."

Gary grabbed the keys to the Thunderbird. "You can take the Camaro."

Jeff made no attempt to hide his satisfaction. "Let's meet at the park. We need a second car close by, in case we go mobile again."

"Good idea," Gary said. He pulled a two-foot stick of solid oak wrapped in camouflage tape from his bag.

"What's that for?" Jeff asked.

"In case we get caught."

"I thought that's what we had guns for."

"If you tell the bad guys you're a cop, dressed like that, they're not gonna believe it. Besides, even if they do believe you, the whole operation is blown."

"So what are you going to do, club them?"

"If I can't run fast enough, yes."

Jeff shrugged his shoulders, deciding he would rely on his martial arts training. He started out the door. "I'll meet you over there."

A few minutes later, Jeff parked next to Gary's car. Gary wasn't in sight, so he tiptoed down the alley. Jeff stopped in the shadows of a large willow tree next to Margo's house. He heard a soft whisper practically underneath him. Shock waves collided with the ends of his fingers and toes.

"If I were a snake, you'd be dead," Gary whispered.

"I might prefer that to a heart attack."

Gary smiled. "I love this job."

Jeff pointed toward the other side of the house. "I'll go hide in the lilac bushes around back."

"Okay, I'll set up by the birch trees."

Jeff used a full ten minutes getting in position. Sometimes he would move only a few inches and then stop to listen. From the lilac bushes, he had a clear view of the alley and part of the birch grove by the circular driveway.

As Jeff studied the backyard, a knot formed in his stomach. *Something's not right.* He studied the birch trees. There was no sign of Gary, but what else was new? He turned his attention to the backyard again. The uneasy feeling persisted.

Then he saw it. A slight movement in the shrubs next to the steps. Before he had a chance to investigate further, the sound of footsteps coming down the alley made him freeze in position. The footsteps soon transformed into a tall figure that vaulted over the chain-link fence.

Jeff felt his heart beat wildly. The new figure paused ten feet away. Jeff squinted to hide the whites of his eyes. The person continued to the back steps, where the earlier movement had occurred. He raised his hand to knock, when someone stepped out from the shrubbery and placed a gun to the intruder's head. Jeff could hear the hammer click back.

"Yo, Dennis, it's me, Randy. Take it easy!"

Margo lowered the gun and gently released the hammer. "Sorry, I get paranoid when I'm dealing."

"No kidding? Man, you need to loosen up!"

Jeff flexed his ears, straining to hear the conversation as they entered the house. He heard something about "office" and "I'll drive" mixed with other words.

A minute later, he heard the garage door opening. He darted around the house and dropped to the ground. A candy-red Ferrari backed out of the garage and drove away.

Jeff sprinted past the birch trees. Gary bolted up and joined him as they raced to their cars. Jeff was first. In one movement, even before the door was shut, he had the engine started and in gear.

Jeff let the engine prove its muscle and gripped the steering wheel with both hands. Diving into the same corner that Gary had nearly blown a week ago, Jeff hit the gas. He slid sideways onto the next street just in time to see the Ferrari turn left on 17th Street several blocks ahead.

Jeff flipped on his portable radio to channel four. "You coming?"

"Give me a direction."

"So far, same as before." Even though the channel was secure, he didn't want to risk it.

The Camaro drove past Boulevard. "Going down hill."

"Okay, I'm with you."

Jeff glanced in his rearview mirror. Gary's car maintained a steady pace two blocks behind him.

The Ferrari signaled to turn right on Yellowstone. "R bender on cowardly rock. You better take the eye."

Jeff bit his lip and hoped that Gary understood. He continued to drive straight on 17th and then turned right on Capital. Gary followed the Ferrari right on Yellowstone. With more traffic on the road, he closed the gap to one block.

"I got the eye. Looks like an L bender for the swimming hole."

Jeff headed for the Broadway bridge.

"Hard right," Gary said. "Look for a stop."

Jeff swung around just in time to see Gary duck into an alley by the B Street Plaza, a three-story brick building. He slid over to the curb, threw the Camaro in park, and ran ahead on foot.

Gary scrambled across the street and motioned for Jeff to follow him inside. They paused only briefly in the lobby as Gary pointed at the far side of the room. "I saw them head for the stairs."

Jeff looked around. Dressed like commandos, they couldn't afford to be seen. He motioned for Gary to follow him up the stairs.

Judging from the muffled voices, Jeff guessed that Margo and the tall newcomer had gone all the way to the third floor. He crept up the stairs and poked his head around the last flight of stairs. They were gone.

Gary huddled next to Jeff's ear. "Where did they go?"

"I didn't see. Let's check the doors."

Twenty feet down the dimly lit hall, Jeff spotted a light glowing under one of the doors. He motioned for Gary and flattened his ear against the door.

"I hear voices, but I can't tell what they're saying."

Jeff could discern Gary's teeth smiling in the darkness

as he pointed above him. He glanced up and saw a small trap door in the ceiling on the opposite side of the hall.

Gary jerked his thumb upward and whispered, "You're the monkey."

He bent over before Jeff could offer any objections. "I'll give you a boost. Then you can help me up."

"Are you sure this is legal—"

Gary cut him off. "Relax, this is a public building."

Jeff started to run fourth amendment court cases through his brain. *Must have found a loophole.* He shrugged his shoulders and put one foot on Gary's bent knee while bringing the other foot to rest on his back. Lifting the square door to one side, Jeff slid upward in an effortless thrust and disappeared into the black hole.

Seconds later, Jeff's arm reached down. Gary didn't want to remain exposed in the hallway any longer than necessary, so he grabbed it firmly and bicycled his way up the wall.

"Sh! Watch your feet."

Gary seized a side brace for support and finished lifting his legs through the hole. "Listen, Tarzan, I'm doing the best I can."

They were forced into a half-squatting, bent posture in the four-foot high crawl space between the ceiling and the roof above. Jeff turned on his flashlight and whispered, "Watch the false ceiling."

Perched on a 2"x4" beam, Jeff surveyed the flimsy tile that ran the length of the hall. He spotted a narrow support four inches wide leading to the room's ceiling.

"Don't put weight on anything but the beam or you'll go through."

Gary nodded in understanding.

Jeff began inching his way down the beam across the hall. By pressing his arm against the ceiling above, he was able to maintain balance. Sweat mixed with face paint burned in his eyes.

Halfway across, he turned to check on the progress of

his partner. Gary reached out with one hand on the tile to steady himself.

Jeff whispered as loud as he dared, "Don't touch it. You'll fall through!"

With a look of defiance that veiled only thinly his true feeling of desperation, Gary teetered and again reached out to steady himself.

This time the ceiling refused to cooperate. Gary's hand pushed through the tile. Reverting to instincts, he lunged like a wild animal scrambling for anything that might support his weight. The entire ceiling—lights, tile, flimsy supports, everything between Jeff and the stairway—collapsed in a heap of twisted conduit, glass, and flesh.

Jeff's first impulse was to laugh. Then he remembered Margo's willingness to use his gun. Instinctively, he drew his Glock and aimed it at the doorway. He expected Margo and his companion to come bursting through with guns blazing.

Gary shook his head and jumped up. He hobbled toward the stairwell, waving for Jeff to follow. Jeff kept his concentration and gun focused on the door. Then he leaped to the floor. At the same time, the door flew open.

Jeff swung around with his finger on the trigger. A middle-aged woman carrying a bucket and a mop froze. Her mouth opened, but nothing came out.

Not able to completely stop his reflexes, Jeff reached out and grabbed her arm. He spun her into the wall and shoved his gun behind her ear. "Don't move. Don't talk." Then, jamming his pistol in his pants, he turned and bolted down the stairs, taking four and five steps at a time. He caught up to Gary going out the door. "Come on. I'll drive. We can get your car later."

Gary grimaced in pain as he stumbled after Jeff. "Let's just get out of here before they show up."

"I don't think they're coming."

"Why?"

"Wrong door."

"What do you mean?"

"A cleaning lady came out. We must have got the wrong office."

"Did she see you?"

Jeff's mind flashed back to the expression of terror pasted on the lady's face. "Yeah, she saw me."

"Don't worry about it. I'm sure she won't be able to identify you dressed like this. Probably thinks you're a terrorist."

Jeff opened the door for Gary. "You okay?"

"I'm fine. Just take me home."

"You want me to take you to a doctor or anything?"

"Look, I said I'm fine. Just take me home so you can get some sleep—and don't forget your appointment with what's-her-face in the morning."

Chapter Five

Bumblebees. Jeff imagined himself on the back of a giant bumblebee as the noise from the Cessna engine droned through his head. The Saturday afternoon sun pierced the cockpit window, making Stephanie's hair appear more blonde than it actually was.

"Climb to 8,500 feet."

Jeff pulled the throttle and gently eased back the control wheel.

"Okay, now watch the instruments. Don't chase it. Excellent! You act like you've done this a hundred times."

"Seems like it," Jeff mumbled under his breath.

"Pardon?"

"I said it seems like I'm getting the hang of it." Jeff's conscience stung. *It isn't actually a lie—technically,* he thought.

"You're doing great. Let's try something a little more interesting."

"Such as?"

"Have you ever stalled before?"

"I've read about it." *Which is true.* "A stall is a loss of lift caused by too great an angle of attack."

"Very good. Let's see if you can recover from one." Stephanie pulled back sharply on her control wheel, causing the nose to rise abruptly. Jeff felt his stomach drive into his pelvis as the plane surged upward.

The controls grew sluggish and the plane started shivering. It seemed to hang in the air, cresting the first pinnacle of a massive roller coaster.

Jeff pushed the nose forward and increased the power as they dove toward the earth. Their bodies tugged upward against seat belts unable to keep up, or rather down, with the plummeting craft. Gently, he pulled back the control wheel, forcing his head into his shoulders. They resumed a gradual climb.

"Okay, superman. This couldn't be your first time. Who taught you that?"

Jeff bit the inside of his cheek for overperforming. "My uncle had a Piper Tomahawk. We did this all the time." Jeff congratulated himself for his response. By telling most of the truth, he could sound very credible. He decided he was good at working undercover without having to lie too much.

Stephanie studied Jeff, apparently deep in thought. He glanced over and caught her stare. She immediately tried to cover her blush with a question. "So what do you do when you're not learning to fly?"

Jeff swallowed hard. "I'm kind of between things. I graduated with a B.S. in accounting from the University of Idaho and worked for a CPA firm for a couple years."

"Accountant?" Stephanie wrinkled her nose. "You don't look like an accountant."

"What does an accountant look like?"

"That was kind of stupid. I guess you just don't seem the type."

Jeff waited expectantly.

Stephanie bobbed her head back and forth as her eyes darted upward. "I mean, accountants are more like . . . oh, I don't know." Then, trying to bring the conversation back on course, "So what do you do now?"

"I guess I just got bored with it. I managed to save up enough money to get by until I decide on something." *Maybe it doesn't hurt to stretch things once in a while.*

"You've got a natural ability when it comes to flying. You ought to do something with it."

"Like what?"

Stephanie shrugged. "If you stay away from your druggie friends, maybe you could get a job as a pilot after you get enough hours."

Jeff pulled a sour face. "Druggie friends?"

"Aren't you the designated driver? And didn't you say you thought drugs were okay?"

Jeff closed his eyes briefly. He regretted his earlier stand, but now he was committed. "What I meant was . . . I think people should be able to choose whether they use drugs without a holier-than-thou society telling them what they can and can't do."

This time Stephanie chose not to get angry. "You think I should be able to use coke before I take you flying?"

"That's different."

"What's different about it?"

"It involves other people then." Jeff felt himself losing the argument.

"So when is it okay?"

"When a guy is alone or when some friends are there to help him."

"And who decides if this criteria is met?"

"The decision should be up to him." Jeff hesitated, then quickly added, "Or her."

"Do you really think a junkie is going to know when he jeopardizes others?"

"You have some good points. I guess for me the bottom line is that I don't do drugs. As for my friends, I've only been here a few months so I really don't have any. Besides, I agree that in general drugs are bad for you. I just think people should be able to choose."

Jeff tried to deflect the discussion. "How about you? Do you have any friends that use?"

"Not really, unless you count my boss."

Jeff's heart raced. "Margo?"

"No, my regular job, the attorney, Mr. Hunnington.

He's the one that introduced me to Margo. And it's not like he's a druggie or anything, but he drinks like . . ." Stephanie blushed. "Look, I shouldn't have said anything. It's none of my business."

Jeff let it drop. "Do you enjoy being a legal secretary?"

"Not really. I mean it's okay, but I'd prefer something more active."

"Like flying?"

Stephanie smiled. "Yes."

They talked about flying and Jeff's days at Moscow. Jeff felt a closeness with Stephanie that he hadn't felt with anyone. He found himself increasingly doubtful that she had anything to do with Margo's drug business. Eventually, the conversation came around to Eagle Aviation. "So what's Margo like to work for?"

"Dennis is a nice enough guy when he's relaxed."

"What do you mean?"

"Oh, sometimes he seems kind of uptight. It's probably just the business pressures."

"Business pressures?"

"Yeah, he's always on the go. Acts like everything is life or death."

"He's lucky to have good help."

Stephanie smiled. "I don't know about that. I wish I could help him more on the business end. He's running himself ragged."

"Why is that?"

"I think he needs more help. Ever since his wife and daughter were killed in a flying accident, he's been kind of drifty."

"Is he hard to get along with?"

"No, he really is nice. I don't think he got along with his wife, but he misses his daughter and I think maybe that's why he's nicer to me than the others. He just gets involved in his work."

"Maybe he's having money problems. Being an accountant, I know what that does to people."

"I don't know. With him, it's either feast or famine. The

guy is loaded, but it's like he doesn't know how to manage his money. One time he pulled a wad of hundred-dollar bills from his pocket. He just peeled one off and handed it to me, apologizing for being late on payroll."

Stephanie's face brightened, "Maybe you should see about getting a job working for him. With a degree in accounting, you could help him manage his money."

Jeff could think of nothing he'd rather do than be on the inside of Margo's dealing. But he realized that Margo probably ran ragged because he couldn't expose his business dealings to anyone—unless that person was a full partner in every sense of the word. "I'm not sure I have the kind of background he needs, but I'd like to meet him anyway."

Stephanie looked at her watch. "It's almost four. Let's go see if he's around."

As they neared the airport Jeff picked up the mike. "Idaho Falls Airport, this is Cessna one niner zero four November, preparing for northeast arrival."

The scratchy voice came over the radio, "Cessna one niner zero four November, follow the twin Cessna turning base."

Jeff looked ahead and saw the twin Cessna.

Stephanie held her hands away from the controls. "You get us close, and I'll take the last three hundred feet."

"Whatever you say, coach."

Soon the radio voice returned. "Cessna one niner zero four November, cleared for landing runway 4."

Jeff banked left twenty-two degrees for the final approach. He looked at the altimeter and waited for Stephanie to direct him to lose more altitude.

"Okay, now aim down a little more. Nose down, increase flaps . . . good. Okay, I've got it now."

Stephanie took the controls and gently coaxed the plane onto the runway.

Jeff felt a slight tug as the wheels touched the ground. The brakes pressed him forward while the plane rapidly lost momentum. "Smooth!"

Stephanie smiled demurely. "I'm glad you approve."

They taxied to the hangar and walked to the office. A brick propped open the door to allow a fresh breeze in. The receptionist sat behind her desk, manicuring her fingernails.

Stephanie cleared her throat. "Have you seen Dennis?"

Ignoring Stephanie, the receptionist eyed Jeff. "He's in his office."

Jeff pretended not to notice. Stephanie just rolled her eyes and gave a flat "Thanks."

Margo's door was shut, so Stephanie knocked. She raised her hand to knock again when the door flew open. "Oh, hi, Steph. What can I do for you?"

"Dennis, I'd like you to meet Jeff Spenelie. He's taking flying lessons from us."

Margo held out his hand. Jeff expected him to be taller. His hands were slender and feminine. He wasn't a handsome man, probably the result of his hooked nose and bulging eyes. The bushy strips that marked the beginning of his forehead overshadowed his thick salt-and-pepper mustache.

Stephanie didn't waste any time. "Jeff has a B.S. degree in accounting and is new to the area. He has a natural ability to fly and is looking for a new career."

Jeff took over. "And this is my agent, Stephanie Evans. She gets 15 percent of the take."

Margo chuckled, "Well, I can always use good pilots, but everything else is covered right now. Let me know when you have enough hours."

Jeff had expected Margo's perfunctory reply and decided to press further. "Seriously though, I am considering aviation, and if you have anything part-time I could do around the place just to get a feel for it, I'd be interested." *Kind of a lie . . .*

Margo stroked his chin. "The night manager is talking about going back to school. Besides doing the books and taking late charters, it includes driving the gas truck and some minor maintenance. If you want to get a feel for late hours and low pay, I might be able to help you out."

Jeff shrugged. "Sounds good." *It's okay to lie to a dirtbag.*

"Fine, I'll give you a call if he leaves."

They said good-bye and left. Jeff stopped before getting in the Camaro and yelled across the parking lot, "Thanks, Stephanie. I owe you one."

She waved it off. "Any time."

About a hundred yards down the road, Stephanie pulled her Ford Bronco over to the side. Jeff stopped next to her and rolled down the window. "Forget something?"

"No, this stupid thing died on me. Did the same thing a couple days ago and I had to call a wrecker. Cost me two hundred dollars, and I thought it was fixed."

"Sorry, I'm no mechanic. But jump in and I'll take you home."

Stephanie hesitated. She looked at the dash of her silent Bronco and then back at Jeff. "Thanks, I'd appreciate that."

Jeff leaned across the seat and opened the door. "If you want, I have another car you can borrow. Do you have anything pressing you need to do?"

"No, that's okay. I was just going to pick up some groceries and go home."

"Do you like Chinese food?"

Stephanie's face brightened. "Love it."

"How about the Hong Kong? We can use their phone to call a wrecker. Then I'll take you to my house, and we can pick up my other car."

"Thanks, but I couldn't take your car."

"Wait till you see it. You might decide you'd rather walk. Besides, I owe you one."

Stephanie ran her fingers through her hair and gave an easy smile. "Okay."

Chapter Six

Dennis Margo closed the blinds on his office windows, but light trickled around the edges anyway. He snatched up a roll of duct tape and pasted the curtain to the wall. He wondered if he could trust his secretary. He fired the last one because she watched him. Now he worried about this one.

Margo got up and checked inside the adjoining bathroom. He knew no one was there, but he checked it anyway. The figure in the bathroom mirror stared back at him. Gaunt skin that stretched over cheekbones formed lines of experience. Margo sniffled and ran his finger under his nose. A constant trickle flowed from his decaying nasal passage. He studied the lines etched into his forehead. There was no going back. He knew that.

But it was more than just his physical appearance. A mental image of his daughter flashed across his mind. She wasn't supposed to be on the plane with her mother. Barely a senior in high school. So much pain.

He remembered how she had looked forward to her eighth birthday and how carefully she had prepared for that special time. She had often said she wanted to be just like him. He vaguely remembered his feelings of warmth. His grandfather smiling at him. He would do anything to feel that way again. But it was too late.

Margo walked back to his desk and sat down. He reached in a drawer and retrieved a large pistol. The blue metal sagged in his hand. He studied the barrel. Sweat beaded up on his forehead and the gun became lighter. It moved upward, up to the side of his head. His hand trembled. He paused—

The gun dropped to his side. He couldn't do it. His fear was greater than his self-hatred. As terrible as life was, he sensed that what waited for him beyond would be worse.

If only there was a way to vanish. Not dead. Not even born. Just gone. Margo shook his head free of the thought.

He used to worry about his health. But now he suspected who his real enemies were. *Perhaps they will try poison.* He ran his hand over the cold metal barrel of the pistol. He would be ready.

At one time, Margo worried about losing his family, but now that was done. Rachel was a witch, and he'd asked Troy to take care of it. But the memory of his daughter haunted him—an unfortunate, horrific accident.

Relief. I need relief.

Margo retrieved a six-inch mirror from the same desk drawer. He reached in his pocket and unfolded a small paper envelope with the picture of a seal balancing a snowflake. He checked his office door again. Still locked.

He meticulously scraped a modest amount of white powder with a gold plated razor blade. *Snow, an interesting name . . . More like Demonic Ruler.* Margo looked at the door again. *I've got to be careful. They're watching.*

His attention returned to the mirror. *Why can't it be like the first time? It's not fair!*

He hadn't intended to become addicted to cocaine. Nervously but unbidden he laughed out loud. *Most people deal to get more coke. But I was too clean. The money—just the money.*

He closed his eyes. *Troy warned me.*

Troy Southwick lived in Las Vegas and knew how to play the game well. When he first set Margo up in business seven years ago, he'd told him, "The reason I feel comfortable working with you is because you won't make mistakes. And do you know why you're not going to make mistakes? Because you don't use. Keep it that way and you'll be the richest man in Idaho."

Margo stared down at the reflection in the mirror and smiled sadly. *If only I had listened.*

It started out as an experiment. One of his dealers wanted to "field test" it. Normally he would have refused and given his standard answer: "No way. That stuff will make you die young." Then he would laugh, "I'm just a businessman. If you want to kill yourself, go for it."

But in a way it puzzled him. He wondered what made the snowy white so alluring that a person would do anything to get it.

Then it happened. He tried it, and it was incredible. Better than anything he had ever experienced—anything. He had to have more.

Margo liked everything about it, the confidence it gave him. But it always took more to get the same high. *Not fair. Not fair at all.*

He had tried to stop. Several times he told himself this would be the last time, but he always came back.

Margo painstakingly drew out two lines of crystal white on the mirror as if building miniature deathbeds of salt for a slug—smooth, even rows. *I've got to get out of this business. Just one more shipment.* But as soon as the thought came, he knew it was a lie. *Too deep. No way out.*

Then, with a gold-plated tube half the length of a straw, he bent over and snorted one line up each nostril. Margo leaned back in his chair and waited for it to come. Soon the blood rushed to his heart. Rushing everywhere. Power . . .

"You will find new romance." Jeff crumpled up the paper and munched on the fortune cookie.

"What did it say?" Stephanie asked.

"Something about new opportunities. What's yours say?"

Stephanie tossed her hair back and laughed. "I will live a long life."

The small Asian waitress appeared with a pitcher of water and asked in broken English, "Is anything okay?"

Jeff studied her thoughtfully as Stephanie repressed a giggle. "Yes. I can think of several things that are okay—"

Stephanie cut him off. "Everything is perfect. Thank you."

The waitress smiled innocently and left.

Jeff leaned back in his chair. "So what do you do for recreation?"

Stephanie rested her chin on one finger. "I like to ski."

"Snow or water?"

"Both, actually. But my favorite is snow. More freedom."

"Kind of tough to do this time of year."

"Maybe that's why I like to water ski."

"I water skied once or twice. I'd like to try it again sometime."

Stephanie sipped on a glass of water. "What do you like to do when you're not tormenting waitresses?"

Jeff popped the last piece of cookie in his mouth and washed it down. "Lots of things. I used to be on a swim team. I like to go skydiving, climb mountains, and listen to Mozart."

Stephanie leaned forward and touched his arm. "You like Mozart?"

"You don't approve?"

She shook her head. "I'm in the Idaho Falls Symphony, and we'll be performing some Mozart next week. It's just that people who do active sports usually don't like . . ." Her voice trailed off as she realized what she was saying.

"You mean like skiing?"

Stephanie shrugged. "I guess I'm different."

"You play the violin, right?"

"Close. I play the cello. How about you? If you like the classics, you must play something."

"My mom made me learn to play the piano, but I'm not very good."

"I'd like to hear you sometime."

"No you wouldn't."

"You're too modest. Probably just like your flying."

Jeff pressed his fingers together "No. If I flew like I play the piano, we wouldn't be here."

"That bad, huh?"

Jeff nodded his head as the waitress returned with the check. Stephanie immediately snatched it off the table. "I'll get it."

"But I'm the one that invited you . . ."

"You're the one lending your car, remember?"

Jeff put his wallet away. "Have at it. My mother told me never to argue over money."

"And you're an accountant?"

"Ex-accountant."

After dining at the Hong Kong, Jeff and Stephanie drove to his apartment. As they entered, Jeff quickly scanned the front room and felt relieved to find no sign of his real identity. He left Stephanie in the front room while he retrieved the keys to the Toyota from his bedroom.

The blinking light on the answering machine by his bed caught his eye. He closed the door and released the message. "Jeff, this is Gary. It's 8:40. I've got great news about our favorite project. Call me immediately. I'm on the pager. Thanks, bud."

Jeff glanced at his watch. 8:50. He scooped up the phone, but was interrupted by the doorbell. He returned to the front room just in time to find Stephanie about to open the door. He reached in front of her. "I'll get it."

Jeff opened the door and came face to face with his home teachers. The older of the two blinked at Stephanie and raised one eyebrow. "Good evening, Brother—"

Jeff coughed loudly, drowning out the rest of the

sentence. He flashed a sideways glance at Stephanie. Apparently, she didn't hear the word *Brother*. *Think fast, Foster.*

"We're sorry if this is a bad time. We tried calling earlier, but Broth—"

In desperation, Jeff cut them off. "Look, I told you I'm not interested. When I'm ready, I'll call you." He pushed the door shut, abandoning the surprised faces on the front steps. A sick feeling developed in his stomach. *Okay, damage control.*

"Who were they?"

Jeff tried to smile as he forced the lie from his lips. "Salesmen. Uh, vacuum cleaner." He looked more worried than happy. "You know how they can be."

Stephanie grinned. "I wish I had the nerve to do that."

Okay, she's buying it. He thought of the distressed home teachers and promised himself that he would call them later tonight to explain. *And tell them what?* He bit his lip.

Stephanie seemed to already forget the visitors as she moved to a cage containing a parrot. "Do you ever let him out?"

"It's a her."

"Do you ever let her out?"

"Occasionally. But she likes to put holes in the drapes, so I have to keep a pretty close eye on her." Jeff remembered the message on his answering machine. "I'll be right back." He disappeared into the bedroom, picked up the phone, and punched in the correct numbers. Within seconds, Gary called back.

"This is Jeff."

The voice on the other end was anxious. "I think we've done it. I think we have enough."

"What happened?"

"Last night after the ceiling fiasco, I ran over to Margo's."

Jeff interrupted, "You mean you hobbled over to Margo's."

"Yeah, right. Anyway, I scooped his garbage. Since it was late I decided to wait and check it today. I found two empty snow seals!"

"All right!"

"I can't believe Margo got that careless, but combined with everything else, I think we have enough for a search warrant. I'm at the courthouse with the prosecutor. The judge is on the way. You'll need to be co-affiant to testify about what you heard Margo say—the part about being paranoid when he's dealing and about the paper you found in his garbage."

"I'm on my way."

"Good. See ya in a few." Click.

Jeff slapped his hand against his forehead as he re-membered Stephanie sitting in his front room. Snatching up the keys to the Toyota, he darted into the front room. "Here's the keys. It's parked right in front of the door out-side. You can't miss it. Important call. Gotta run."

Before she could respond, Jeff was outside the door and heading for the Camaro.

Stephanie's cheerful expression sagged into an I-must-have-really-scared-him gaze.

Jeff paused before entering his car and called out, "Sorry about this. Don't worry about the car. Just keep it for a few days. I'll call you." He left.

Stephanie shook her head and opened the door to the blue Toyota. "He's right. It is a junker," she mumbled. "At least it's clean."

She glanced at her watch. 8:52 P.M. "Cat food!" Stephanie urged the miserable clunker forward.

Coasting through a stop sign, she looked up in time to see a black-and-white patrol car parked at the corner. "Oh no!" she groaned. The police car flashed its lights at her. She pulled over to the side and rolled down her window.

The cop had graying hair and a square jaw. "May I see your driver's license and registration?" It sounded more like a command than a question. "You know why I stopped you?" Again another statement.

Stephanie didn't try to act dumb. "Yes, I know." She opened the glove compartment, found the registration, and handed it to the officer. "It's not my car. It belongs to a friend of mine."

The cop studied the paper. "What's your friend's name?"

"Jeff Spenelie."

"It says here 'Jeff Foster.'"

"What?"

"Foster. It shows the last name of Foster."

"No, that must be his middle name. Let me see it."

Ignoring her request, he walked back to his car mumbling something about checking the computer.

The weathered cop spoke into the microphone. "8B52."

A female voice squawked a return, "52, go ahead."

"10-28 on license number 8B30880."

In a few seconds the voice returned. "Local 30880, registered to Jeff Foster, 221 Saturn, apartment number 3, on a '78 blue Toyota 2-door."

Jeff turned into the courthouse parking lot when his heart slammed into his throat. Grabbing his radio, he identified himself. "This is 8B27. Who requested the twenty-eight?"

The female voice returned, "8B52."

Jeff continued, "52 from 27."

The cop answered, "Go ahead."

"Do you have that vehicle stopped?"

"Affirmative. Is it yours?"

"Can the driver copy this transmission?"

"Negative."

"Vehicle in question is involved in UC operation. If possible, keep owner identity from driver."

"10-4, I'll do what I can to salvage."

"Thanks." Jeff rubbed his fingers through his hair. He decided there was nothing he could do about it now, so he parked the Camaro and dashed into the courthouse.

Stephanie's eyes followed the returning policeman through the rearview mirror. "Ma'am, I'm just going to warn you this time, but next time make sure you come to a complete stop for all stop signs. Also, there's a mistake on the registration. The computer shows a different last name. This isn't the first time the DMV messed up. I'll take the registration and have them send a corrected copy."

Stephanie took a large breath of air and let it out slowly. "Thank you so much. I'm sorry, and I promise to be more careful."

The officer threw a quick nod and returned to his car. He shook his head and chuckled.

Jeff arrived shortly after Judge Glenford. He liked Glenford. Most judges were stiff and formal all the time. Glenford acted the pompous tyrant only in court.

Gary had just finished giving his statement. The prosecutor motioned Jeff in and punched the tape recorder. "Please state your full name for the record."

"Jeffrey Foster."

The prosecutor proceeded, "And how are you currently employed?"

"As a detective for the City of Idaho Falls in Bonneville County, State of Idaho."

Jeff outlined how he had overheard Margo, Margo's paranoid behavior, and the writing on the paper in the garbage. Finally, the judge approved the search warrant, and Jeff and Gary headed for the office.

"You ready to go camouflage?" Gary asked.

"My stuff's in the trunk of the Camaro. Why?"

"I don't think we ought to search until Margo gets home. If we camy up, then we can get him as he goes in. Maybe we'll catch him dirty. Besides, it'll be safer. Don't forget the knock and announce rule. Who knows what kind of weapons or booby traps he'll have inside."

Once at the office, Jeff applied the face paint meticulously and inspected his extra magazine of ammo. He felt the familiar tingling in his stomach return.

Gary picked up a notebook. "Okay, we have the camera, extra film, garbage bags, sacks, gloves, paperwork . . . You want the AR15 or the shotgun?"

"I'll take the shotgun." Jeff liked the sawed-off shotgun. Pistol grips, stock, and barrel totaled only twenty-one inches. It was attached to a bungie cord that he strapped to his shoulder under his jacket. This freed his hands while still allowing the gun to be concealed under his windbreaker. An AR15 assault rifle looks intimidating, but nothing like the sound of a shell being racked into a twelve-gauge shotgun.

They parked a block and a half away from Margo's house. Jeff sneaked into the backyard to see if Margo was home. This time he spent a full half hour examining the yard. Meanwhile, Gary looked through the garage window. The Ferrari was gone. They met back at the pine tree.

Jeff pointed toward the garage door. "I'll hide in the shrubbery. When he comes home, I'll grab him."

"What about the garage door opener? He'll probably go directly inside the garage."

"As the door comes down, I'll slip under it and lie down beside the car. When he opens the door, bingo, he's mine."

Gary scratched his head. "And what if there's trouble?"

"Then I'll call 911."

"Okay, Batman, I'll be by the birch trees in case he leaves it parked in the driveway and goes in the front door. As soon as you get him under control, hit the garage door opener." Gary paused and then quickly added, "If you're not out in three days, I'm calling the fire department."

Jeff took his position and hunkered down in the shrubs, happy that they were only juniper bushes instead of the prickly beasts that grow around churches. His mind flitted to Stephanie. *What will happen if we bust Margo? No more flying lessons. Maybe she'll go out with me.* For the first time, it occurred to Jeff that he would eventually have to tell Stephanie who he really was. He wondered how she would react.

He rehearsed several scenarios.

Stephanie, I'm not who you think I am.

Uh, Stephanie. You remember that time you were stopped by the police?

Uh, Stephanie. Guess what. You're never going to believe this, but . . .

Stephanie, this is going to sound crazy, but . . .

Stephanie, please don't be angry with me, but . . .

He was jarred back to the business at hand by an ant that had lost its way in his pant leg. He gently reached up the pant and shooed the trespasser away.

For now, he would wait. But he didn't have to wait long.

Chapter Seven

The constellation Lyra arched high overhead. Light from Vega, its brightest star, turned twenty-seven years old as it reached the earth's surface. Some of it collided with the camouflaged shirt and pants worn by Jeff Foster. Some of it penetrated the windshield of a Ferrari, and blasted onto the blue jeans and pullover shirt worn by Dennis Margo. Neither seemed to care.

Margo glanced down at his speedometer—38 mph. Not too unreasonable, but not worth the risk of being picked up for speeding. Not when he carried this kind of load.

Margo eased off the gas until the Ferrari slowed to 34 mph. He had purchased the Ferrari against Troy's advice. Troy had told him to hide his wealth until it could be laundered and then justified through other business enterprises. Troy said it brought too much attention. At first Margo exercised caution. But he'd started getting careless about two years ago, when he had started using.

As the Ferrari coasted into the garage, Margo punched the garage door opener a second time. He waited for the door to close and then took a deep breath.

He felt tired, yet restless. He fingered the tiny envelope of cocaine in his pocket. Almost empty. A craving swelled inside his breast. He thought of the stash in his bedroom. He threw open the car door, intent on satisfaction.

At the sound of the car door, Jeff sprang the trap. "Police, don't move!" He stood with his Glock pointed directly at Margo's chest. Margo's jaw worked but nothing came out.

In an instant, Margo recovered and reached behind his back. Almost simultaneously, Jeff lunged forward. He pinned him between the open car door and the steering wheel. Jeff held Margo's right elbow against the door. Margo's hand squirmed behind his back, but couldn't get free. With the gun in his other hand, Jeff used the barrel to activate the garage door opener under the dash. Meanwhile, Margo's free hand managed to find Jeff's throat.

Jeff shoved the working end of his Glock into Margo's right nostril, forcing his head back, and whispered in a hoarse voice, "Let go or die."

Margo opted for the former and released his grip on Jeff's throat.

Gary dashed inside with his AR15 trained on Margo's head. Jeff, still holding Margo's arm behind his back, turned his head toward Gary and forced a smile. "Hi, I think he has a gun behind his back."

Gary reached behind Margo and retrieved an S&W 40 automatic pistol. Popping the magazine out, he ejected a round from the chamber and disengaged the hammer. Gary paused to mold his empty hand into a gun and pointed it at Margo's forehead. "One shot between the eyes, and pow!" His hand jerked back with the imaginary blast. Then he stared at Margo with contempt as he spoke to Jeff. "Why didn't you dump him?"

"I don't know. Maybe it's not too late."

Gary shook his head and quickly handcuffed Margo while Jeff continued to press the barrel against his nose.

Jeff jerked his head, motioning toward the concrete floor. "Okay, let's prone him out and search." Releasing the pressure on the gun, Jeff shoved it into his holster and lowered Margo to the floor.

For the first time, Margo spoke. "Who sent you? Are you going to kill me?"

Mockingly, Jeff said, "You don't get it, do you? Like I said, we're the police."

"Dressed like that?"

Gary pulled out his wallet, flipped open his badge, and stuck it in Margo's face. "We have a warrant to search this place. You want to save us some time?"

"I don't know what you're talking about."

"Fine." Gary grabbed his portable radio and called for a patrolman to assist.

Jeff searched Margo's pockets and pulled out two thick wads of hundred-dollar bills along with a small paper envelope with the picture of a seal balancing a snowflake. Carefully, he unfolded the paper revealing a glistening white powder. "That's a start."

They raised Margo to a standing position. Sweat dripped off his face. "Look, you can keep the cash. There's over ten thousand dollars there. It's yours. Just let me go."

Jeff smirked. "Yeah, right, and maybe you could set us up with a couple hookers and a houseboat."

Margo turned white. After a few seconds, he stammered, "Wh-what do you want?"

"Nothing. You're busted." Jeff turned and began searching the Ferrari, leaving Margo in Gary's custody. When the patrolman arrived, Gary instructed him to take Margo to the interview room at the station and hold him until they arrived.

Jeff did a quick once-over on the car and found nothing. Promising himself that he would return for a more thorough search, he moved into the house. After a walk-through, they divided up the house. Jeff hit the master bedroom first while Gary worked on the living room and kitchen.

Jeff whistled softly. The master bedroom could easily contain Jeff's front room. To the right of the door was a walk-in closet. Just past the closet, a door opened to a bathroom. Other than a king-size bed and two dressers, the only other pieces of furniture were a rolltop desk and a short overstuffed couch on the far side of the room. Everything appeared to be made of oak.

The bathroom looked as large as the bedroom. A heart-shaped spa on a raised platform overshadowed the shower and toilet.

Jeff started with the dresser. The first thing he found was a fully loaded Tech 9 submachine gun buried under a woman's negligee. Jeff pulled a leather case with the initials D.M. from the lower drawer of the dresser. He unzipped it cautiously. A heart-shaped mirror surrounded an intricate design made of gold fastened to one side. The remaining contents consisted of a gold-plated tube and a gold-plated razor blade.

Jeff moved on to the bathroom. He turned the brass handle on the spa. Hot water spewed out from the nozzle. He turned the water off and opened a side panel. Jeff scratched the side of his head. He spoke to no one in particular. "Why two heaters?" He scrutinized them closer. The lettering on one of them read "Culligan." *Water softener.*

Jeff lifted the lid and shoved his hand into the coarse rock salt. *Tight quarters.* Jamming his shoulder up to the edge, he thrust his hand into the salt as deep as it would go.

A glimmer of hope trickled through his chest as he sensed something smooth and rounded. He twisted his hand and detected two more. Carefully, he extracted a plastic bag weighing about an ounce. The end was doubled over and sealed with a rubber band. After recovering the other two, he peeled off the rubber band and opened the bag. Sparkling white powder. "Yes!"

Gary bounded into the room. "What did you find?"

"See for yourself." Jeff shoved the bag at him, not even trying to contain his excitement.

Gary's eyes grew with his smile. He looked at the

cocaine and then back at Jeff. "All right!" He quickly checked the other bags and found them to be the same. "Margo is history. There must be about three ounces here. That's about five thousand dollars." Gary glanced at his watch. "Two o'clock. I'm about done. How much you got left?"

"Just the desk."

"I'll help you. That's probably where we'll find any kind of paper trail." Gary opened his folder. "On second thought, you're the accountant. Why don't you search the desk, and I'll process the evidence."

"Sounds good." Jeff started on the desk. He pulled out a black ledger book from the first drawer and started to read out loud. "January 7, 2 key, $45,000. January 14, 1 key, $26,000. January 21, 2 key, $38,000. . . . Yowza! We're onto something here."

Gary returned with a paper sack. "Whatcha got?"

"Dates and amounts. Look at the kind of volume and cash he's doing! Here's an address book."

Gary snatched up the book and thumbed through the S-section.

"What are you looking for?"

"T.S. Remember from the garbage?"

Jeff blushed with understanding. "Margo's connection."

Gary mumbled several names going down the column. "Christie Shoemaker, Gayle Simmons, Debbie Snyder, Jerry Sorenson, Troy Southwick—that's gotta be it. Troy Southwick!"

Jeff grabbed the book. "Troy Southwick, 5922 Merida Drive, Las Vegas, Nevada." Jeff let out a slow breath of air and fought the temptation to rush through the rest of the search. Letting his training as an accountant take over, he examined each piece of paper.

One hour later, Gary returned with all the evidence packaged and ready to go. "How are you doing?"

Jeff closed the desk drawer. "Done. I was just double-checking."

Gary rubbed his finger against his thumb. "Let's take off. If we don't get Margo interviewed pretty quick, they'll kick out the confession."

"You think he'll talk?"

"They always talk. My best cases come from pukes turning on pukes."

Jeff stretched and let out a long yawn. "I think we have everything covered. I'll go get the Camaro."

Minutes later, Jeff returned with the Camaro. They loaded the last of the evidence into the trunk.

Jeff remembered the car. He rubbed his eyes and looked at his watch. "We still need to do the Ferrari."

"I thought you already checked it."

"Not really. Just gave it a once over."

Gary yawned and nodded. Jeff popped the hood open, revealing the twelve-cylinder engine with three carburetors. Gary let out a soft whistle. "Should we see if he wants to trade this for your Toyota?"

Jeff winced as he remembered Stephanie with his car. A new surge of acid flowed into his stomach. *Relax, Foster, she's only a connection.* He pushed the thought from his mind, unsure if he wanted to deal with the feelings he was experiencing. "Nothing doing, my car's an antique. It's probably worth three times this piece of junk."

"Then you won't mind if I drive it? 'Cause if we find dope in it, we'll be able to seize it."

Jeff had forgotten about the Rico law and began searching with renewed vigor.

Gary continued, "Course, if we do get it, there's no way the captain'll let us keep it. They'll sell it to fund your exorbitant salary."

"Right."

While Gary partially dismantled the engine, Jeff shifted his attention to the trunk. He pushed on the spare tire. It seemed flat. *Why would Margo be driving around with a flat tire?*

Jeff twisted off the wing nut holding it in place and

flopped the tire over. He probed against the side of the tire. To his surprise, a six-inch square of rubber folded inward like a door. Jeff pulled his hand back and the rubber door popped back into place. Two thin lines marked the opening.

The nerves in his hands tingled with energy as he mashed down the tire again. He shoved his hand through the aperture and groped around the hollow interior. At first, he felt only dusty rubber. He turned the tire on end. A familiar object collided with his hand. It felt smooth and round—like the bag in the water softener. But this one was much larger.

Jeff eagerly withdrew a two-pound plastic bag bulging with white powder. "Looks like I get to drive."

Gary jerked his head up. "Whatcha got?"

Jeff held up the prize. "A bill of sale for my new Ferrari."

Gary gave Jeff a high five. "Whoa! Check it out! I'd say Margo's definitely history. Let's see, there's about a kilo here, and with the bags you found inside . . ." Gary counted on his fingers.

Jeff saved him the mental anguish. "About two and a half pounds."

Gary packed up the cocaine and took the keys to the Camaro from Jeff. "Drive careful, that's a lot of car."

Jeff eased into the driver's seat of the Ferrari and bobbed his eyebrows. "Trust me!"

"I wish you hadn't said that."

Jeff quoted from memory, "You have the right to remain silent. Anything you say can be used against you in a court of law. You have the right to an attorney. If you cannot afford one, one will be appointed for you. You can decide at any time to stop talking. Do you understand these rights?"

Margo sat stooped over in a chair next to the table. He nodded, his eyes staring at the floor.

Jeff proceeded. "We found the stash under the hot tub and the kilo in your spare tire."

Margo visibly flinched but still stared at the floor.

"It looks like you'll be spending the rest of your life in prison."

Margo grunted with a sneer, still not looking up.

Gary pressed, "You're not getting out of this one. We've covered all the bases. You're had."

Margo's stare finally raised to Gary's eyes. "On the contrary, you're the one that doesn't understand."

"Look, man, with this much dope, you're likely to get at least fifteen years, if not life!"

Margo formed a gun with his hand and raised his finger to his own head. "Pow." Drops of sweat ran down his forehead as his lips forced a pitiful smile. "So you see, if you put me in jail, my stay will be brief. That's the way it works."

"Suicide?" Jeff asked.

"No." Margo laughed nervously and placed his palm over his throat. "No. They call it risk management."

A satisfied smile materialized on Gary's face. "So. How does it feel?" Pausing for his last statement to sink in, Gary questioned, "Who's gonna kill you?"

Margo's face was ashen grey. "I can't tell you. I'd be dead before tomorrow."

"Looks like you've got a problem."

Margo leaned forward, his attitude clearly changing. "Please. I can't go to jail."

"Guess what. You don't have a choice."

Margo gripped the edge of his chair. His knuckles turned white. "They'll kill me! You have to help me."

Gary straightened. "We don't have to do anything. You made your bed. Sleep in it."

Jeff sat down directly in front of Margo and leaned forward. "Remember me?" Face paint still covered his face.

Margo's jaw dropped as a look of recognition came over him. "Pilot?" He shook his head.

After noting his recognition of Jeff, Gary drew his attention. "Here's your only way out, the only way to live. You tell us everything we want to know—your connection, your organization, everything—and you help us bust your connect with at least five keys. In return, we let you walk."

Margo howled, "Five keys! I can't get that much. Why I—"

Jeff cut him off. "You forget. I'm an accountant, remember? I saw your records."

Margo buried his face in his hands. Silence. Finally, he raised his head. "Okay, I'll do it."

Gary said, "Fine, prove it. Who's your connection?"

"A guy named Troy Southwick. He lives in Las Vegas."

"How much and how often?"

"In the past, I only got an ounce or so. This is the first time I ever brought this much."

Gary snorted in disgust. "That's it. You're going to jail."

"Okay, okay. I average about three keys a week. I'm scheduled to pick up a delivery in Vegas on Monday. It'll be two keys."

"Okay, that gives us a few days to figure things out. Where's the records of your organization?"

"You saw everything. I don't have any records to speak of." Margo pointed at his head. "It's all up here."

Gary rolled his eyes back as Jeff folded his arms and stared at Margo. "Try again."

"Uh, I guess there is some stuff on a disk."

"Where?"

"I'll have to go get it."

Jeff punched out the words distinctly, "You will tell us where it is, and we will get it."

"There's a safety deposit box at First Security Bank downtown."

"Where's the key?"

"In my left shoe." Margo was still handcuffed, so Jeff reached down and pulled off Margo's shoe.

"Pull the heel, then twist."

Following his directions, Jeff watched as a small compartment materialized in the instep. He tipped the shoe, and the key clattered against the tile floor.

"Any ideas?" Gary said to Jeff.

Margo stood up and answered for him. "Here's what we'll do. Send me down with a hundred grand. I'll get him to make the transaction personally. I bring it back and then—"

"Sit down and shut up." Gary stared Margo back into his seat.

Jeff ignored Margo. "I could go with him. I flew commercial for over a year. Maybe I could be his pilot."

Margo nodded. "I almost always take someone down with me when I go to Vegas."

Gary shook his head. "Too risky."

Margo snapped back, "What am I supposed to do—bring him up here with five keys and a signed confession?"

Jeff cut in. "It would be the perfect cover. We could have the Vegas narcs pick up the tail."

Gary took Jeff by the arm and led him into the hall out of Margo's hearing. "Fowler would never go for it."

"Then how are we supposed to get him? If you've got a better idea, I'm all ears." Jeff waited while Gary rubbed at his chin in silence. Sensing his indecision, Jeff launched another appeal. "We could borrow a bird dog from Western States. They're always telling us how good their surveillance equipment is."

"Based on what we know about Troy Southwick, he probably has plenty of countersurveillance. What are you going to say when he finds it—'Gee whiz, I wonder how this got in here'?"

"He won't find it. We'll use the kind that shuts off automatically at lower elevations. We would only be tracked in the air, but where else can a plane go?"

Gary bit down on his lips and nodded. "Then there's the bigger question. What if Margo tells Troy?"

"No way. What's he going to say? 'Troy, you know that

pilot I brought with me? Well, actually he's an undercover cop. I hope you're not upset with me for bringing him here.'"

"What about right now? If we don't put him in jail . . ." Gary let the words hang.

"I think he's dangerous and would do anything to get out of his predicament. But we can't put him in jail, or word will get out."

"Do you think he'll run?"

Jeff pondered that thought. "I don't think so. He's already given us too much information. He'll be afraid that Troy will find him. I think the only option he has right now is to take out Troy."

"I agree, though there is one other option."

"What's that?"

"Take out us."

"True, but he'd have to get both of us at the same time, and our records. The only real chance he has at that is to get us tonight."

Gary scratched his head. "Well, I guess we'll just have to be careful."

Chapter Eight

Stephanie ran a comb through her hair and dashed on a touch of blush. As she scrutinized her face, her eyebrows furrowed in disapproval. The slender remains of a scar memorialized a run-in she'd had with a barbed-wire fence while sledding fifteen years ago. After she had made the transition from tomboy to young woman, she always made it a point to carefully conceal the scar with makeup. Later she learned that no one could see it but her—with or without makeup.

Stephanie considered her deep-blue eyes and then shifted her attention to her prominent cheekbones. It felt good to know that men noticed her.

She flushed with embarrassment and chided herself for such vain thoughts. Annoyed by some women's constant primping, she suddenly felt a bit hypocritical.

She focused on a red spot near her ear that hadn't decided if it was a mole or a freckle. "Defect," she muttered, hoping to relieve some guilt.

Stuffing a towel and sunscreen into a bag, Stephanie donned her Oakley sunglasses and headed for the door. She still had plenty of time, but she doubted her little sister would be as prepared.

It's not a date. Stephanie remembered her mother's warnings, which had begun over a decade ago, about dating non-Mormons. She rehearsed what she would tell her. "It's not like a real date. Besides, he's just a friend."

At first, she had been disappointed when Margo told her the Cessna 152 was in the shop for repairs. This meant she had to cancel the Saturday morning flight lesson with Jeff.

But then Jeff invited her to go water skiing instead and even suggested she bring her sister to staff the warning flag. *Besides, I have to return his car anyway,* as if water skiing with Jeff Spenelie really wasn't a date but merely some odd ritual connected to the borrowed car.

Jeff finished hooking up the boat to the truck just as Stephanie wheeled into the parking lot. He was thankful that Gary had loaned him both the boat and truck, though when Gary found out who Jeff was taking, his enthusiasm had waned. Gary seemed to accept it, but he reminded Jeff not to blow his cover, especially now that he would be flying to Vegas as Margo's pilot on Monday.

Until now, the thought had never occurred to Jeff that Stephanie could be LDS. But for some reason, now he wondered.

Stephanie tossed him the keys to his Toyota and flashed an enthusiastic smile. "Hi! You ready for this?"

Jeff studied her for a moment. Her baggy white pants and pullover shirt hid her well-proportioned figure. As usual, her hair looked great. He decided her hairstyle could come out of a wind tunnel and still look right. "I don't know. I've only done this a couple of times."

"Well, if you ski anything like you fly, you'll do fine."

Stephanie's seven-year-old sister peeked around the edge of the car. "Jeff, I'd like you to meet Holly. She's my favorite sister."

The young girl blushed and turned away, pressing her shoulder and cheek together. "I'm your only sister."

Jeff squatted down to Holly's height. "How was the ride?"

She shrugged an I-don't-know expression.

Stephanie turned toward the old Toyota. With hands on hips, she cocked her head. "Are you sure you want to know?"

Jeff stood next to the clunky auto and rubbed his hand over the hood. "Come on now, I don't let just anyone drive this finely tuned machine."

"Only those you want hurt?"

"Ouch!" Jeff turned to his car. "Don't listen to her. She just doesn't understand quality."

"Seriously though, I appreciate your letting me use it." She looked pensively at the rust bubbling through the fender and shrugged. "At least it's clean."

After picking up a bucket of chicken from KFC, they made the hour drive to Calamity Point in the Palisades Reservoir and began unloading the eighteen-foot turquoise ski boat. Jeff backed down the ramp while Stephanie gave directions.

"Hold it!" Stephanie yelled.

Jeff hit the brakes. "What's wrong?"

"There's some old rope caught in the prop."

They took turns trying to pull the rope out, with no success. Finally, Jeff pulled the belt from his pants and cautiously removed a razor blade from its zippered compartment. He made it a point not to let Stephanie see the handcuff key still inside the belt.

Stephanie arched her eyebrows. "You always keep a razor blade in your belt?"

"You never know when it might come in handy."

Jeff cut the rope free and backed the boat into the water. Stephanie tied it to the dock while Jeff parked Gary's truck. When he returned he picked out the pink-and-black wet suit belonging to Gary's wife and handed it to Stephanie. "You first. I want to see how this is done."

Stephanie silently accepted it and slid off her outer clothing. Underneath she wore a modest but very attractive rust-colored swimsuit. Jeff gained a new respect for her. Most of the women around the docks wore high French-cut swimsuits. But none of them were more beautiful than Stephanie.

Jeff secured Holly in a life vest and handed her the warning flag. "When she wrecks, you hold this flag up, okay?"

Holly nodded in excitement.

Jeff called out to Stephanie. "The water awaits you, me lady."

Stephanie fit one ski to her foot and left the other ski in the boat. Jeff released the tether while she made a few coils with the tow rope. She stood ready on the dock. "I'll dock-hop it."

Jeff started up the engine and putted slowly away from the dock. The throaty sound advertised the power seated in the rear of the boat. When the ski boat neared the end of the rope, Stephanie called out, "Hit it!"

The boat surged ahead as she tossed the remaining two coils into the water ahead of her. The rope snapped tight, and Stephanie stepped onto the water while leaning back slightly. Her 110 pounds seemed to make little difference as the ski pushed downward a few inches and shot across the water with its master firmly in control.

Jeff adjusted the angle of the prop and regulated the speed at 30 mph. Wasting no time, Stephanie cut back and forth, completely clearing the wake at times. Abruptly the boat surged forward, signaling that the pursuer was no longer in pursuit. The orange warning flag shot up in Holly's hand high over her head. Jeff wheeled around and pulled alongside Stephanie. "You okay?"

"I caught an edge. No big deal."

Stephanie signaled for another run. When the boat straightened, she called out, "Okay, hit it."

Jeff shoved the throttle forward and glanced over his shoulder in time to see Stephanie pop out of the water. They got up to speed and she leaned hard, forcing a wall of water taller than herself. After a while, she signaled her intention to stop. She let go of the rope and slowly coasted down into the water.

Jeff eyed Holly and with a smile flipped his wrist, reminding her to raise the flag.

"Oh!" She grabbed the flag and held it high.

"Your turn," Stephanie said as she climbed into the boat.

Jeff stared at her streaks of wet hair pressed against her shoulders, already drying in the warm sun. If she felt self-conscious, she gave no sign of it.

"All right, now you'll see a real pro in action." Jeff peeled off his shirt. His stomach flexed with anticipation, dividing his muscles into a checkerboard. "Uh, which foot should I put in front?"

Stephanie threw her head back and laughed. "I use my left in front, but some people prefer their right. I don't think it really matters."

She tossed him a life jacket. "Don't forget this."

"What I need is an electric blanket." Jeff threw himself into the reservoir with a rescue jump to keep his head above the water. "Turn up the heat!" He stuffed his right foot in the ski boot. "Okay, get me out of here."

Wasting no time, Stephanie turned the boat into position and devoured the slack in the rope.

"Hit it!"

The engine spewed water with power, dragging Jeff forward. The tip of the ski plowed through the water as if some shark had mysteriously learned to swim sideways. Then the gurgling wake revealed a mouth attached to a head desperately fighting for gasps of air. Suddenly, the shark's fin corrected itself and swam at a ninety-degree angle from the wake. Jeff clung to the rope without the ski for several yards before giving up.

Holly proudly displayed the warning flag while Stephanie circled around and pulled up next to him. In a sober tone she leaned over the edge and whispered, "Save some of the water to ski on."

Jeff swam back to his ski. "I just wanted to make you look good."

Stephanie raised her eyebrow. "How many times have you tried it on one ski?"

"Counting this one?"

Stephanie nodded.

Jeff held up his hand and started ticking off fingers. "Well, on one ski, I guess this makes . . . once. So what's the trick?"

"Drag your other foot behind you and push it into the water like a rudder. Think of it as doing a hurdle."

A moment later, Jeff tried her advice. The rope tightened while he got in a hurdler's position. He pushed the top of his left foot against the water and rose up onto the ski. Sliding his free foot into the boot, he immediately cut across the wake. He didn't have the finesse Stephanie did, but he put on a show.

On the next cut, Jeff tested the length of the ski's rudder, somersaulting twice before diving into the water head first. He took a couple more turns before they decided to have lunch.

Jeff climbed into the boat and threw on a T-shirt. They found a sandy beach, parked the boat, and pulled out the bucket from KFC.

After gulping down a couple pieces of chicken and a biscuit, Holly wandered down the beach a few hundred feet and began constructing a sand castle.

A gentle breeze from a distant shore carried the mild odor of beached seaweed mingled with decaying minnows. Stephanie sat in the sand, unconcerned that her white pants might get dirty. Wrapping her arms around her knees, she peered across the water at the mountains to the east. "It's beautiful here."

"Yes, it is. It reminds me of camping with my family." Jeff sat with his legs crossed, a few feet away. The white trunks contrasted with his tanned legs.

Stephanie wiped drying sand from her ankle. "Tell me about your family."

"Well, I have three sisters and one brother. My mother lives in Mesa."

"And your father?" Stephanie turned back to the scenery. "Uh, I don't mean to pry."

Jeff looked longingly across the water and took a deep breath. "He died when I was eleven."

"I'm sorry." Stephanie leaned over and put her hand on his shoulder.

"That's okay." Jeff closed his eyes and took another breath. "He drowned saving my sisters and me."

They sat in silence for a moment. Stephanie broke the quiet. "What happened?"

Jeff hesitated. "We were forced off the road into a river by a truck. My dad and me and my two little sisters were in the car." Jeff paused for a moment and then looked into Stephanie's eyes. "The car was almost full of water, and I lost it. I was in a complete panic. I remember this strong arm pulling me through the window and pushing me up toward the surface. It was kind of dark, but then I saw my sister pop up next to me. My dad . . . he came up and shouted, 'Where's Becky?' That's my other sister." Jeff glanced down the beach. "She was about Holly's age."

He cleared his throat. "Anyway, he took a deep breath and went back down. I dragged Sheri to the bank and waited. It seemed like forever and then Becky came up. I pulled her to the bank and waited. I wasn't a very good swimmer at the time. We all screamed out 'Dad! Dad!' sitting there on the bank holding each other." Jeff's head dropped as he ran his fingers through the sand. "But . . . he never came up."

Both of them were silent for a long time. Finally Stephanie spoke. "That must have been tough."

"Yes, it was." Then, sitting up straighter, "So here I've monopolized the whole conversation. Tell me about your family."

Stephanie gave his shoulder a soft squeeze. Then she leaned back and rested her hands against the sand. "I have five brothers and one sister. I'm the oldest and Holly is the youngest."

She's got to be LDS. Jeff gave her a nod to continue.

"I was raised more or less in America, most recently in Mountain Home. My father was stationed at the air force base. He retired last year and is now a consultant."

"So what brings you to Idaho Falls?"

Jeff noticed a hint of distress on Stephanie's face. "I moved here because of a guy."

At first Jeff flattered himself that somehow she referred to him, but then she continued. "We were engaged to be married."

Jeff blushed. "So what happened?"

Stephanie's voice turned bitter. "He was killed by a drunk driver a couple years ago."

Jeff didn't know what to say, but now he understood at least part of the reason she took such a strong stand against legalizing drugs.

They both seemed content to bask in the noon sun without speaking. Stephanie was the first to break the silence.

"Do you ever wonder what it will be like after you die?"

Jeff fought his old missionary instincts and maintained his undercover role. He wondered how he would ever tell her about his true identity. "Yeah, I think about it all the time, especially when I'm flying with you."

Stephanie tossed a fistful of sand at him. "I thought you did that 'cause you're a thrill seeker."

Jeff nodded in agreement. "It's a thrill, all right."

Stephanie's smile turned thoughtful. "But don't you ever wonder what comes next?"

He thought about his mission in Peru for the LDS church and ventured cautiously, "I believe there must be something."

Then Stephanie took him completely by surprise.

"Would you like to go to church with me tomorrow?"

Jeff stammered, "Uh, what church is that?"

"The Church of Jesus Christ of Latter-day Saints."

"Oh, you mean the Mormons?"

"Have you heard much about them?"

Jeff flushed uncomfortably. He wanted to tell her he was a member. He wanted to hug her and tell her how glad he was that she was a member, that he had a firm testimony. But he knew he couldn't. At least, not until the case with Margo was finished. "Yeah, I've heard some things."

Deciding to make the most of it, Jeff continued, "Are you going to have lots of husbands?"

Stephanie giggled. "No, that's wives, not husbands."

"You mean if I go to your church then I get to have lots of wives?"

Stephanie feigned offense. "Get to? You'd be lucky to find one that will have you!"

Jeff fell back onto the sand groaning, his hands clasped tightly over his heart. Stephanie grabbed the empty chicken bucket and scooped it full of water. As Jeff realized what was happening, he charged, trying to reach her before she could bring the bucket up, but it was too late. The chicken bucket blasted a punishing wall of water squarely at Jeff's chest. As the water hit, he accelerated his pace and snatched her off her feet. Twisting as if preparing for a shot put, Jeff flung her toward the water. At the last second, Stephanie gripped his shirt and dragged him after her. Laughing, they both crawled onto the beach and collapsed to catch their breaths.

Holly ran down the beach toward them with an eager smile. Jeff grabbed her by a leg and one arm and swung her over the water. She squealed in delight. He set her back on the beach safe and dry. "If all Mormon women are this tough, then I guess I better see what this is about."

Stephanie flashed a wide smile, drops of water glistening on her face. "Pick me up tomorrow at 8:45."

"Can we make it next week?"

"Sure."

"Okay, a week from tomorrow at 8:45."

On the way home, Jeff's thoughts turned to Margo and Troy Southwick. He felt that familiar feeling, the tight knot, return to his stomach. He worried about what might happen with Margo, but right now, he worried more about what Stephanie's reaction would be when he told her the whole truth.

Chapter Nine

Jeff adjusted the tinted visor to block the late afternoon sun as the Cessna 310 twin-engine plane descended into Las Vegas. Hundreds of tiny blue specks dotted the ground below them.

Jeff whistled softly. "Check out the swimming pools!"

Margo appraised him curiously. "Haven't you ever been here before?"

Jeff blushed and tried to cover his naivete. "I drove here once a few years ago, but I've never flown in."

Captain Fowler had accepted Jeff's proposal to be Margo's pilot only after the Vegas narcs assured him they would maintain constant surveillance. Apparently, they already had a team working on Troy Southwick.

The Cessna taxied down the runway to Southwick's private hangar. Jeff applied the brake for the last time as he noticed a bright red Mercedes pull up. An attractive brunette wearing leather boots with a matching leather miniskirt and an expensive low-cut blouse stepped out from the driver's seat and waved at Margo as he and Jeff climbed out of the plane. "Dennis!"

"Tracy." Margo smiled.

The way she dressed reminded Jeff of the first time he had visited Las Vegas. He had been stunned by all the glamour and flash of the women. But when he had looked closer, what looked attractive initially turned out to be nothing more than plain women exposing more of their bodies.

He decided that in Tracy's case, it wasn't just flash. Jeff briefly wondered if she had any physical defects he couldn't see. He suspected not. She was beautiful, and she gloried in it. He quickly censored his thoughts and turned to Margo.

Tracy gave Margo an embrace that let Jeff know they shared more than just a passing friendship. She turned to Jeff. "And who is this?"

"He's one of my pilots." Then, lowering his voice for emphasis, "One of my most trusted pilots."

Tracy nodded with understanding as she studied Jeff. Then, leering provocatively, she asked Margo, "Are you going to share him?"

Jeff felt his ears burn red. His gaze dropped to the ground and then returned to Tracy. She caught his discomfort and watched with pleasure as he stood flustered.

Margo spoke with the same sad smile that had accompanied his resignation to work with Jeff. "Perhaps, my dear, perhaps."

On the drive over to Troy's, Margo and Tracy exchanged some small talk. To Jeff's relief, none of it involved him. He let the chill from the air conditioner envelop his body. The Mercedes provided a welcome reprieve from the dry desert heat.

Jeff mentally noted the street sign, Merida Drive, as they approached a long row of palm trees positioned just inside a twelve-foot concrete fence embedded with decorative rock. Halfway down, a large iron gate with a security booth confronted visitors.

They pulled next to the booth, facing the gate. Jeff's pulse picked up. The guard nodded at Tracy and triggered the gate opener. After another one hundred yards of manicured gardens, lawns, and ponds, the Mercedes stopped in front of an extravagantly adorned house constructed of adobe.

A doorman with muscles filling a tailored suit escorted them through a solarium and into a greeting room. Jeff studied the doorman for the weapon he knew he wouldn't see. A sudden panic began to well up inside him. *Maybe they already know. Maybe they're all just playing along until the right moment.*

The doorman seated them in overstuffed chairs. An assortment of nuts and fresh shrimp lay on a glass table in front of him. Not waiting for an invitation, Margo dug into the pecans and motioned for Jeff to do the same. Tracy sat opposite Jeff with her legs crossed elegantly.

Jeff glanced across the table to her. She stared at him with salacious eyes. He fought the impulse to look away and matched her stare with defiance. She winked at him. Color again flooded his cheeks. With great decisiveness, he snatched a shrimp by the tail, held it out for inspection, and popped it into his mouth.

Crunch. Jeff realized that he'd neglected to peel off the shell. He continued to munch on the crusted mess in his mouth, unwilling to admit defeat.

Drawn like a magnet, Jeff's eyes raised to Tracy's. She gave him a knowing smile. He chastised himself for playing her little game and tried to focus his attention on a vase on the table.

The doorman returned to the room following a man in his early thirties. Jeff copied Margo's and Tracy's example and stood up.

"Troy, how are you?"

Troy took Margo's hand warmly. "Business is favorable." His blond hair and brilliant white teeth contrasted handsomely with his year-round tan.

Troy turned to Jeff expectantly. Jeff nodded a sideways glance at Margo, but it was Tracy who did the introduction. "Troy, this is Jeff, Margo's pilot."

Troy raised one eyebrow and looked at Margo.

"He's my most trusted business associate," added Margo.

With his easy smile, Troy nodded and gave Jeff a firm hand-shake. "I hope you enjoy your stay. Please let me know if there is anything I can do to make you more comfortable."

Jeff forced a smile. He remembered a DEA instructor telling him that some major drug dealers liked to appear well bred, as if big money had always been a part of their life.

"Please, sit down." Troy motioned for the servant, who poured wine into small glasses.

Jeff courteously accepted it. *Great, Foster. Now what are you going to do with this?*

Troy raised his glass, interrupting Jeff's thoughts. "I propose a toast."

Jeff's throat tightened.

Troy surveyed the room. His eyes landed on Jeff. "To a prosperous business and trustworthy friends."

Margo nodded in approval. "I'm all for that."

With the soft tinkling of glass, everyone raised their cups. Jeff sealed his lips tightly against the glass and feigned a sip. He'd never drunk an alcoholic beverage in his life and he wasn't about to start.

A large jade plant surrounded by brick stood inches from Jeff's chair. Keeping his eye on the doorman, Jeff rested his arm on the brick. Then he nonchalantly poured his drink into the bark-covered soil surrounding the plant. No one seemed to notice.

Troy stood up and faced Jeff. "Tracy needs to run an errand. With Margo's approval, I hope you wouldn't mind escorting her?"

What are you up to? Jeff glanced nervously at Margo. *No, he won't turn back now—not after leading me to Troy.* "Fine with me."

"Let's meet back here at nine o'clock," Troy said. "That

will give Tracy enough time to show you some of the sights in Vegas."

"Okay," Jeff responded with a little less than enthusiasm.

"Hey, don't be so excited," Tracy said.

Jeff stammered, "No, really, I mean it's no problem, I, uh, think it sounds great." Jeff didn't know if he was more worried about leaving Margo or being alone with Tracy.

Tracy slipped her arm through Jeff's and began escorting him back to the car. Just before they got to the car, Jeff pointed to Tracy's other hand. "Are those the car keys?"

Tracy looked puzzled. "Yes, why?"

Jeff snatched the keys and escorted her to the passenger side. "I'll drive, you navigate."

For the first time since Jeff arrived, Tracy looked flustered. "Okay, whatever."

Margo could barely see Troy through the steam.

"I think I'm about ready for the pool again," Troy said.

Margo pushed open the redwood door. "Yeah, me too."

Settling into the warmth of the spa, Troy set the timer on the jets for fifteen minutes. Margo stared down into the swirling foam with his back against a jet of water.

As if sensing Margo's unspoken resentments, Troy said, "You need to buy into some other businesses. That way you can live better without attracting attention."

Margo shrugged it off. "Hunnington's been working on a package for me."

"What's eating you, Margo? You seem a little out of it. You're not using, are you?"

"I've got this bug I've been fighting."

Troy seemed to accept his answer and moved on. "Speaking of being sick, my pilot is in the hospital with appendicitis. How would you like to fly me over to Newport Beach tomorrow? It's a new contact, and I could use your help."

A subtle smile crept over Margo's face, a smile too small for anyone to see. Margo acted disappointed. "I'm grounded."

"What?"

"I'm grounded. I flunked the last physical. That's why I brought Jeff with me."

Troy leaned back against the side with his arms hooked over the edges and paused thoughtfully. "So what's this Jeff like anyway?"

"He's good—real good."

"Can you trust him?"

Again, an almost invisible smile. "If it wasn't for him, I'd be in a whole different world."

"What do you mean?"

"The guy flies great and makes no mistakes. He seems to have an uncanny way of knowing when a deal isn't right. I swear he's kept me out of jail. Yup, trust him completely."

"I'll use him tomorrow."

"You're not going to steal him, are you?"

"You can come along if you want to."

"If you don't mind, I'll stay here." Then Margo added quickly, "With Tracy."

"Fine, then it's settled." Troy rubbed his chin and developed a smirk on his face. "Depending on what happens tonight."

"What did you have in mind?"

Troy pushed his wet hair back and locked his fingers together behind his head. "Tracy."

Margo nodded his head and grinned. "I understand."

Jeff seated Tracy at the table. His manners seemed out of place in the smoke-filled room. Even the Mercedes parked outside didn't fit the atmosphere. A single sign plastered across the front of the business outside simply read "Jackie's."

The bar counter formed the nucleus of the room. It was

surrounded by scattered tables. The outer layer consisted of slot machines lining the walls.

A cocktail waitress appeared at their table. "What can I get ya, honey?" Her already too-long legs were accented by high-heeled shoes and a skimpy miniskirt.

Tracy didn't hesitate. "Coors Light."

Jeff quickly added, "Bud . . . no, make it a Heineken."

Tracy called after the waitress, "We're expecting two more. Forget the Coors and bring a pitcher of Bud, and while you're at it we'll take a basket of chicken wings." Tracy turned to Jeff. "You'll love their chicken. The sauce makes it."

The waitress shifted her attention to Jeff. "You still want the Heineken?"

His eyes narrowed at Tracy. "Yes."

They were alone in the bar except for a group of men gathered around one of the slot machines, shouting vulgar remarks.

After feeding several quarters into the machine, one of the men started watching Tracy. He jabbed his burly companion in the ribs. The two of them began walking toward their table. Jeff stiffened. *What am I doing here?*

The burly man stood with his arms folded, glaring down at Jeff. The other man planted both hands on the table and leaned over Tracy. "Hey, babe, how'd you like to join us for a little blackjack?" The odor of beer permeated the air.

Before she had a chance to respond, Jeff said calmly, "She's not interested."

Tracy raised one finger. "I'll speak for myself. Maybe I am interested."

Jeff's mouth opened in surprise.

Tracy continued, "Why don't you two gentlemen have a seat and we'll discuss it?"

The intruders eyed Jeff coolly as he sat speechless. Then Tracy broke into a wide smile. "Jeff, I'd like you to meet two of my friends, Barry and Reed."

Laughter erupted from everyone except Jeff. Finally, Jeff leaned back in his chair and folded his arms to hide his trembling hands. He grinned. "Cute."

The long-legged waitress reappeared with their order. The others guzzled the pitcher of beer while Jeff pretended to drink from the green bottle of Heineken. Painfully aware that his bottle was still full, Jeff excused himself to the bathroom.

Once there, he poured the beer into the urinal—a trick he'd learned from Gary. Except for the suds, Heineken looked clear. Gary had taught him to mix it with water as a way to keep from getting drunk. Jeff took Gary's idea one step further, dumping the whole thing and refilling it with water. Then he added a drop of soap to recreate the suds.

Too much soap. He dumped the sudsy water and filled it again. A thin layer of suds rimmed the glass.

When Jeff returned to the table, his heart jumped. A fresh release of acid boiled into his stomach. Barry, the smaller of the two, was drawing lines of cocaine on a mirror. Barry leaned over the mirror with a rolled-up twenty-dollar bill. Reed followed.

He pushed the mirror to Jeff. "Your turn."

Jeff steadied his hands on his knees. "No thanks, I never use while I'm on business." *No backup. Think, Foster.*

Tracy nudged him. "Lighten up. This is how we do business here."

He shook his head. "I never let myself get messed up when I'm out of town." Even as he said it, he realized how dumb it sounded.

Barry leaned forward. "Look, man, if you wanna do business, have at it."

Jeff rested his left hand on the table and hooked his right thumb on his pants pocket. His face turned to stone. "I don't mix coke with business." *This is getting bad. Take control.*

Reed produced a switchblade and began cleaning the dirt from behind his nails. Barry stuck his finger in Jeff's face. "You want our business? This is business. Now do it!"

Tracy placed her hand on Jeff's arm. A touch of nervousness showed through her voice. "Just do it."

Jeff sighed. *Fine, now we'll play it my way.* In a blur of motion, he pulled his hand from behind his back and stuck a pistol into Reed's left ear. His voice was steady. "Put the knife down and live."

Reed obeyed.

Jeff picked up the knife with his left hand and drove it into the table, giving it a quick twist that snapped the blade in two pieces. He grabbed Tracy's arm while still pressing the gun to Reed's head. "Come on, Tracy, we're leaving." Then he backed away to the door and out to the Mercedes. They were several blocks from Jackie's before he put away his gun.

"Okay, what's going on?"

Tracy looked at Jeff naively. "What do you mean? Other than the fact that you just blew a perfectly good deal and nearly got us killed, nothing's going on."

"Troy's not going to send me out with you to make some two-ounce deal in a dump like that. What's going on?"

Tracy just shrugged her shoulders. "You'll have to ask him."

Jeff's jaw tightened. "Count on it."

Chapter Ten

"Orange County Airport, this is Cessna November two niner three zero with information bravo requesting landing instructions."

"Roger, two niner three zero, maintain two thousand feet. You are number three behind Delta six zero, over."

Again, Jeff found himself piloting a twin engine Cessna, but this time it belonged to Troy Southwick. *Margo is right. This is the opportunity of a lifetime.*

Troy sat in the copilot's seat. His bodyguard sat behind Jeff. Troy referred to him as Sidney, his "travel companion."

A thin smile grew over Jeff's lips. The only Sidney he ever knew was a wimp in grade school. But this Sidney's six-foot four-inch frame looked too short for his stocky build.

Sidney carried a black briefcase that looked puny in his ample hands. Troy called it "the papers," but Jeff felt sure it contained cocaine.

Jeff reflected on the events of the past day. The Vegas narcs had never made contact with him, nor did he have an opportunity to phone Captain Fowler. He thought about trying to slip away to make a call, but he didn't want to risk detection. He tried to forget he was an undercover police officer, forget about trying to gather evidence. The only goal now was to get through the ordeal safely.

Jeff eyed the needle of the altimeter as it slowly wound backwards. *Fowler wouldn't have let me go anyway. Hard enough to get to Vegas.*

He began plotting a plausible excuse to give Fowler when he returned. *I didn't have a choice. They kidnapped me. You don't approve? Oh, I'm sorry. It will never happen again.*

Jeff stretched his neck and looked toward Troy, who was immersed in a calculator and planner. Jeff caught glimpses of his notes, but the writing was too small to see clearly. He wondered if it contained evidence that would someday put Troy away.

Troy glanced up from his calculations. "How are we doing?"

"Turning final now."

Troy didn't fit Jeff's image of a drug lord. He looked and acted more like the CEO of a major corporation.

The Orange County Airport lay opposite the morning sun. Beyond it loomed the Pacific Ocean on the horizon, hinting of a vast wasteland hoping to swallow up the un-prepared.

Jeff turned for the final approach.

"So where do you think you'll be in five years?"

The question startled Jeff. "What do you mean?"

"You impress me as someone who knows where he's going. That can be good, depending on how you get there, or it can be incredibly dangerous."

"How so?" Jeff responded casually.

"Ambition must be tempered with loyalty. If you're loyal, you can go anywhere."

"Loyal to what?"

"Not what—" Troy paused for emphasis. "Who."

Jeff wondered silently who Troy was loyal to.

"Are you loyal, Jeff?"

Jeff decided Troy would make a great bishop if he weren't such a slime. "Yes, I guess I am."

"I believe you are loyal. The only question is to who."

Jeff tried to hide the nervousness he felt as he pondered Troy's insight. He tried to focus on landing the plane.

A black limousine, complete with a driver, waited at a private hangar. Troy spoke privately with the driver and then returned to the plane. "Jeff, if you don't mind, I would like you to be the driver. This man says he'll be happy to watch the plane for us."

"Sure." *Yes, I mind. I'd rather stay here. Come on, Foster, don't be a coward. This is the opportunity of a lifetime, remember!*

"Would you mind wearing his jacket? He says it's company policy."

"No problem." *What's he up to?*

They pulled away from the airport with Sidney and Troy in the back seat. "Thanks, Jeff. This is an unproven business contact. Even though Sidney is very capable, I like the idea of extra assistance if it is required."

So that's it, Jeff realized. *He's establishing a new dealer and wants extra protection in case it's a rip-off.* Tracy probably told him about what happened in the bar last night.

Rip-offs were a far greater risk than getting busted. He remembered Gary telling him about a local dealer who drove to Portland with two kilos of cocaine, hoping to turn over a big profit. He was gunned down by his would-be dealers. The local newspapers called it a drive-by shooting and went on to describe how one of their hometown boys was victimized in the big city.

"Pull into that used car lot."

Jeff turned into Griffin Motors. Jeff and Sidney stood in the heat beside the air-conditioned car while Troy spoke to a salesman.

After some unheard words, the salesman handed a set of keys to Troy. Troy then motioned for Jeff and Sidney to come over. Speaking to the salesman, Troy handed the keys to Jeff. "If my driver likes it, you've got a deal."

The three of them climbed into the Ford Taurus and

left the limousine with the salesman. Following Troy's directions, a fifteen-minute drive took them to Fashion Plaza in Newport Beach.

Fashion Plaza stood two stories high and consisted of dozens of small shops. They were interconnected by open cobblestone walks that reminded Jeff of a European village with alleys for roads. The entire borough connected like spokes on a wheel. At the hub, a food court overlooked a large fountain that sent forth bursts of water intermittently.

Troy motioned for them to be seated at a table near the fountain on the second story. Jeff watched below as a little girl reached her hand into the fountain. The fountain shot up and the girl ran away squealing in delight. This process was repeated several times before her mother led her to other adventures.

Looking down one of the cobblestone walks, Jeff watched as an acne-faced man with long black hair greased into a ponytail approached them. He wore a thin, black, New York–cut suit with a white T-shirt and white shoes. A Nike gym bag hung from his arm. For the first time, Jeff noticed that Sidney was no longer carrying the black briefcase.

Troy stood up and greeted the man. "Hello, I'm Troy. These are my companions, Sidney and Jeff."

The stranger's eyes darted back and forth. "You got the merchandise?"

Troy offered the stranger his easy, relaxed smile with forced patience. "Everything is in order. As soon as you present the necessary paperwork, I believe we can transact business."

"Paperwork? What paperwork?"

Troy sighed, his patience beginning to wear thin. "Cash, show me the cash."

"Uh, yeah, the paperwork."

The long-haired man cautiously looked around him. He parted the gym bag, exposing several packets of fifty- and twenty-dollar bills. Troy reached toward the bag.

Ponytail snatched the bag shut. "No way, man. First I want to see the cola."

Troy turned to ice. "As agreed, after I see the cash, we'll transact business at the approved location. That is where I will have it."

"Okay, you saw the cash, so let's go."

"I saw what looked like cash."

"Look, dude, you saw the money. If you want to deal, meet me at the turnout at twelve o'clock." Without giving Troy time to respond, he left.

Troy turned to Jeff. "What do you think?"

Jeff hid his trembling hands under the table. "Maybe there's nothing in the middle of those packets of money. Maybe it wasn't even real cash on the outside. Could be a rip-off." *Maybe I never should have become a cop.*

Troy faced Sidney. "Well?"

Sidney spoke for the first time Jeff could remember. "He's just a punk—a little nervous, that's all."

Troy sized up Sidney and grinned. "Yes. I guess I'd be nervous too if I were him looking at you."

Jeff looked at his watch. "It's almost twelve now."

Troy looked unconcerned. "I believe you're still on Idaho Falls time."

Jeff shrugged with embarrassment and corrected his watch.

"Gentlemen, shall we enjoy a bite to eat while we're here?"

Stephanie's hands flew across the word processor. Pausing, she looked up at the clock. *Twelve-thirty—that should give me plenty of time to finish it before lunch.*

Returning her attention to the keyboard, she began the spell check.

"*Effluviate?*" Stephanie mumbled to herself, "Where does he come up with these words? It's probably not even in the dictionary." Grabbing her Webster's desk dictionary, she started thumbing through the *E* section. "*Effluence, effluvium,* hum . . . close." Setting aside the desktop dictionary, she lugged the unabridged dictionary onto her desk with both hands. "*Effluent, effluvial, effluviate!*" Quickly she scanned the meaning: "To emit or throw off effluvium." Then checking under *effluvium:* "1. a real or supposed outflow in the form of a vapor or stream of invisible particles. 2. a disagreeable or noxious vapor or odor."

Stephanie read the document to herself again. "*Thus, when Mr. Scoresby began to verbally effluviate, my client had no option, but to—*"

Mr. Hunnington strolled into the office. "Hi, Steph. You gonna make it?"

Stephanie slammed the dictionary shut, nearly knocking it off her desk. Then, blushing, "I'm just finishing the spell check."

"You mean to tell me that you, Stephanie Evans, make spelling errors?"

"No, of course not. I just run a periodic check to make sure the machine is functioning properly."

"Good, just leave it on my desk when you're finished." Mr. Hunnington sat on the edge of her desk. "Are you still in the chartering business?"

"Yes, if you supply the plane."

"We just lost a pilot to Delta. We might be calling you for help if you don't mind."

"Are you kidding? I'd love to."

"Good, I'll let you know."

After Mr. Hunnington left, Stephanie leaned back in her chair. A strange feeling started working in her stomach. It was as if something was wrong—dreadfully wrong. The last time she had had this feeling was over two years ago, just before the accident.

She picked up the phone and called her mother. A mature woman's voice sounded on the line. Stephanie responded, "Hello, Mom?"

"Is that you, Stephanie?"

"Yes. Is everything okay?"

"Everything is fine, dear. How are you doing?"

"Fine."

"Are you still dating that young man you told me about—the one you were teaching to fly?"

Stephanie's heart followed the action from her stomach. "Yeah, Mom."

"Do you think that's wise, dear, him being a nonmember?"

"He's going to church with me next Sunday." The feelings inside her intensified. "Look, Mom, I just wanted to see how things were going. I have to go now, okay?"

"All right, love you."

"Love you too. Good-bye, Mom."

Stephanie hung up the phone. Her brow furrowed. She shook her head in silent prayer. *Please, Heavenly Father, not again.*

Stephanie tried to push the thoughts from her mind. She glanced at the clock and spoke aloud, "One o'clock, time for lunch." But she didn't feel like eating.

She sat back in her chair. *Why do I like him anyway? He's not even a member of the Church.* She stood and tried to force a smile. *It's probably nothing.* But the feeling persisted.

Stephanie walked over to the window. She absently watched an old man cane his way down the sidewalk. Her thoughts were far away. *Jeff Spenelie, where are you?*

Jeff gazed out across the ocean. The sun beat down on him, leaving no shadow. "So do you think he'll come?"

Troy leaned against the Taurus. "He'll be here. It was in his eyes."

"What was in his eyes?"

"The greed." Looking back at Sidney, Troy tapped his fingers nervously. "He'll be here."

They were parked at a dead-end road at a turnout overlooking the ocean. Seventy feet of rock and an occasional bush clung to the cliff between them and the sandy beach below. A gentle breeze helped cool Jeff's perspiration-soaked shirt.

Then he felt it. A heavy sensation above his stomach. Jeff looked around him, surveying the landscape 360 degrees. Nothing. The sensation persisted, a foreboding that Jeff had learned not to ignore.

A dark blue Cavalier motored up the road toward them. Jeff recognized the passenger as the ponytailed man at Fashion Plaza.

Sidney turned to Jeff with an I-told-you-they'd-come expression. Even Troy seemed too confident.

The car stopped thirty feet away, turned at a slight angle to protect the driver. It reminded Jeff of the way patrol officers park during a traffic stop, the car and door providing a shield. It worked great for the driver, but didn't leave any protection for the passenger.

The ponytailed man stepped out of the car and glanced over his right shoulder. He stooped back into the car and nodded. Then the driver opened his door and stood by the car.

Jeff didn't like the way the driver seemed to be using the door as a shield. Instinctively, Jeff stepped next to the Taurus for better cover.

The ponytailed man walked up to Troy—this time without the gym bag. "Let's see what you got."

Troy folded his arms. "Where's the money?"

"You saw the money. Now where's the cola?"

Troy shrugged his arms and motioned for Sidney to bring the briefcase. Sidney opened it on the hood of the Taurus, exposing several tightly wrapped bags of cocaine.

Ponytail retrieved a small pocketknife and a plastic test kit with three ampules inside.

Jeff studied the plastic pouch. *Scott Reagent Modified Test—same one we use.*

Ponytail stabbed the knife into one of the packets of cocaine and tapped a small measure of white powder into the plastic pouch. He popped the first ampule and shook the kit gently. The acid turned blue. Thirty seconds later, he broke the second ampule. Instantly a blue flash surged through the liquid and it turned pink. He broke the last ampule and watched blue separate from pink and rise to the top. A big smile grew across his face.

"And the money?" Troy directed patiently.

"Yeah, the money," the man smiled with new confidence. A confidence that relaxed everyone, even Sidney. Everyone except Jeff, who now sensed that something was wrong. Dreadfully wrong.

Chapter Eleven

A sharp crack pierced the salty air. A look of profound shock covered Sidney's face as he watched a tiny red spot on his white shirt swell to a large disk.

"Rip-off!" Jeff yelled as he dove to the ground, knocking Troy with him. Simultaneously, the driver of the other car produced a Tech 9 and directed a shower of bullets in Sidney's direction.

Sidney jerked out his .45 automatic, firing two shots into the driver's neck and head. Unaware the first shot had come from an unseen sniper, Sidney stiffened and fell forward like a falling tree.

The hostile driver collapsed backward, spraying bullets harmlessly into the air while the ponytailed bandit ducked behind his car to await for the massacre's end.

Another crack from a rifle sent Jeff and Troy scurrying for cover behind their car.

Jeff's training took over as he caught a glimpse of shiny metal only a hundred feet away. "Bolt action," Jeff whispered to Troy. "Too long to reload. Next time he fires I'll take him. You cover the other one."

Now Jeff was propelled into a world he understood and was expertly prepared for—a firefight. Tearing off the limousine driver's jacket he was wearing, Jeff gingerly set it on top of the car. The rifle rang out again, this time punching a neat hole through the jacket.

Almost before the bullet left the jacket, Jeff leaped on top of the car for a clear shot. He quickly identified his target and fired a burst of three shots. The second two found their target.

The only threat left was Ponytail, hiding behind his car. Before they could take action, he yelled out, "I give up, man! Don't shoot."

Jeff barked out a succession of orders. "Put your weapons down and walk out backwards with your hands over your head." Realizing he sounded like a cop, he added awkwardly, "Or I'll blow your face off!"

The outlaw complied.

Jeff searched him while Troy went to the back of the car where Ponytail had been hiding. He came back with a sawed-off shotgun. As if lecturing a naughty child, Troy sneered at Ponytail, "Were you going to use this on me?"

Looking down at Sidney's bullet-ridden body, Troy ordered Ponytail to the edge of the cliff. "Now you need to fly."

Jeff's eyes widened as he watched Troy raise the shotgun. His mind screamed too late as his body twisted toward Ponytail.

The blast of the shotgun caught Ponytail squarely in the face, causing him to somersault twice before hitting the beach below.

Jeff whirled around to Troy, gun ready. "Wh—"

Not seeing Jeff, Troy peered over the edge and spoke in sarcastic wonder, "Fool, thought he could fly."

Jeff stood dumbfounded. *Murder . . . I'm an eyewitness to murder.* He quickly ran his options through his head. *I can make an arrest right here and now. This will be better than any drug charge. Or I can keep playing along and we can arrest him later. But the physical evidence . . .*

Jeff decided that now was the time. He gripped the handle on his pistol and took a step toward Troy. Warning bells went off in the back of his brain. He paused.

A second later, a car squealed around the corner. Jeff

pivoted with his gun. Troy held his hand up. "They're with us."

Four men armed with automatic weapons raced to Troy's side. Troy walked up to the leader and slapped him across the cheek. "You fool! You were supposed to have a sniper in place."

The leader stuttered, red faced. "We did—"

"Then they had a counter sniper." Troy pivoted on one foot and snatched the briefcase from the hood of the car. "Send in a cleanup crew immediately. I want absolutely no traces left."

The leader nodded respectfully. "Understood."

Jeff's heart sank. *The physical evidence—soon to be gone, and there's nothing I can do about it.* He surveyed the scene before him and felt his knees go weak as the events of the last five minutes caught up with him. *So much death.* Unable to contain his emotions any longer, Jeff dropped to his knees and vomited until there was nothing left.

Troy watched with amusement. "First time?"

Jeff nodded.

Troy slapped Jeff on the back. "You saved my life." Then, hesitating, "I owe you."

But there were no tears. No tears for Sidney, his trusted bodyguard. No tears for the others. Dark clouds hovered over the ocean's surface as if summoned to the grisly site.

"Rip-offs can be more dangerous than the feds." Jeff was jerked back to reality by Troy's voice. Troy picked up the black briefcase and put it into the trunk of the car. "Let's go."

The numbness he felt began to wear off. An idea crept into Jeff's mind. In spite of the fact that all the physical evidence of Ponytail's murder would be destroyed, Jeff had an incredible opportunity. He had saved Troy's life in a shoot-out and had won his confidence. Perhaps he could get Troy's connection.

Either way, time was on his side. He could always do another deal with Troy with probably more dope.

He would wait.

Jeff glanced at the Tech 9 driver. Something caught his eye, and he examined the driver closer by turning his body over. An exit wound came from his chest. Jeff studied the surrounding countryside.

"What's wrong?"

Jeff decided to keep the information to himself. "Nothing."

On the way to pick up the limousine, no word was said about what had happened. As far as Jeff could tell from Troy's demeanor, Sidney never existed.

Later, after they were in the air, Troy asked casually, "So how would you like to work for me? I could use your talent."

"I work for Margo," said Jeff matter-of-factly. The discomfort he had felt with bending the truth had long since vanished.

"But if you weren't working for Dennis, would you be interested in working with me?"

"Sure."

"I'll pay you twice as much as he's paying you."

"No."

Troy waited, expecting more. Then he grew impatient. "What do you mean, no? You don't know what I can do for you."

Jeff smiled. It was obvious that Troy wasn't in the habit of being told no. "I work for Margo." Then Jeff lightened up. "I really would like to work with you, Troy, but I couldn't do it without Margo's blessing."

Troy smiled. "That's what I like about you."

Beep beep . . . beep beep . . . beep beep . . . Jeff looked up just in time to see a massive yellow tractor backing over him. He yelled, but there was no noise. Then, as soon as it had appeared, it vanished. Anesthetized, now all he could see were numbers, big red numbers—6:00. Then the periodic beeping returned. Reality enveloped him as his hand came crashing down on the snooze button of his alarm clock.

It felt good to be in his own bed. *Okay, get up, Foster.* Jeff rubbed his eyes. *Okay, on the count of three: one, two . . . maybe just ten more minutes. Uh-uh, get up now, you slug.* The memory of dropping off Margo at the airport last night slowly came into focus. His full memory returned and Jeff bolted upright. *Troy . . . the firefight.*

Nausea surged through his stomach as he remembered the shots he fired into the sniper. *It was justified. He tried to kill me.* He shook his head and looked into the mirror. He felt different but didn't have time to analyze it.

He cleared it from his mind and dashed into the shower. *You've got a lot of explaining to do. Maybe even some job hunting after you get done talking to the captain.*

Shifting into high gear, Jeff gulped down a glass of orange juice and a bowl of granola. As he headed out the door, the phone rang. "Hello?"

"Foster?"

"Yeah."

"This is Captain Fowler. Why didn't you report when you got in last night?"

"It was late and I thought—"

"We've got company."

"Who?"

"Drag your tail down here and find out."

"Yes sir, I'll be right there."

"We'll be in my office." Click.

Jeff groaned. Visions of the FBI waiting for him with an arrest warrant for drug dealing and homicide swam through his brain. He pushed the Camaro faster than usual, wanting to get it over with. The dull ache in his stomach threatened to become an ulcer.

Jeff tapped on the captain's door gingerly. A short man wearing wire-rimmed glasses and a dark blue suit opened the door. Captain Fowler sat behind his desk with his arms folded. "Come in." Gary sat next to the door.

Jeff briefly turned his head and saw two other men sitting in the office. His head jerked back to the men. *Reed and Barry from the bar in Vegas.*

Reed smiled broadly. "I want a new knife."

The wire-rimmed man took over. "I'm Special Agent Empy with the United States Drug Enforcement Agency, and I believe you've already met detectives Goldberg and Denning."

Barry extended his hand. "Barry Denning. This is my partner, Reed Goldberg, Las Vegas Narcotics Division."

Jeff sputtered, "You and him, cops? If I had known, I wouldn't have—"

Reed interrupted, "Don't worry about it. I'll be more careful next time."

"Yeah," Barry grinned sarcastically. "We learned not to mess with the Idaho Falls Narcotics Division."

Jeff's mind raced back to the night at the bar. "But what about the cocaine?"

"It was just Procaine, a mild—and legal—stimulant."

"But why?"

"Credibility," responded Reed. "As far as Tracy is concerned, we're the last ones in the world that she needs to worry about getting busted from."

"But wouldn't she have realized that it was Procaine instead of the real thing?"

"Hers was the real thing."

"And mine?" Jeff asked.

Barry nodded. "Yours was real too, but you've got to understand that we didn't know who you were at the time. The team that was tailing you told us who you were right after you left the bar with Tracy."

Special Agent Empy continued, "Detectives Denning and Goldberg have been working on the Southwick case for three months now. The DEA took an interest in him about two years ago when he was connected to a large shipment of cocaine received from Peru. It's Troy's source that we're primarily interested in."

Barry jumped in. "Actually, we've known about Troy Southwick for some time. We just recently made a connection with someone on the inside."

"Tracy?" Jeff asked.

"Cute, isn't she?"

Gary looked at Jeff. "Foster, are you chasing another druggie?"

Captain Fowler eyed Gary quizzically.

Gary wiped his hand over his face. "Private joke."

Empy went on, "It seems that you've managed to fall into an incredible opportunity, Detective Foster."

"What do you mean?"

"Well, we at the agency have expended a considerable amount of resources toward interdicting and apprehending Mr. Southwick and his organization, but—"

Reed interrupted, "What he's trying to say is the DEA with all its manpower and superior intellect has not been able to accomplish in two years what you've accomplished in two weeks."

Special Agent Empy stiffened. "We have joined forces with the Las Vegas Narcotics Division to mount a special task force to interdict and arrest Troy Southwick and his connection. I'm coordinating this campaign, but Barry is supervising the field operations. After what happened with your little side trip to Newport Beach, the Orange County task force has decided to join us."

Captain Fowler cleared his throat. "What side trip?"

Jeff took a deep breath. "I ran into a difficult situation. Troy asked Margo to lend me to him as a pilot to fly down to Newport Beach for a deal. Margo figured it would be a great opportunity to connect me with Troy—and it was."

Barry helped. "The problem was, Jeff had no way to contact anyone and couldn't really refuse. We put a bird dog on Troy's plane and took a lateral flight. The narcs there picked up the tail for us and ended up following them to a mall. Then they lost them. A few hours later, Jeff showed up back at the airport and flew back to Vegas."

Captain Fowler shook his head. "I should never have let you go. This is getting out of hand."

Jeff swallowed hard. "That's not all."

"What's not all?" Captain Fowler asked.

"The deal." Jeff squared his shoulders. "It went bad. At least four men are dead; one of them I killed in self-defense."

The room was silent. Reed almost laughed, but for some reason didn't. Gary put his hand on Jeff's shoulder. "What happened, buddy?"

Jeff related the whole incident, starting at the first contact with the ponytailed man in the mall. He ended "Troy trusts me and wants me to be his personal bodyguard and pilot."

Barry shook his fist in excitement. "Yes!"

Special Agent Empy tapped his pen on his palm. "If what you say is true, this is better than any of us envisioned. Imagine! Troy Southwick's personal pilot and bodyguard."

"No."

All eyes focused on Captain Fowler.

"Captain, this is the opportunity of a lifetime. I'm sure the agency will provide any resources necessary to—"

"No. Jeff is a good man, and I won't risk him getting killed three states away by some dope-selling maggot."

"But the agency would skillfully—"

"Like the Orange County Task Force skillfully lost Jeff in a mall?"

"I didn't say it is without risk. But I believe this is a different situation. Orange County didn't know what they were dealing with."

"No, the captain's right." Barry drew an imaginary line with his hand in the air. "It's *not* worth getting killed for. Reed and I can tell you stories of dumb things we've done just to put the bad guy in jail. It's not worth it."

Reed nodded in agreement.

"Unless . . ." Barry said.

Captain Fowler looked up, willing to listen. "Unless what?"

"Unless he had backup next to him all the time, twenty-four hours a day. Backup that could be next to Jeff even in Troy's presence. And then make sure we have the resources to call in the troops on a second's notice."

Captain Fowler folded his arms. "Okay, what are you thinking?"

"Well," Barry said, "the cavalry and heavy support can be provided without too much problem. I mean, look, we have the DEA here."

Special Agent Empy wrinkled his forehead and pushed his glasses further up his nose. "Between the Las Vegas Narcotics Division and our agency, we should be able to provide the necessary support."

Gary chimed in, "So how do we get this magic backup that Troy will unquestioningly accept?"

Barry smiled. "All we need to do is get Jeff a girlfriend. We've got a new agent from Dallas on the division who has the street experience but hasn't been burned yet. She'd be great." Then, glancing at Jeff, Barry winked. "She's a looker too!"

"I don't know." Captain Fowler scratched his chin thoughtfully. "There's just too much that can go wrong. What do you think, Gary?"

Gary looked at Jeff and then back at Captain Fowler. "There's risk, but that's our business. This is a chance to hit them hard. I say do it."

Captain Fowler turned to Jeff. "Well?"

Jeff scratched his head and faced Barry. "How cute did you say she was?"

Chapter Twelve

The conductor raised his hand, and a hush fell over the audience. Suddenly the music came crashing down in a grandiose opening, launching into the intense but meticulous lead by the violins. Then a run by the cellos in a totally different direction complemented the bass. Individually, their sounds pleased. Together they enthralled.

Eine Kleine Nachtmusik by Wolfgang Amadeus Mozart. Jeff loved Mozart, but he had a special reason for being at the Idaho Falls Civic Auditorium tonight.

Fifteen feet to the right of the conductor sat Stephanie Evans, laboring over her cello with noble finesse. Jeff had managed to get a seat close enough to see Stephanie's features clearly.

Her eyes showed a power and intensity that revealed something much deeper than desire to perform well. The simple grace that flowed from her seemed to suggest all that was good in life—something that Jeff yearned to be a part of.

Two boys were seated next to Jeff. He guessed their ages to be eight and ten. The older boy watched the conductor in awe, as if imagining himself majestically wielding the conductor's wand with exalted authority. Incredibly, the younger boy had fallen asleep and sat curled up next to his father.

At the close of the concert, Jeff waited by the side door for Stephanie. Soon she appeared. Her wavy hair clung gently to her moist cheeks. She momentarily stood in the doorway, refreshed by the night breeze. Jeff watched as she ran her fingers back through her hair and stretched.

She caught his gaze and gave him a big isn't-it-great-to-be-alive smile.

Jeff waved. "You sounded great!"

"Thanks, but I believe it was a team effort."

"No, I think you definitely carried the show. I mean, it was incredible. Everyone around me was saying, 'Who is that gorgeous cello player? She plays so exquisitely!' They all wanted your autograph."

Stephanie's eyes widened in mock amazement. "You really mean it!"

Jeff brought his right arm to the square. "Scout's honor."

"Then it's a good thing I escaped out this side door. I wouldn't want to get mauled by the crowd."

"Fear not. I'll be your knight in shining armor."

Stephanie curtsied. "Oh, kind and valiant one. So brave."

"Come, me lady, there is a festive treat awaiting us at Baskin-Robbins."

Stephanie formed a small circle with her lips. "Ooo, ice cream." Then, tugging slightly at her black dress, "That should help cool me down."

A teenage girl greeted them as they walked into Baskin-Robbins. "Hi, we're having a special tonight on licorice."

Stephanie wrinkled her nose. "Yuck! How about lime sherbet in a dish."

The high school girl shrugged her shoulders. "Small or large?"

"Large," said Stephanie without hesitation.

Jeff laid a five-dollar bill on the counter. "Do you have any banana cream pie?"

"No, I'm sorry. We just have ice cream."

"Well, do you have any coconut cream pie?"

The girl gave him a questioning stare. "No, but we do have thirty-one flavors of ice cream and all kinds of ways to fix 'em."

"Okay, I think I'll just have a small piece of banana cream pie."

"We don't *have* any pie, sir."

"Maybe just a taste of banana cream p—?"

Stephanie elbowed him in the ribs and rescued the girl. "Just fix him a banana split."

Jeff winced. "Yeah, that's what I meant. A banana split."

The girl shook her head at Stephanie in pity. "I'll bring it out to you."

Jeff smiled politely and directed Stephanie to a table opposite the door.

"So, how was your trip?" Stephanie asked casually.

Jeff stuttered, "What trip?"

"The one you said you were going on last Sunday."

"Oh, that trip. Yeah, it was good to see old friends."

Stephanie changed the subject. "So, where do you think you'll be five years from now?"

Jeff nearly choked on an ice cube. It was the same thing Troy had asked him only three days ago. "Why do you ask?"

"I don't know. I guess I wondered if you think much about it." Not waiting for further response, Stephanie added, "Jeff, do you ever feel like something's wrong?"

Jeff looked around the room, surveying its contents.

Stephanie shook her head. "No, not now, I mean do you ever feel something strange and then find out later that something happened?"

Jeff shrugged his shoulders. "One time I felt prompted to slow down before I drove around this corner. There was a—"

"Prompted? You said prompted. Why?"

Jeff stammered, "Uh, I don't know. I mean, that's how I felt. Why?" Jeff silently chastised himself for his choice of words and wished he could tell Stephanie who he was.

Stephanie's eyes sparkled. "It's just a different choice of words. Anyway, I'm sorry I interrupted you. Go ahead."

"Well, anyway, there were two cars racing side by side. It was a narrow road and if I hadn't slowed down . . ." Jeff gazed out the window.

"How were you prompted?" Stephanie asked.

"It was like this voice—no, it was more like this feeling. A feeling to slow down." Jeff tossed his hands open. "I don't know. Maybe my subconscious heard the cars coming and warned my brain."

"Maybe not."

"Huh?"

"Maybe something else warned you to slow down."

Jeff gazed into Stephanie's eyes. He saw a deepness of character, of faith, that mirrored his mother's. Jeff recalled how his mother gave credit to the Lord for everything good that ever happened. At the time, he had thought it foolish. His mind flashed to a scripture he had memorized on his mission: *Trust in the Lord with all thine heart; and lean not unto thine own understanding. In all thy ways acknowledge him, and he shall direct thy paths.*

"What are you thinking about?"

Her voice jerked him back to the present. "I was just reflecting on what you said."

Stephanie glanced down at his hands and then into his eyes. "While you were gone, I felt that way."

"What way?"

"Like something was wrong. I even called my mother to see if everything was okay. She asked me how you were doing and I—"

"She asked about me?" Jeff winked.

Stephanie blushed. "Yes, I had told her about the

water ski trip. Anyway, when she said your name, I had this feeling like something was wrong."

"Like I'm a bad influence?" Jeff smiled, but Stephanie stayed serious.

"No, not at all. It was like you were in danger or something. Maybe that sounds dumb to you."

Jeff flashed back to his feelings of apprehension just before the rip-off on Wednesday. "When did you feel this way?"

"A couple of days ago; let's see, I was just finishing a letter that had to go out in Wednesday's mail.

Jeff leaned forward in his seat. "What time?"

"Just before lunch. Why?"

Jeff remembered the carnage that day and pushed it from his mind. Speaking softly, he looked down. "I don't know. I guess I was just curious."

Stephanie studied his face and then whispered, "You can tell me when you're ready."

"What was that?" Jeff leaned forward, not sure he had heard her correctly.

He was interrupted by the waitress. She set a bowl in front of Stephanie and announced, "One lime sherbet." Then, turning to Jeff nervously, "And one banana cream p . . . uh, I mean split."

Jeff showed no pity. "A banana cream split?"

"No, a banana cream pie. No!" The girl shook her head vigorously. "I do mean split." Then, punching out each syllable distinctly, "A ba-na-na split."

Jeff looked up innocently, "Okay, fine."

Stephanie rolled her eyes. "Do you treat all waitresses like that?"

"Only the ones that don't have banana cream pie."

Stephanie giggled and then dug into her sherbet. "Are we still on for Sunday?"

"Tomorrow at 8:45."

"Good."

Jeff picked out the bananas, carefully saving them for last. "Have you ever been spelunking?"

Stephanie cocked her head. "Isn't that cave exploring?"

"Yes, there's a world-class cave near the Tetons, in Darby Canyon. How would you like to go spelunking next Saturday?"

"You mean with ropes and everything?"

"It all depends on what you want to do. We can explore the wind cave aways without ropes, or we can go into the ice cave side and use crampons, ice ax, Jumars—the works."

"So you've been there before?"

"A couple of times last year."

"From Moscow? That's a long drive."

Crimson filled Jeff's face. "Yes, very long. I had a room-mate at college that was a real fanatic." He bit down hard on his cheek.

Stephanie nodded. "Let's do the ice cave, but you'll have to show me how. I've rapelled a couple times, but that's about it."

Jeff breathed relief, "No problem. With the way you ski, you'll catch on fast."

"Oh, so now skiing is part of it. Do I need to bring a swimsuit?"

"Actually, there is a small lake we'll need to wade across if we want to go all the way through."

"Are you serious?"

"Yeah, but don't worry about it. The water's always at least thirty-four degrees."

Stephanie raised her eyebrows.

"I have a pair of chest waders I used to cross the lake when I went a few weeks ago." Jeff held up his hand. "It's only three or four feet deep and a few hundred feet long. I'll carry you across on my shoulders."

"And if you slip?"

"I won't."

Stephanie grew more excited. "This sounds fun. What time are you going to pick me up?"

"Is five o'clock too early?"

"A.M. or P.M.?"

Jeff grinned. "A.M."

Stephanie shrugged. "I can handle it."

Margo looked down into the swirling water. The heart-shaped spa in his bedroom had been designed for company, but now he was alone. No one really cared whether he lived or died. Even his mother was gone. Not that he cared; in fact, he hated her. He hated her for marrying the drunken derelict. He hated her for what she had done to him. No matter now. She was gone.

Jabbing one finger in the water to test the temperature, Margo caught the sleeve of his velvet robe. *Nice and hot.*

He reflected back to the first time. He remembered the night well. He was at the office while his wife and daughter were home waiting for him. It sat in front of him, laughing at him, taunting him. What had been so powerful that people would give everything they owned for just one more hit? What could be so fantastic that people would kill for . . .

The memory of his daughter momentarily pricked something deep inside. He chased it away. His thoughts returned to the first time. *Yes, the first time.*

He never made the decision to use. But yet it was made. At least, his body had decided, for he was drawn to it like a magnet. Inside he knew he was going to use, but his brain teased him, hinting that he would somehow back out at the last minute.

Then, as if someone else forced the cocaine up his nose, it was too late. But too late for what? The sensation was spectacular. And from that day, nothing would ever be the same.

Over time, sores developed inside his nose. Once his heart felt like it would explode. Several times, he promised himself that he would quit—especially after the heart episode—but he didn't.

Any rational hopes of quitting had faded long ago. He felt as if he were in someone else's power, someone who wished him evil.

Margo squeezed at the wetness on his sleeve. His hand trembled in anticipation. He wiped his moistened finger on his robe and retrieved a leather pouch from the bedroom dresser. Then he sat down at the table and unzipped the pouch. The contents spilled onto the table.

A tiny brown vial bounced gently and then rolled carefree until it bumped into a bronze tube. Margo picked up the vial and examined it at eye level. Gazing past the vial, he watched the figure in the wall mirror, the man who held his treasure—the treasure he worshipped—his god. The man he had learned to despise.

In a fit of profane rage, Margo threw the vial into the reflection.

The vial burst, sending a fine spray of crystal white powder into the air. Some of the larger chunks fell rapidly onto the carpet below.

Margo stared at his trembling hand. The reality of what he had just done swelled through him. In a panic, he dropped to his knees and frantically searched for tiny specks of gleaming white embedded in the carpet. Picking out the pieces he could find, Margo scraped the powder with its accompanying dirt onto a small silver tray.

He licked his hands like a savage dog and grabbed the razor blade. Sweat covered his body. He used both hands to help steady the blade and carefully made two fat lines composed of dirt, lint, and cocaine.

Grabbing the metal tube, he quickly snorted a pile up each nostril. Then he shed his robe and entered the warm surging water. Leaning back on a jet of hot liquid, Margo rested his head on a built-in dish and waited for it to happen.

It started. His heart pumped faster, the torrent of blood

rushing to go nowhere special, the sensation and sense of well being. *Rush*, Margo pondered. *An appropriate description.*

Yes! There were no thoughts now about his murdered wife and daughter. No thoughts of the future. Only right here, right now.

The blood began coursing faster. The cadence of his heart picked up. Soon it pounded in great throbs, straining to supply the life-sustaining fluid. The lungs expanded and collapsed, struggling to keep up.

True to form, the blood vessels began clamping down. His blood pressure continued to rise higher. *Yes!* Margo gloried with hedonistic gratification.

What? Something new—something exciting. His heart raced faster. *Perhaps a new high?*

The strange new sensation abruptly tightened inside him. Margo's elation turned to apprehension. His left arm clung to his body, refusing to obey his commands. He gaped at his open palm in horror. "No!"

He felt the weight of a thousand sins pressing down on his chest. Harder and harder, punishing him cruelly, pinning him against the bottom of the pool.

The furor in his chest exploded, ripping the aorta from his heart. Massive amounts of blood gushed into his chest cavity.

Margo's eyes bulged in terror, transfixed in their new and permanent position as he lay face down, turning slowly with the spiralling water.

Chapter Thirteen

"You look nice in a suit and tie."

Jeff pulled up the corners of his mouth and blushed as he opened the car door for Stephanie. "I think it's more like Beauty and the Beast."

Her white dress hung loosely around her shoulders, accenting the natural color of her face. "As long as you turn into a handsome prince."

"Then you don't think I'm handsome now?"

Stephanie pursed her lips. "Hum. Let's just say I see lots of potential."

Jeff grabbed at his heart. "Ouch!" His face grew thoughtful. "Maybe if I shaved my beard."

"Then you wouldn't be the beast."

"And I'd be the handsome prince?"

"Or at least a handsomer beast."

"Handsomer? Is that a word?"

"Of course it is. I'm a legal secretary, you know."

"Sounds like an illegal use of the word."

"Perhaps you'd prefer—you'd be a *more* handsome beast."

"But not a more handsome prince?"

Stephanie tilted her head in contemplation. "Lose the beard and we'll see."

"Then you don't like it?"

"You'd definitely look different."

"A skillful answer, but you avoided my question."

Stephanie shook her head. "I don't know. Seeing you in a suit and tie with a beard. It works for some people, but . . ."

He finished the sentence for her. "Not for me."

She nodded her head and shrugged.

"Great. You don't mind if I swing by my apartment and pick up a sack to put over my head, do you?"

Stephanie laughed. "Don't worry about it. You look nice—for a beast."

"It's been awhile since this beast has been in a church." *About a week*, he mouthed the thought to himself as if that would somehow alleviate the lie. "Do Mormons have beards?"

"Not too many, but you'll fit in fine."

"I don't care if I fit in. I just don't want to scare anyone."

Stephanie studied Jeff's face. "I see what you mean."

He repressed a grin. "Okay, your ladyness, where do I turn?"

Stephanie directed Jeff to her ward's chapel. As soon as they entered the building, a thin man carrying a two-year-old girl greeted Stephanie.

"Hello, Sister Evans." He shifted the toddler to his left arm and stuck his hand toward Jeff. "And you're . . ."

Jeff grasped his hand. "Brother Foster." Jeff coughed violently. "Uh, brother! fostering new relations is good. I mean, oh brother! I like to foster new friendships." Jeff's face turned crimson as he vised cheek between teeth.

Stephanie's brow flexed a brief concern. "This is Jeff Spenelie. He's a friend of mine. Jeff, this is Brother Mike Ryan."

"Wonderful. The elders meet in the multipurpose room next to the kitchen." Mike Ryan pointed down the hall.

He looked at Stephanie for guidance.

"Jeff's not a member of our church."

Mike Ryan's eyes widened as a broad smile spread

across his face. "Oops, sorry." He proceeded to give an overview of the meetings and their purpose and left Stephanie to explain the rest.

"Seems like a nice guy." Jeff meant it.

"Yes, he is."

After sacrament meeting and Sunday School, Mike Ryan escorted Jeff to the elders quorum meeting. He introduced him as a special friend of Stephanie Evans, which caused a small stir of chuckles.

As the lesson progressed, Jeff settled into a trance. He rehearsed, as he had a dozen other times, how he would tell Stephanie who he was. He pushed the problem from his mind and tried to think of something more pleasant. It didn't work. He pictured the ponytailed bandit being blown off the cliff by Troy. The shots he fired into the sniper who had tried to kill them.

"So when do we turn the other cheek?"

The teacher's question brought Jeff back to the lesson. An answer came from behind him. "Christ said that whoever hit us on the right cheek, we need to turn and let them hit the other cheek."

"That's dumb," came another answer.

Another hand shot up. "So we can't defend ourselves?"

A man with bulging shoulders said, "I think it means that we should just try to be patient in our afflictions with other people."

The instructor thumbed through his scriptures. "Does anyone have that verse?"

Another man started to read, "'But I say unto you, That ye resist not evil: but whosoever shall smite thee on thy right cheek, turn to him the other also.'"

The verse stung Jeff. He had never questioned using violence if the cause was just. Had he missed something along the way?

The man in the back spoke again. "We live in an imperfect world, but the higher law is clear. We should never use violence against our fellowman. You know, like the

121

people of Ammon. They lay down and let their enemies slaughter them by the hundreds and still wouldn't defend themselves."

A heavyset man with a wide, flowery tie nearly shouted. "What about when the Lord told Seth to kill all those men, women, children, flocks, everything?"

"I think that was Saul, not Seth."

"Yeah, whatever. But they got in trouble with the Lord for not killing enough."

Another voice chimed in, "That's because they wanted to keep the spoils for themselves."

The teacher spoke up, "But back to the issue at hand. Should we turn the other cheek instead of defending ourselves?"

Jeff spoke softly, "Or others."

All eyes turned to Jeff, curious that he would take part in the discussion. The teacher cupped one hand behind his ear. "Pardon?"

"Or others. Is a man justified in using force to defend others against evil?"

The man from behind defended his position. "I don't think so. It's not our place to judge. The Lord will be the one to exercise vengeance."

The large man rebutted, "He's not talking about vengeance. If your wife was being attacked by a gang of hoodlums, would you stand by and wait for the Lord to execute judgement?"

"He who lives by the sword, dies by the sword," mumbled another voice.

The man in the back opened his Bible. "In Luke, the Savior told the soldiers to do no man violence."

"What about the Nephites? They were commanded to defend themselves against the Lamanites."

The instructor raised his hand. "This is a difficult question. Perhaps it just depends on the circumstances. Shall we move on?"

"Can I make one more point?" the man in the back spoke.

The teacher nodded.

"Violence is a terrible thing. When we're violent, we can't have the Spirit with us. For example, King David wanted to build a temple and the Lord told him no because, and I quote"—he raised the scriptures to his face— " 'Thou shalt not build an house for my name, because thou hast been a man of war, and hast shed blood.' "

Jeff raised his hand. "So you're saying men of war, like police officers, can't also be men of God."

The man nodded and pointed at the scriptures. "I'm not saying it, the Lord is."

The teacher shifted from one foot to the other and then leaned forward, anxious to move on, but a man wearing a light grey suit joined the discussion. "Was Moroni a man of God?"

"Yes, but—"

"And was he a man of war?"

"He tried to avoid shedding blood."

"But he did kill, by his own admission, correct?"

"Not wanting to, and avoiding it whenever he could, but yes, he did kill. But he was an exception."

"Like Nephi killing Laban?"

"Only when commanded by God to do so. And even then, he almost didn't do it."

"What about when Alma fought with Amlici? He asked for mercy from the Lord for his people's sake and was strengthened to the point that he could kill Amlici." He paused for the words to take effect. "Was Alma a man of war?"

"Yes, but—"

"Then there's Gidgiddoni, another prophet-general who commanded his armies to slay everyone until they came to the borders of the wilderness. And isn't it true that the Lord actually commanded the Nephites to defend themselves—to shed the blood of their brother Lamanites—as long as they weren't guilty of the first or second offense?" Not waiting for an answer, he proceeded. "As for King David, he shed innocent blood. But yes, Brother Hurley, you're absolutely right. Violence is a terrible burden on our society, and men who enjoy violence can't have the Spirit with them. But let's not connect evil violence to the righteous use of force as exercised by men of war like policemen or prophets of God, bloody though it may be." The grey-suited man sat down.

Brother Hurley, the man in the back, broke into a large grin. "As King Agrippa said to Paul: Almost thou persuadest me." Then he winked. "Besides, I can't argue with a lawyer."

Jeff turned and studied the man who had defended his profession and mused silently. *A lawyer.*

After Jeff dropped off Stephanie, he grabbed a bite to eat and headed for his own ward. He entered the chapel and waved at a young man he had taught before being called to the Primary.

"Hi, Jeff."

Jeff grabbed at the teenager's hand. "What's happening, Rex?"

The gangly teen pinched his neck. "Meyers just conned me into giving a talk next week."

"That's *Brother* Meyers," his father corrected.

"Yeah, whatever."

Jeff repressed a smirk. "How's driver's ed coming?"

The teen flashed his braces. "Next week I take the test."

"Scary."

"Terrifying," his father added.

Jeff folded his arms. "Think you'll pass?"

"Of course."

"Then I'd better alert the guys on shift."

The teen smiled confidently. "Watch all you want. You won't get any tickets off *me.*"

His father agreed. "He knows that tickets and safe driving are connected to driving privileges."

"He blackmailed me."

"Yup," the father nodded. "No wrecks, no tickets: he lives."

The teen complained to Jeff, "Isn't that extortion?"

"Sorry, I'm on your dad's side."

"You wouldn't write me a ticket anyway. Would you?" The teen paused and studied Jeff's face. "Hey, you working undercover or something?"

Jeff forced a nervous laugh. "Right. I have a special assignment to guard the president."

"Cool." The teen waved it off as his attention shifted to a girl entering from the back. "Put in a good word for me." He disappeared around the bench.

After sacrament meeting, Jeff set up chairs for his class in the overflow section between the chapel and the cultural hall. None of the eleven-year-olds had arrived yet. He reached across the table to latch the metal curtain leading to the chapel, and stopped. The voices of two women carried through the crack in the curtain.

"At least he's coming to church now."

"But should he be teaching Primary? I worry about the example it sets for the children."

"You mean the beard?"

"It's not just the beard. Did you notice the ponytail?"

"I didn't see a ponytail."

Jeff tucked the two-inch lock of hair into the collar of his white shirt. When his hair had been trimmed a few weeks ago, he had deliberately left the narrow lock of hair to help his new image. He smiled grimly. Evidently, it was working.

"It's not a regular ponytail. It's like the kind you see on MTV."

"You watch MTV?"

"Of course not! But my sister's son, the one with the drug problem, had his hair just like that, and she told me it was like the guys on MTV. Anyway, I think it's wonderful that he's coming out to church, but what kind of message is it sending to the children?"

Jeff had heard enough. Without any effort to hide the noise, he slid the locking mechanism shut. He closed his eyes and massaged his forehead. *What kind of example am I setting for my students?*

Chapter Fourteen

"Urgent but not important," Jeff mumbled to himself as he bent over to pick up the ringing telephone. He thought about not answering it at all. *What's more important—a* Star Trek *rerun or answering the phone?*

The call turned out to be both urgent and important.

"Hello?" A hint of irritation bled through the line.

"Jeff, this is Gary. Are you alone?"

"Yeah, why?"

"I can't talk about it over the phone. Meet me at the office in fifteen minutes."

"Is it that important?"

"It's that important. You don't have company, do you?"

Jeff glanced over at the TV just in time to see a reptilian creature beaming aboard the *Enterprise.* "No." He rubbed his hand over his nose. "I'll be right over."

Jeff threaded his gun through his belt and scooped up the gym bag containing his extra gear. Wondering what could possibly be so pressing, he tossed the gear in the trunk and accelerated his pace.

With the dark clouds threatening rain, many of the cars on the road employed their headlights early. Jeff parked illegally in front of the undercover office.

He swung the door open and found Gary staring out the window. His countenance was somber.

"What's so important?"

Gary swiveled his chair to Jeff. "Margo's dead."

"What?" Jeff stared in disbelief.

"They're doing an autopsy now. They found him face down in his bedroom spa."

"Who's they?"

"His maid."

Jeff's mind raced to the time Troy had asked him to work for him. *Is Troy responsible?* "Any idea on the cause of death?"

"There was no sign of a struggle, and no obvious suicide evidence. But here's the kicker—a broken vial with cocaine residue was found with some paraphernalia spread out on his bedroom table."

Jeff rubbed his chin. "Maybe an overdose or heart attack."

"Maybe someone put something in the coke." Gary stuck out his thumb southward. "The vial's at the lab being tested now."

Jeff's thoughts returned to Troy and how he coolly walked away from the massacre last week.

Gary punched out the title in mock reverence, "Special Agent Empy is flying in with the Vegas narcs first thing in the morning. We'll meet them with Captain Fowler at the Little Tree Inn, room 215, at nine-thirty. By then we should have a report on the vial and the cause of death." Gary leaned forward and spoke with a softer voice. "We need to take extra precautions now. From now on, don't talk about anything on the phone that you don't want Troy to hear."

"You think it's bugged?"

Gary shrugged. "Troy didn't get where he is by trusting people and being a nice guy."

Jeff detected the familiar anxiety return. He pressed his palm into the top of his stomach and stood up.

"One more thing."

Jeff stopped in the doorway and glanced back at Gary.

"Make sure you're not being followed, and it may not hurt to wear your vest for a while. It won't stop a sniper, but it could save your bacon in a drive-by."

Jeff waved his trembling hand and smiled grimly. "Yeah."

Visions of the ponytailed man being blasted off the cliff haunted Jeff throughout the night. The scenario repeated itself several times. Each time the faceless man struggled back up the cliff. Each time Troy blasted him back over the cliffs to the beach below. At five-thirty, Jeff pulled on his sweatpants and headed out the door.

Birds began their morning singing ritual. They reminded him of sleeping outside in his backyard as a child. He used to curse them for waking him up so early. Now he enjoyed the memory of an easier time.

The dew-soaked grass persuaded him to perform his brief stretching routine on the sidewalk. Unable to coerce his abdominals into lifting his trunk one more time, Jeff stood and vaulted into a slow jog. He labored for the first mile, but finally caught his rhythm and picked up the pace.

His thoughts shifted to Stephanie. He studied her features carefully in his mind. He imagined her running with him, her eyes teasing him as her hair bounced with each step. Three miles later, the sluggishness left him.

Jeff glanced down at his watch. Six-thirty. He realized for the first time that he was several miles from home. *Way to go, Foster. Looks like you're in for a long one.* Jeff settled into his run again, oblivious to his surroundings. *Lachoneus.* The word entered Jeff's head unexpectedly. *Who's Lachoneus? Let's see . . . oh yeah, the Book of Mormon governor.*

Jeff recounted reading the story ten years ago, the first time he had read the Book of Mormon cover to cover. The Gadianton robbers who infested the mountains were becoming stronger each day. Their wicked leader, Giddianhi, wrote a letter to Lachoneus, demanding that the Nephites surrender all their land and property or die. If they cooperated, they were told, they'd be treated like brothers. Giddianhi told him that if he refused, Giddianhi's army of robbers would come the next month and kill everyone without mercy.

Jeff recalled how he had at first hoped Lachoneus would comply. *For who could stand against such a terrible army? Wouldn't servitude be better than the death that was sure to follow?*

But Lachoneus didn't comply. He would not be terrorized. He told the people to ask the Lord for strength and then prepared for battle. The good guys won.

Jeff rounded a corner absentmindedly. *But what if the good guys lost?* Jeff thought of Christ's words to the Apostles, *"Fear not them which kill the body, but are not able to kill the soul."* And his words to Joseph Smith as he sat incarcerated in Liberty Jail, *"Fear not what man can do, for God shall be with you forever and ever."*

Jeff felt a silent power prick his heart and spread throughout his body. Energy surged through his legs and chest as he picked up his pace. *Runner's high? Maybe.*

A young mother gathered her children into the family car as she prepared them for the morning ritual of traveling to the baby-sitter. Her four-year-old daughter looked at Jeff and hollered, "Why's he wunning?"

Jeff's mind raced back to the first undercover buy and the accompanying apprehension. Gary's face flashed in front of him. *"Remember, kid, they can kill you, but they can't eat you."* Jeff smiled and repeated it aloud, "They can kill you, but they can't eat you!" unaware that he was absently staring at the little girl as he ran toward her.

The mother gave Jeff a threatening stare and hurriedly locked the doors as he passed by.

Jeff finished the run and dashed into his apartment to prepare for the day. He arrived at the Little Tree Inn twenty minutes early. Jeff went into the restaurant for a glass of orange juice and saw Reed and Barry still eating breakfast. "You guys know where a man can score a little cola?"

Reed held out his hands in mock trepidation. "Anything you want, Batman. I'd give you my knife, but you know how it is."

Jeff rolled his eyes and smiled good-naturedly. "Mind if I sit down?"

Barry drew back a chair and motioned for Jeff to be seated. "Don't pay any attention to him. He was abused as a child."

"Anyone else here yet?"

Reed pronounced with false respect, "Special Agent Empy is probably practicing his speech, even as we eat."

Barry censored Reed. "Empy is a good man. He's a little strange, but when it comes to the bureau, there's none better."

Reed stood rebuked. "True, the guy knows his stuff. No way he could work as the UC, but he's a pro on strategy."

The waitress approached their table smiling at Jeff. "Can I get you anything?"

"Do you have any banana cream pie?"

"I'm sorry, the only pies we have are apple and cherry. We have strawberry shortcake, blueberry cheesecake, rhubarb crisp, hot fudge sundaes, ..." The waitress went on listing several more desserts.

Jeff smiled innocently. "How about coconut cream pie?"

The waitress took a deep breath and spoke slowly as if talking to an old man who was hard of hearing. "The only pies we have are apple and cherry."

Jeff maintained a sober face. "Maybe just a small piece of banana cream?"

The waitress shook her head with a hint of frustration in her voice. "Sir, we don't have any pies except cherry and apple."

"Perhaps I could have just a *taste* of banana cream pie?"

Dumbfounded, the waitress struggled for something to say. Jeff was content to let her squirm.

Finally, Barry leaned over and whispered to the waitress, "He was traumatized during the war. It was a special operation in Central America. The only thing he had to eat for six weeks was bananas."

The waitress looked at Jeff and then back to Barry. Both appeared dead serious. Backing up, she stuttered, "I, uh, will bring your check right out."

The motel room contained a table with several chairs next to the bed. Captain Fowler and Gary were waiting with Special Agent Empy when Jeff arrived with the Vegas narcs.

Jeff sat on the edge of the bed next to Reed. Empy stood with one elbow propped on top of the TV and announced the beginning of their meeting. "Gentlemen, shall we begin?" Not waiting for a response, he continued, "Margo's death changes things dramatically. It creates some problems, but it also provides us opportunities. Gary, would you fill us in on the autopsy and lab reports?"

Gary opened a manila folder. "The cause of death is listed as a massive coronary failure precipitated by the severing of the aorta from the heart."

Reed offered an unsolicited interpretation. "His heart popped."

Gary continued, "The broken vial contained cocaine and trace amounts of inositol, hydrochloric acid, and strychnine."

"Strychnine?" repeated Captain Fowler.

Barry responded, "It's occasionally used as cut. When they dilute the coke for profit, they sometimes add strychnine to give it more kick."

"Hopefully they don't throw in too much," Reed added.

Gary went on, "In this case, it wasn't significant. He

could have tooted the whole vial and not been affected much by the strychnine."

"So what happened?" Jeff asked.

Empy answered succinctly. "Simply put, Margo had a heart attack—probably from using cocaine."

"There was cocaine in his blood," added Gary. "So it looks like he may have accidently done it to himself."

Captain Fowler raised his eyebrows. "May have?"

"There's no way of knowing for sure; I mean, who knows what else could have caused the heart attack that just didn't show up in the autopsy, but they're almost positive he died from a heart attack caused by cocaine."

Captain Fowler looked satisfied. "So where do we go from here?"

Empy held his glasses in one hand. "We have Jeff contact Troy. With Margo gone, we now have a reason for Jeff to work with Troy directly."

Fowler interjected, "Will Troy suspect Jeff killed Margo?"

"Perhaps." Empy wasn't reassuring.

"What if he wants me to take over Margo's business?" Jeff said.

"Then tactfully decline. It will help dispel any thoughts that you were responsible for Margo's death. We need you working directly with Troy, preferably as his pilot or bodyguard." Empy paused to wrap his hand around his glasses for emphasis. "We need to be with him, in tight. To be there when he connects with Mr. Big."

Gary held up his hand like a respectful student. "Do we have any idea who Mr. Big is?"

Empy shook his head. "Not a clue."

"What about backup?" This time it was Gary who was concerned.

Barry smiled. "It's all set. Melonie will arrive tonight. You two will have to get to know each other quite well to pose as lovers."

"Lovers?" Jeff squirmed.

"Relax," Reed said, "the key word here is *pretend.*"

Empy held up his hand for attention. "With your captain's permission, we have made some special arrangements. Given the present circumstances, it will be most prudent to establish a lifestyle and conditions consistent with your cover."

Reed interjected, "What Einstein is trying to say is that you're going deep cover."

"What does deep cover consist of?" Jeff asked.

Barry picked up the slack. "Your whole life becomes your undercover identity. Jeff Foster does not exist, only Jeff Spenelie. Everything you say, everything you do, is Jeff Spenelie."

Empy cleared his throat. "This is where you have to decide if you're willing to proceed. We have taken extraordinary measures to protect you and give you a credible cover, but there's always a chance that something will go wrong."

Reed looked Jeff in the eye. "There's nothing that says you have to go through with this. No one would blame you if you just said it's not worth it." Captain Fowler nodded in agreement.

Jeff searched his feelings carefully to check the answer he already knew. "They can kill me, but they can't eat me."

Empy quizzically examined Jeff. "Does that mean you accept?"

Jeff paused, looking at Gary. "Yes."

Empy rubbed his hands together. "Good! We have already taken the liberty to relocate you in a duplex under your assumed identity."

"What if they check with the manager and find I just moved there?"

"There is no manager and the owner is out of town. We have temporarily changed his phone and address to ring directly to one of our people first."

"What if they talk to the neighbors?"

Empy was confident. "Your neighbors are snowbirds

that live in Arizona during the winter. They decided to stay there all summer this year. The only other residence is across the street. It's being used by our people as the safe house and is ideal for surveillance."

Reed turned to Jeff. "Don't sweat the details. Believe me, this is where Empy shines. The agency will take care of your houseplants and parrot in your old apartment until this thing is over. They'll even take care of your bills."

"How did you know I had a parrot?"

Empy showed an unusual demonstration that surprised even Reed. Putting his hand on Jeff's shoulder, he spoke like a reassuring father. "Jeff, before we put these kind of resources into a person, we check them out thoroughly. It has got to be this way for your protection. Mr. Big is not worth an agent's life: not yours, and not Melonie's."

Jeff nodded in understanding. "So what now?"

Barry threw a set of keys to Jeff. "Here's the keys to the duplex. It's complete with clothes, personal items, everything. Melonie's things are already there—"

"Say what?"

"You two will be living together."

"Wrong."

Barry leaned forward. "Excuse me?"

Jeff mouthed the word with precision. "Wrong."

"We're not asking you to sleep with her. Just share the apartment and pretend you're live-ins."

Jeff folded his arms. "I'm not living with a woman."

Reed smirked, "You'd prefer a boyfriend?"

Everyone laughed. Even the corner of Empy's mouth turned up slightly—everyone except Captain Fowler. "I'm not going to ask a man to compromise his principles. Work something out he can live with."

Empy sighed patiently. "Look, Jeff. If anything went on between you and Melonie, it would be very unprofessional. And I, for one, knowing your background, would be disappointed. Publicly, as part of your cover, you pose as girlfriend and boyfriend. Privately, we expect you to maintain the highest principles. I know this looks like a difficult situation, but—"

"No."

Barry became impatient. "What do you mean, no? Help us out here, Jeff. Give us some solutions."

"I can understand the necessity for us to be together when we see Troy, but I don't think it would be that unusual for us to have separate apartments and play the dating game."

Not wanting to make a bigger issue of it, Empy accepted Jeff's position. "That will work. We'll just get her an apartment." Then, reaching into his briefcase, he pulled out a pile of papers. "These are checks, bills, and documents under your assumed name going back to the time you attended college at Moscow. Sign them. Our people will put them in the system.

"Your mother died two years ago from a stroke. Instead of becoming a cop, you maintained your job as a pilot until three months ago. Everything else, including your Mormon heritage, will be the same as your real life.

"You met Melonie two months ago in the Teton Mall where she works as a hairstylist at Third Dimension Cuts. Tomorrow she will be there. You need to go in and meet her for real. She will cut your hair at 11:00 A.M.

"Remember to act the part. That way if anyone ever checks your story against hers, both of you will have it down to the last detail—because it really happened, except for the fact that the meeting was two months late. The key to working deep cover is to change as little as possible. Any questions?"

Jeff's head was spinning. "What if they check and find that Melonie hasn't been there two months?"

"The manager is on vacation. The other three employees are new. They think Melonie did work there and left for a few weeks to—"

Barry interrupted Empy. "Jeff, you can 'what if' this

thing to death. Nothing is foolproof, but we've spent a lot of resources to make it work. Empy did it right. This isn't deep cover in the traditional sense. It's only going to be good for two or three weeks. But in that time . . ."

Barry let it hang, so Empy continued. "Melonie is thoroughly briefed on your story. If you have any questions, she will probably be able to help. We will not initiate any contact with you unless it's an emergency. Therefore, you will need to contact us regularly. If you need to contact us, go to the Corn Dog Factory in the Teton Mall. That's where our base station is for now. You need not worry about who's there. Everyone you see will be on the team."

Special Agent Empy relished his assignment, belching out information like a volcano. "Okay, that takes us down to the call. After you finish your haircut, it's time to tell Troy the news. We already made sure that Margo's secretary knows about his death. Call down to Eagle Aviation and ask to speak to Margo. When they tell you what happened, hang up the phone and immediately call Troy. Do this from your new apartment.

"Gentlemen, I think this concludes our business, unless any of you have anything else?"

But Jeff was deep in thought—not about the specific mission but on how it would affect his relationship with a flight instructor named Stephanie Evans.

Chapter Fifteen

The muffled clamor of a hundred footsteps clicking on the cobblestone tile confronted Jeff as he strolled through the double glass doors into the food court. A profusion of odors lay in wait to invade his unsuspecting olfactory nerves—pizza, fresh cookies, and corn dogs. The Teton Mall featured a dozen eateries, all vying pleasantly for their share of the market.

Jeff passed the Corn Dog Factory, glancing nonchalantly behind the counter. A middle-aged woman who looked like someone's mother stood next to the cash register. *DEA? Maybe they haven't set up yet.*

Jeff casually rambled back to the counter and his eyes eased up to the menu. The plump woman looked up from her work and smiled. "Hello, may I help you with something, young man?"

Jeff squinted his eyes for a moment and then reacted to his stomach. "I'll have a corn dog."

Without comment the woman pulled out a wiener and dipped it into the batter.

Jeff gave a quick glance around the food court and ran his hand through his hair. "You work here long?"

"Long enough to know I should have finished my degree when I had the chance." She shrugged. "But I do enjoy watching people."

Jeff doubted her DEA connection. *Just a lady trying to get by.* But he decided to ask one more question. "Do you ever wish you could do something more exciting?"

The woman sighed and gazed into space. After a pause, she turned to him. "Son, I'll just be satisfied when my youngest daughter gets married." With a little twinkle, she added, "Are you married?"

Jeff chided himself for believing she could be connected with the operation. "No ma'am."

"I have a daughter that's quite lovely, you know."

"Oh, uh, well, I . . ."

"In fact, she works here." She handed him the finished corn dog with a napkin.

Not wishing to offend her, Jeff offered a closing remark, "Oh really? Well, I need to go now." He turned to walk away. "I need to get a—"

"Haircut?" The woman finished his sentence.

Jeff jerked his head up, but the lady was already taking someone else's order.

"Spenelie, Jeff Spenelie," Jeff echoed to the young blonde.

"I show an appointment with Melonie. Is that right?"

"Yes."

She escorted Jeff to a turn chair closest to the back of the salon. The aroma in the air changed from pizza and corn dogs to a piquant strawberry and peach.

A phone call interrupted Jeff's wait. The blonde answered, "Third Dimension Cuts, may I help you?"

Jeff's attention shifted to a young teenager two chairs away, trying to hide her head full of curlers from his view. Jeff winked at her, causing shades of pink to flood her cheeks.

Closing his eyes, he reflected on his own little sister, now a young woman. But he remembered her best as a gangly teen. When he opened his eyes, a young woman stood in front of him with her arms folded.

Her dark skin and high cheekbones hinted at Polynesian ancestry. The brunette hair was rich and flowing with a pronounced schoolgirl puff in front. Overall, she would be considered a good catch by anyone's standards.

"Catching up on some sleep?" Her voice was deep with a full and vibrant tone, typical of a singer or disc jockey.

"No, I, uh, was just . . ." Jeff fidgeted as he tried to think of a way to end his sentence. "I just . . ." But nothing came.

The woman ignored his pleading eyes, content to let him strain for something to say.

Finally, he just shrugged his shoulders. "Are you Melonie?"

"Yes," she smiled, "and you must be Jeff. How would you like it?"

"Like what?"

"Your haircut."

"What do you think would look good?"

Melonie studied Jeff carefully. "Let's dump the beard, shorten the sides, and give you a perm."

Jeff hesitated. "I don't do perms."

"It'll look great. Trust me."

"Trust you? I hardly know you."

Melonie winked. "I think you'll find me quite trustworthy—someone you can count on."

Jeff grinned. "Okay, do what you want. This will be a test to see how trustworthy you really are."

Melonie held up a pair of scissors like a sword. "You shall not be disappointed." Then she motioned toward a small basin with a guillotine curve for his neck. "Come on. We'll start with a shampoo."

Jeff hopped out of the chair and leaned back onto the porcelain sink. The spray of water sent a warm shiver through his body. Spicy peach assaulted his nostrils as Melonie massaged shampoo into his scalp.

Satisfied to enjoy the tingling on his crown, Jeff half

closed his eyes. But as soon as he did so, the water turned off and a towel attacked his hair.

"How long have you been cutting hair?" *What a dumb question, Foster.*

"I've been in Idaho Falls about a year. Before that, I lived in Seattle, where I was a beautician with my mother. I guess I started when I was about sixteen."

"How old are you now?" Jeff scolded himself mentally. *Dumb question number two.*

"Twenty-three."

Melonie stood near his front, working diligently on his bangs. With her hip pressed against his leg, she was close enough that he could smell her perfume—stronger than Stephanie's. Continuing the comparison, Jeff noted the heavy makeup. *Stephanie wouldn't use that much.*

"How about you?"

"Huh?"

"How old are you?"

"I'm twenty-five." *This conversation is going nowhere.* He took a deep breath. "So, how about if we elope to Vegas? We'll have a passionate honeymoon, raise eight kids, and grow old together living happily ever after."

Melonie snorted involuntarily and doubled over laughing.

"I'm sorry." Jeff threw his head sideways. "All this is kind of new to me."

Melonie paused and put her hand on his shoulder. "You're sweet; don't worry about it. How about if we get together tomorrow night for dinner?"

Jeff raised one eyebrow. "Are you asking me out, Miss . . . ?"

"Hathaway, Melonie Hathaway. And yes, I would like it very much if you would consider gracing me with your presence for dinner. I hear the Sandpiper has good seafood fettucini."

An hour later, Jeff looked into the mirror.

Melonie stood with her hands on her hips. "Well, what do you think?"

His hair was trimmed tight against the sides and back. The top spilled over his forehead in curls. "I look like a high school kid."

"More like a model out of *Gentlemen's Quarterly*." She turned to the blonde employee. "What do you think, Terry?"

Terry scrutinized Jeff as if he were an item on a menu. "Oo, aah, gorgeous if you ask me."

Melonie hooked her arm through his and led him toward the front of the shop. "Sorry, he's mine."

After paying for the haircut, Jeff drove directly to his new apartment and phoned Eagle Aviation.

The receptionist answered the phone. "Eagle Aviation, may I help you?"

"This is Jeff Spenelie. Is Dennis Margo around?"

"Jeff, I just found out this morning that Dennis died. You'll have to talk to Stephanie about your flight lessons."

Surprised at her coolness, Jeff tried to act the part. "Died? What happened?"

"They said he died of a heart attack. It's no wonder, the way he ran himself, always on the go."

"Who's running the place?"

"I really don't know. His attorney called me, a Mr. Hunnington. Said to continue on for now."

"Okay, I'll see you later." Jeff hung up the phone and began dialing Troy's number. His pulse quickened as he punched in the last digits.

A polite female voice answered on the other end. "Southwick Enterprises, may I help you?"

"This is Jeff Spenelie. I'd like to speak to Troy, please."

"Mr. Southwick is in conference now. May I take a message?"

"Yes, give him a note that I will call back in ten minutes with very urgent business. I'm sure he'll want to be interrupted, whatever he's doing."

"Please hold, Mr. Spenelie. I'll see if Mr. Southwick is available now."

Jeff waited on the phone while a smooth voice crooned "Raindrops keep falling on my head" in the background.

The voice returned. "Mr. Southwick will speak to you now."

A short series of clicks interrupted the silence. "Hello, Jeff?"

"Hi, Troy. I'm afraid I've got some bad news."

"What?"

"Dennis is dead." Jeff spoke softly.

There was a long pause. "What happened?"

"I'm not sure. I called over to the airport, and they said he died from a heart attack."

"I'll have my people check into it." On the other end of the line, Troy reached for a pen and wrote the name *Jeff Spenelie* on a piece of paper. "Are you okay?"

"Yeah, I guess so."

Troy wrote down *Dennis Margo* next to Jeff's name. "Can you hold on a minute?"

"Sure."

Troy pushed the hold button and handed the paper to his assistant. "Get the details on Margo's death. And check this other name out. I want to know everything there is to know about him."

Troy returned to his conversation with Jeff. "Would you call me back in an hour? I should have some information by then."

"Okay."

Without further comment, Troy hung up the phone.

Exactly one hour later, Jeff dialed Troy's phone number. Again the polite female voice, "Southwick Enterprises, may I help you?"

"This is Jeff Spenelie."

"Yes, Mr. Spenelie, Mr. Southwick is expecting your call." Click.

"Jeff, I'm sorry about what happened. It looks like he died from a heart attack Tuesday night."

"Any idea how?"

"There's some preliminary indications, but it will take more time before we know for sure." Then, changing the tone of the conversation, "I know this is kind of sudden, but would you be willing to service his accounts?"

"I'm sorry, but I'm really not interested in that end of the business."

"Jeff, I'm not sure you realize how lucrative this could be. Before you make up your mind, will you do me one favor?"

"Sure, if I can. What is it?"

"Accompany me on a business trip this weekend. We could discuss our options then."

"I promised this girl that—"

"Bring her along. We'll mix business with pleasure."

Jeff thought about his date Saturday with Stephanie. He knew this would be a perfect opportunity to bring Melonie. He bit his cheek. "Okay, when do we leave?"

"Let's see, tomorrow's Friday. Meet us at the airport at three o'clock tomorrow afternoon. We'll leave directly from there."

Jeff hesitated. "Where are we going?"

"I really don't want to discuss this over the phone. If you don't mind, I'll fill you in on the details when we arrive. But trust me, you'll have a good time."

Jeff gritted his teeth. *Why is it that every time someone says "Trust me," I feel like a guppy in a shark tank?* "Sounds good, I'll plan on it."

"Fine, and don't forget your suntan lotion. There'll be a lot of water."

"I'm looking forward to it."

After the dial tone, Jeff absentmindedly hung up the phone and leaned back in his chair. *Things are happening too fast.* Two months ago, Jeff Foster arrested drunks and caught burglars. Now he was being suctioned into the

144

black hole of hardcore drugs and violence. He closed his eyes. *Too fast.*

Unaware of Margo's death, Stephanie stared at the computer screen with her brow furrowed. It stared back in silence. Then the wrinkles were replaced by a lifted chin as her fingers flew across the keyboard.

Stopping to admire the feat, her thoughts were suspended by a young man standing by her desk. "Jeff! Is that you? What happened?"

"Hi, I just got a haircut." He squirmed uncomfortably.

"Wow! You look gorgeous."

"Sure, that's what all the women are saying." Jeff's face turned serious as he laid a single red rose on her desk. "I came by to tell you that something came up. I'll be tied up all weekend."

Stephanie's heart sank. She had been looking forward to a day of cave exploring with Jeff. Trying to hide her disappointment, she just questioned, "Oh?"

"I'm really sorry. I have this job opportunity, and this guy needs me the whole weekend."

Stephanie forced a smile. "That's okay. I'm sure I'll find plenty to do." *I have nothing to do.* For a moment, she wondered if he was trying to get rid of her. She pushed the thought away.

"I'll call you when I get back."

Stephanie nodded her head in agreement. "Uh-huh."

Jeff paused before leaving. "I'm sorry about this. I was looking forward to spending the day with you."

Stephanie held her hands in her lap. "Maybe another time."

Jeff turned to leave and then stopped. "Stephanie?"

"Yes?"

"There's something I want to talk to you about . . ."

"You're married."

"Very funny." Jeff sat on her desk, leaned over, and took her hand. "I want you to know that I care deeply for you, but there is something I have to do." Jeff hesitated. "I'll call you when it's over."

"When what's over?"

"Please, just trust me. I'll call you when I get back." He opened his mouth and then closed it and walked out the door.

After he left, Stephanie again stared at the computer screen. Her mother had warned her about dating non-Mormons. At first it had seemed harmless. Now she sensed a longing that she hadn't felt for over two years.

She made herself a promise. *Next time I see him, I'm going to ask him if he wants to take the missionary discussions. If he does, great. If not . . .*

She shook her head and tried to concentrate on work. Feeling heavy footsteps pressing through the carpet, Stephanie looked up, expecting to see that Jeff had returned. Instead it was the senior partner in the law firm, Marvin J. Hunnington.

"Good afternoon, Stephanie."

"Hello, Mr. Hunnington."

"How are things going?"

"Fine."

"Are you still interested in doing a charter for the firm?"

"Sure, you know I love to fly."

"How about this weekend? We thought we'd have our regular pilot back by now, and we need someone right away."

Stephanie thought about her canceled date with Jeff and decided this would be a good opportunity to sort things out. "I'd love to."

"Splendid. Roger will be going with us to Spokane. We'll be staying at the company's lodge on a lake. Let's leave about eight o'clock Saturday morning."

"Fine. I'll go about an hour early to make sure the plane is ready."

"Excellent." Mr. Hunnington paused at the door. "Don't forget your swimsuit and suntan lotion. You might as well enjoy yourself while you're there."

Chapter Sixteen

Darkened glass doors filtered the afternoon sun. The now familiar aroma of pizza and corn dogs wafted through the air. This time, instead of the middle-aged woman, Jeff spied a familiar burly figure behind the counter.

Reed winked at Jeff. "May I help you?"

"Not if you're the cook."

"Oh, come on, corn dogs make for a great appetizer before you get down to the serious stuff!"

"I'll pass. But you can get me a Sprite."

"Coming right up." Reed leaned over the counter and scooped some ice into a paper cup. "What be happening?"

"I'm going for a plane ride tomorrow afternoon with Troy."

Reed moved closer. "Where?"

"I don't know. Sounds like it'll be somewhere on the coast where it's warm and sunny. Maybe California or even further south."

"If it's California or further south, why is he coming all the way up here to pick you up?"

"I don't know. I guess it could be about anywhere this time of the year." Jeff shrugged his shoulders. "He told me he'd tell me when he got here. Didn't want to say over the phone."

"What about Melonie?"

"Troy invited me to bring her along."

Reed stared at Jeff with a friendly smirk. "Your first honeymoon. How special!"

Jeff rolled his eyes back. "You moron, just tell the others." Then he paused. "Where are the others anyway?"

"Special Agent Empy and Gary are at the safe house with Melonie. Barry is in Vegas. He'll be back Saturday morning."

"Got any ideas about backup?"

Reed rubbed his chin. "We can't risk a wire."

Jeff's face brightened. "How about putting a bird dog on his plane when he refuels?"

"No, he's probably got fairly high-tech counter-surveillance; same problem as with the wire. Besides, we'll already know his flight plan before he leaves the ground."

"If he follows it," Jeff added soberly.

Reed shrugged. "We do have the Lear, and it's equipped with radar. As soon as we know where you're going, we'll do our best to get there first. But don't count on us too much. You know how dicey surveillance can be."

Jeff thought back to the time Gary lost him when he made the buy-bust at Circle K. That seemed years ago. "Yeah, I know."

"As soon as you can, try to contact us. We'll do what we can, but your primary backup will be Melonie."

"Can she shoot?"

Reed chuckled. "As good as she cuts hair."

Jeff rubbed at the side of his head. "So am I supposed to be impressed?"

"I don't know. Are you?"

"You're just jealous. All the women think I'm gorgeous."

Reed nodded his head in agreement. "Yeah, you're gorgeous, all right." Then he feigned seriousness. "But hey, don't put yourself in a bad situation if you can help it. If it doesn't feel right, just pull your gun out and call 911."

"And if we're in Mexico?"

"Then don't call 911."

"Thanks for the advice. You're so reassuring."

Reed handed Jeff a cup of Sprite. "Listen, don't worry about it. Empy really shines with this kind of stuff. I'm sure he'll surprise us with some great master plan."

"I'll go home and call Melonie."

"Give us one hour before you call her. Then act like it's a date. If we need to get ahold of you between now and the time you leave, we'll do it through her."

Jeff paid for the Sprite and left. He drove directly to his apartment and turned on the CD player. A half hour went by before he picked up the phone.

A deep but feminine voice answered. "Hello?"

"Melonie, this is Jeff."

"Hi!" Her voice sounded genuinely thrilled to receive his call.

"About tomorrow night . . ."

"You're not going to cancel out on dinner, are you?"

"No, I have something better. How would you like to go away for the weekend?"

"Sounds exciting! Where?"

"It'll be a surprise, but I'll give you a hint. Bring plenty of suntan lotion."

Melonie spoke in a flirtatious tone. "I don't know. Will you behave yourself?"

Jeff blushed even though no one could see him. "Trust me. It will be everything you've ever hoped for."

"Whoa, I can't pass up an offer like that! What time do you want me ready?"

"I'll pick you up at two o'clock tomorrow."

Melonie laughed. "It's a date."

Jeff carried Melonie's bags out to Troy's plane. She had three to his one. His attire was simple—Levi's and a turquoise shirt. Melonie wore designer pants and a white sleeveless top that emphasized her dark complexion. Everything fit so well that Jeff wondered where she kept her gun.

Troy waited inside the Cessna 310 while the pilot took care of refueling and flight plans. He was busy making calculations when Jeff opened the door.

"Jeff! How are you?" Then, scrutinizing him closer, "Is this a new look for you?"

A touch of pink coursed briefly through Jeff's cheeks. "Troy, meet Melonie, my personal hairstylist."

Troy stepped out of the cabin and extended his hand. "Hello Melonie, I'm happy to meet you. I can see why Jeff was so anxious to bring you along."

Melonie flashed a full set of white teeth. "I'm excited. It was very kind of you to invite me."

"The pleasure is mine." Then turning to his pilot, who had just arrived, Troy motioned at the luggage. "Robert, would you see that the bags are packed?"

"Yes sir, and then I believe we'll be ready."

"Fine." Motioning for Melonie and Jeff, Troy climbed back into the airplane.

As the Cessna pushed away from the ground, Jeff turned to Troy. "So, where are we going?"

"North."

Jeff wrinkled his forehead. "North?"

"To Sandpoint."

Melonie pulled in her chin. "Sandpoint? Where's that?"

"It's about sixty miles under the Canadian border." He added quickly, "Still in Idaho, but we'll be flying over Montana to get there. We'll stay in a company cabin on Lake Pend Oreille."

"With a friend?" Jeff questioned.

"Yes." Troy paused, staring out the window. "A friend." He opened his notebook, indicating that he was through with the conversation. Melonie reached over and took Jeff's hand, gesturing at the same time out the window and acting well the part of the excited girlfriend off to spend the weekend with her man.

Three hours later, they were preparing to make the final approach to the Sandpoint airport.

The radio popped, "Cessna 310, follow the Lear turning base." The pilot acknowledged the radio voice and proceeded to land.

As they taxied to park, Jeff looked out the window and saw two men in casual dress waiting by a red and yellow seaplane only a few yards away. Not waiting for the propellers to come to a complete stop, one of them immediately began unloading the baggage. To Jeff's surprise, they carried it over and loaded it into the seaplane.

Troy pointed at the seaplane. "It's only a few minutes in this thing. Much better than the hour drive."

Jeff glanced around the airport and headed to the seaplane. Melonie followed.

The total time on the ground was less than three minutes. As soon as they left the runway, they turned left over the lake, away from the sun.

Troy acted as tour guide. "What you see is only a small part of the lake. It looks like a big hooked earring. Most of it is over there." He pointed toward the southeast. "When we get higher, you'll see it over those mountains."

But rather than fly over the mountains, the seaplane followed the lake around to the east and then due south. Already they were beginning their descent.

Harrison Bay, enclosed by mountains on three sides, stands as a snare for unsuspecting pilots. The innocent blue-green water fuses into the lush vegetation covering the shoreline. The earthy mass then abruptly stretches upward, eager to thwart any attempted escape. Too narrow to turn around in, the landing has to be done right the first time.

Troy pointed to one side of the bay. "That's it."

What initially looked like a beach house slowly transformed into a mansion. As they got closer, Jeff noticed a helicopter landing pad. A fifty-foot cruiser lay nose to nose with a two-masted sailing vessel, too large to be called a boat.

"You call this a cabin?" Jeff asked open-mouthed.

Troy smiled. "The company purchased it two years ago. As you can see, Mr. Tinaco appreciates water sports."

Tinaco. Jeff caught Melonie's eye and cataloged the name for future reference.

Committed for landing, the seaplane slowed to near stall speed. First it skipped lightly, then slid effortlessly along the water, still cruising at a swift pace.

For one accustomed to water landings, everything would seem normal. For one who knew nothing of flying, like Melonie in her ignorant bliss, everything seemed fine. But for Jeff, a pilot who hadn't landed on water before, a pilot who was accustomed to using brakes to slow down, and a pilot who knew there were no brakes on seaplanes, they were proceeding much too fast.

He judged they would impact the dock in about five seconds. While he pondered the inevitable explosion that would surely follow the crash, a strange thing occurred. The slower the plane traveled, the quicker it slowed down, due to the increased drag from the water as it settled deeper.

Finally, they moved into a slow taxi about a hundred feet from the dock. Jeff took a deep breath and let it out slowly. Then he aimed his attention at the beach and accompanying hillside.

A man wearing a white polo shirt and shorts grabbed at the plane and swiftly lashed it securely to the dock. Without waiting for instructions, he began unloading the plane's cargo, half of which belonged to Melonie.

Melonie appeared to forget why she was here. "This place is beautiful! Check out the water. You can see all the way to the bottom."

Jeff peered over the side of the dock. "It must be twenty feet deep already."

Above the dock, beyond a patch of neatly trimmed lawn, a chateau made of stained cedar boards complemented the forest setting.

An overdressed servant wearing a white dinner jacket

and black tie met Troy at the end of the dock. "Mr. Tinaco will be with you shortly, sir. Please come in."

Melonie and Jeff followed Troy's lead and climbed up several rock steps past a fountain. A series of private gardens surrounded the estate. Many of them were lined with decorative fences, and all held a profusion of shrubbery.

Once inside, the usual courtesies were offered. Without hesitation, Melonie accepted a glass of chardonnay. Jeff took a glass of freshly squeezed orange juice.

Mr. Tinaco strolled into the room, dwarfed by two six-foot four-inch bodyguards. Shorter than Melonie, he looked like a South American version of Napoleon. A white polo shirt and teal shorts covered his swarthy skin. Deep lines etched a pockmarked face.

Without warning, the closest guard waved a hand-sized metal detector around Jeff. The buzzer identified Jeff's Glock tucked behind his waist. With lightning speed, the other guard whipped out a pistol and trained it directly at Jeff's head. Almost as fast, the first guard retrieved Jeff's weapon.

"Gentlemen and lady, you will have no need for protection here. My associates are quite competent." A slight accent could be detected in Mr. Tinaco's voice.

With the gun still trained on Jeff's head, the other guard proceeded to check Melonie. Jeff braced himself for the inevitable discovery. But it didn't come.

Tinaco's head gave a quick jerk and the guards retained their original positions as if nothing happened.

Troy made the introductions. "This is my good friend Jeff Spenelie and his companion, Melonie. I trust him with my life." Then, motioning toward the host, "This is Mr. Tinaco, a trusted business associate."

Tinaco nodded with no smile. "You are hungry." He turned to the servant. "Richard, a tray of fish." Tinaco addressed Melonie with his stony face. "Do you appreciate fish, Miss Melonie?"

"I love seafood."

"I captured them myself," Tinaco said.

Troy smiled thinly as if he knew something the rest of them didn't.

A moment later, the servant reappeared with a large silver tray adorned with Kokanee salmon. Some were smoked and some were raw. All had their heads still tenaciously clinging to their bodies.

Tinaco picked at one of the fish. "Try it. You will be impressed with the flavor."

Jeff flaked off a small chunk. "This is great!" Then, turning to Melonie, "Here, I'll save the head for you."

Melonie stared at the head and swallowed hard. "Thanks, I'll pass."

Without hesitation, Tinaco scooped one of the raw fish off the tray. He held it firmly behind the gills. "In some South Pacific islands, the eye is a delicacy." Pressing his lips against the fish's head, Tinaco made a quick sucking sound.

Melonie gawked with open disgust when she noticed the fish head was missing one eye.

Tinaco swirled the contents in his mouth and swallowed. Then in one swift motion, he slipped the remainder of the head into his mouth and bit down. There was a definite crunch that made Melonie turn pale and shudder.

Troy appeared content to watch.

"Try it." Tinaco's eyes challenged Jeff.

Jeff shrugged his shoulders. "Why not?" Selecting the largest raw fish he could find, Jeff repeated Tinaco's performance. "Not too bad. The texture takes a little getting used to though."

Melonie stared at the tray and then at Jeff. "You're sleeping on the couch!"

Jeff pulled down the corners of his mouth and tried to act hurt.

Tinaco grunted in satisfaction. "Richard, prepare dinner for them. One that Miss Melonie will appreciate." He turned to face his guest. "You may leave. Troy and I have business to attend to."

After the meal, the servant escorted Jeff and Melonie through the gardens to a small cottage outside the main house. He opened the door. "Your belongings have already been put away for you. If there is anything I can do to make your stay more comfortable, please pick up the phone. It will automatically ring to us."

"Thank you." Jeff felt like he should tip him, but the servant turned and left.

The cottage consisted of a single large room. Even the bathroom was only walled off on three sides. A couch and table were on one side and a large king-sized bed was on the other. All their clothes had been neatly folded in the dresser next to the bed.

Jeff faced Melonie. "So where did you hide y—"

Before he could finish, Melonie slapped him across the face. "Where do you get off eating fish heads in front of me like that? You only did it to show off."

Jeff just stood there with his mouth open.

"I'm sorry," Melonie said as she put her arms around him. She whispered in his ear, "Don't say anything that will get us in trouble. The room is probably being monitored."

Jeff mentally chastised his rookie error and gave her arm a quick squeeze to show his understanding. "Let's go outside and cool off." Melonie nodded and followed him out the door.

Jeff looked around and saw that they were alone. "So where *did* you hide your gun?"

"I dumped it in the water after we got off the seaplane. I was hoping you would see it when you looked over the edge. I had no idea the water would be so deep."

"But why?"

"I knew it would be just a matter of time before they checked us for weapons. For you, it would seem natural, but for me—your girlfriend . . ."

Jeff rubbed his nose with a sinking feeling that he was in over his head. "I guess it was the right thing to do."

Melonie looked over to the dock. "I'll go swimming later

and get it." She stared thoughtfully at Jeff. "We'll have to be careful to act the part."

Jeff glanced toward the cottage. "Yeah, uh, what about sleeping arrangements?"

Melonie raised one eyebrow. "What about it?"

"Well, if they have hidden cameras and, well, you know."

Melonie took Jeff's hand. "They told me why I was in a separate apartment. I understand your religion isn't real keen on people living together. Don't worry. I'll do everything I can to make things easier for you."

"Thanks, but what about tonight?"

Melonie wrinkled her forehead in thought. Her face brightened. "We'll continue our fight!"

Jeff rubbed his cheek and grinned. "Okay, but no more slaps or I'll dunk you in the lake."

"Fair enough," Melonie smiled.

As they reentered the cabin, Jeff walked directly to the bed and yanked off the top cover. "Fine! Take the bed." Then he stomped over to the couch, lay down, threw the blanket over himself, and closed his eyes.

"If that's the way you want it, that's the way it'll be." Melonie turned off the lights, undressed, and slid into bed.

Chapter Seventeen

The Green Monarch Mountains plunge four thousand feet before meeting the waters of Lake Pend Oreille. They continue their descent over a thousand feet, seemingly intent on driving to the earth's core, making Pend Oreille one of the deepest lakes in the United States.

Stephanie's attention was riveted to the deep blue expanse below, surrounded by mountains covered with alpine fir and bear grass. Sheer north slopes ended with snowbanks protecting pockets of fish-filled lakes.

"God's country," Stephanie mumbled.

"What?"

Stephanie jerked her head up from the trance to face Mr. Hunnington's quizzical stare. "God's country," she repeated a little louder. "That's what my friends call this part of Idaho. I heard it was beautiful, but I had no idea."

Mr. Hunnington nodded in understanding.

A tailwind had helped the morning flight from Idaho Falls to Spokane go quickly. Mr. Hunnington had spent most of the time going over briefs for court next week. When they arrived in Spokane thirty minutes ago, they were picked up in a red and yellow seaplane. Now they were on their way to a remote location on the lake. Stephanie, no longer in the pilot's seat, leaned back, content to enjoy the scenery.

Tiny cometlike streaks posing as boats frequented the lake in areas where the fish were more abundant. The seaplane circled over the lake from the west in order to make the only possible landing into Harrison Bay.

Mr. Hunnington leaned forward to the pilot. "How do you land when it's windy?"

"I've made it when there's whitecaps on the lake. Unless the wind comes from the east, the bay's almost always calm."

Hunnington grunted a note of satisfaction and settled back into his seat.

As they neared the final approach, Stephanie raised one eyebrow. "Looks interesting. You've done this approach before?"

The pilot turned his head back and smiled. "Works every time."

Stephanie felt the country rapidly closing in from both sides. "Ever try to abort landing?"

"Never."

"Oh."

The pilot kept his eyes locked forward. "I don't think it would work. Do you?"

Stephanie watched the head wall of earth rushing at them. "No, I don't suppose it would."

First a skip, then glide, and then settle. The seaplane plowed through the water up to the side of the dock and was quickly secured.

Tinaco looked across the table at Troy. They were alone. "How do you know he's safe?"

"Well, for one thing, he saved my life in a rip-off. If he was heat, something would have happened then."

"Not if he's deep cover."

"No cop would risk his life to save mine. He could have just ducked down and taken cover, but he didn't. He threw his body over mine."

Tinaco leaned forward. He had the disturbing habit of

tilting his head forward and looking at people through his eyebrows. "Did you check him out?"

"We did a quick study two days ago. Everything looked good."

"But can you trust him? What about this thing that happened to one of your dealers?"

Troy's eyes raised in surprise. He had not expected Tinaco to know about Margo's death.

Tinaco arched his finger together. "Dennis Margo, was not this his name?"

"Jeff had nothing to do with that. Margo was stupid. He started using and it caught up with him. I merely accelerated the inevitable. Besides, Hunnington is tying up the loose ends."

"Is this Jeff desiring Margo's business?"

"I don't think so, unless he's playing hard to get. I offered it to him, and he said he wasn't interested."

Tinaco's servant entered the room. "The attorney from Idaho Falls is here."

"Make Mr. Hunnington comfortable."

"Yes sir."

Tinaco returned his attention to Troy and folded his arms. "Trust. You trust him too much. Always you should have an alternate plan. Always prepare for the worst." Then emphasizing the first and last words that followed, "*This* is the basis for *trust*." Tinaco reached over the table and popped some nuts into his mouth. "Do what you want. Test him further. I will have a real—how do you say it—study done on this Jeff."

Troy nodded. "I think you'll find him quite satisfactory."

Tinaco leaned on one elbow over the table and pointed his finger at Troy. "Before you give him too much credit for saving your life in the rip-off in Newport Beach, you should check the bullet holes in the driver's body. I think you'd find that the one through his heart entered from the back."

"But how did you know—"

Tinaco interrupted him. "That was a stupid chance you took. Fortunate for you, I take a personal interest in your continued survival." Without further comment, Tinaco strolled out of the room.

Troy shook his head and mumbled, "No wonder he got where he is. No one would dare challenge him." Troy put on his sunglasses and walked outside to find Jeff.

The conversation between Jeff and Melonie shifted to swimming as Troy walked up from the garden path.

Troy called out. "Did you try the boat yet?"

Jeff waved with excitement. "They took us for a quick cruise. What a ride! It's loaded."

Troy turned to Melonie. "Would you mind if I talked to Jeff about some business matters?"

"Not at all." She glanced up at the sun and nodded. "I think I'll catch some rays."

Troy unabashedly stared at Melonie as she sauntered down the path. He smiled at Jeff. "Are you enjoying yourself?"

"I could get used to this kind of lifestyle fast."

"You have what it takes to have this kind of lifestyle—if you want it." Troy stepped closer.

Jeff felt his steely gaze. He shoved his trembling hands into his pockets.

"Do you want it?" Troy's stare brought an icy chill down Jeff's spine. The memory of the ponytailed bandit flashed in front of him. "Yes. If the conditions are right." Jeff tried to steady his nerves.

"And what would be the right conditions?"

"I know you want me to take over Margo's business, but I don't want it." Jeff picked a leaf from a lilac bush and began shredding it. "Remember when you asked me to work directly for you?"

Troy nodded.

"At that time I wanted to, but I couldn't just walk out

on Margo. Now I don't have those ties. If the offer is still open, I'm interested."

Troy smiled. "You know if you took over Margo's accounts, you could retire a rich man in two years."

Jeff shrugged and then nodded his head. "Maybe someday that will interest me, Troy, but I have a feeling that I'll be much more successful if I spend a few years working with you first. I like your style."

Troy sighed. "I am pleased with your choice. I can get any number of people to take Margo's position. Consider yourself hired." Troy turned to leave. "As for the money part, I think you'll be pleasantly surprised."

Alone, Jeff sat down on the grass and stretched out his legs. Taking in a deep breath, he propped himself up with his arms and gazed up at the occasional puffy clouds floating by. *It's working.*

"This is Bob Burtenshaw with KUPI on this sunny Saturday morning. Coming up on the hour is Paul Harvey news and commentary. The temperature is 92 degrees here in Idaho Falls, with a 95 in Pocatello and 91 in Rexburg."

Barry punched the seek button until it stopped on Classy 97. Miami Sound Machine filled the air. "That's better."

He pulled into the safe house and met Special Agent Empy at the door. Empy cleared his throat, clearly pleased with the news he was about to announce. "You'll be delighted to know that our strategy has culminated in a workable plan that is currently being implemented."

"What?"

"Jeff left with Melonie to take a business trip with Troy."

Barry grinned. "So Troy took the bait?"

"Yes."

"Where did they go?"

"Initially we theorized they would travel to California.

This supposition was based on the prior trips Troy took and on Troy's comments to Jeff."

"So where did they go?"

"North."

"North?" Barry's voice tightened. "Where north?"

"As near as we can tell, it's by a lake in northern Idaho called Pend Oreille. There's a house in a bay that—"

Barry interrupted, "Why wasn't I notified? Where's Reed?"

"Reed's there now with the surveillance team."

"What have they found out? Who is involved?" Barry spat out questions faster than Empy could answer.

"Take it easy, Barry. Is something wrong?"

Barry laughed nervously. "No, I guess I'm sorry to miss out on all the action." Then, glancing back at the car, Barry snapped his fingers in remembrance. "I left my luggage at the airport. I'll run back and get it."

"Curt's already there. I'll phone and have him bring it."

Barry protested loudly. "No!" Then, lowering his voice, "I mean, I would rather just do it myself."

Empy put on his glasses and peered through them at Barry. "Are you feeling okay?"

Barry jumped back in the car. "I'm fine. I'll be back in a few minutes." Not waiting for further argument, Barry slammed the door and drove off.

Instead of turning on Skyline Drive toward the airport, Barry stopped at a pay phone. He leaped from the car and snatched up the phone receiver. "Operator, I'd like to make a collect call . . . "

Stephanie walked toward the dock toting a towel and suntan lotion. The host had been very courteous, but it was obvious he didn't want her involved in the meeting. After being warned about the cool lake water, Stephanie accepted the challenge, changed into her swimsuit, and headed for the waterfront. She thought about Jeff and decided a little sun might make her more attractive.

162

A deck constructed over the water next to the docks accommodated a variety of chairs, awnings, and tables. Stephanie stepped onto the deck and discovered she wasn't the only one ready to take advantage of the sun.

A woman who needed no further tanning lounged on her back with small reflective patches shielding her eyes. The high-cut sides of her swimsuit and skimpy top exposed more than they covered.

The soft tap of the suntan lotion being set on the table brought the woman up with a start. Stephanie apologized. "I'm sorry. I didn't mean to startle you."

The woman flashed her TV-perfect teeth. "That's okay. Sometimes I get kind of jumpy." She extended her hand. "Hi, I'm Melonie. Do you live here?"

"No, I just came up for the weekend. My name is Stephanie."

"Well, I'm glad to meet you, Stephanie. Are you here for business or pleasure?"

"Both, I guess. I'm a pilot for Mr. Hunnington. Do you know him?"

Melonie shook her head.

"He's an attorney. Actually my regular job is as a legal secretary, but my boss lost his pilot and asked me to fill in."

"Lost his pilot? Sounds exciting."

Stephanie laughed. "To Delta, not a crash." Stephanie decided they could become friends if they lived closer. "Are you vacationing?"

"Kind of. My boyfriend is here on business, and he invited me up with him." Melonie pointed her finger in the direction of the cottage. "We're staying in the cabin over there. It's kind of like a honeymoon for us."

Stephanie beamed. "So you just got married?"

"No, actually we're not even living together yet. But the way things are going, we might get married some day—if we decide to have kids."

"Oh."

Melonie redirected the conversation. "So are you and this Mr. Hunnington, you know . . . "

Stephanie flushed. "No, he's old enough to be my father. With him it's strictly business."

"Then there's someone else?"

Stephanie paused for a moment, and Melonie blurted out, "I'm sorry. I forget my manners sometimes. I didn't mean to pry."

"No, that's okay. I was just thinking. I do have someone. In fact, I was supposed to be with him today, but he had some business come up."

"Too bad. I'll bet you wish he could be here."

Stephanie reclined, and then hopped back up. "Darn! I forgot my sunglasses."

"Do you want to borrow mine?"

"Thanks anyway, but I have them in my luggage. I'll just run up and get them."

"I think I'll go with you. I could use a drink."

As Melonie accompanied Stephanie up the garden paths, they came across the figure of a man sitting on the grass facing the other direction. A look of recognition came across Melonie's face as she saw the tightly trimmed hair on the back of his neckline. Strangely, Stephanie sensed something familiar too, but couldn't quite place it.

Melonie put her finger over her lips, signaling silence, and crept up to where he sat. Standing almost directly over him, Melonie bent over, spilling her dark hair into his lap. Nose to chin, she pressed her lips against his for a brief moment and then whispered something in his ear. Then she kissed him harder.

Stephanie cleared her throat and turned away. Then she looked back expectantly as Melonie's boyfriend stood up and turned to face her.

Chapter Eighteen

"Stephanie, I'd like you to meet Jeff. Jeff, this is Stephanie. She's spending the weekend here too."

Stephanie's eyes widened while Jeff froze in place. Neither spoke for several seconds.

"Jeff?" Her voice quivered. Her eyes spilled over with tears. Swinging her head around, she staggered blindly down the trail.

Melonie cocked her head and stared at Jeff. "Boy, you really know how to make a good impression!"

Ignoring Melonie, Jeff took a step forward and shouted, "Stephanie, wait!"

"I take it you've already met?"

Jeff sunk to the ground and pressed his hands to his head. He looked up at Melonie. "Why is she here?"

"She said something about flying her boss here—an attorney. Something about his regular pilot being out of commission."

Jeff cocked his head back and stared at the sky. His mind raced to Stephanie's connection with Margo. He remembered Gary warning him about how clever a plant could be. *Could she be a plant by Tinaco? Someone to keep an eye on Margo? No way. It just doesn't make sense.*

Melonie gently placed her hand on Jeff's back. "We need to talk."

Jeff nodded. "I was dating her."

Melonie raised her eyebrows. "You mean *that* Stephanie? The one connected to Margo?"

"How did you know about her?" Jeff snapped.

"I was briefed on everything. Remember?"

"I suppose you think she's part of this."

"No."

"Then you think she is being duped?"

"No."

"Well, what then?"

"I think she is a nice girl who has fallen for a nice guy." Jeff's shoulders sagged.

Melonie took a long breath. "I'm sorry. It looks like I truly messed things up for you."

"It's not your fault."

"I didn't have to kiss you like that."

"It's not your fault."

Melonie shook her head. "No, there's no excuse. I don't know what got into me. I just—"

"Really. It's not your fault." Then, with a mischievous grin, he added, "It's been a problem all my life. I guess it comes with being so gorgeous."

Melonie nodded in agreement. "You are truly gorgeous."

Jeff laughed. "So now what? I can't very well tell her that I'm a secret agent working for the government to uncover a major drug connection. That I only kissed you for love of country and queen."

"Why not?"

"What do you mean why not? I mean, look at you! Am I supposed to tell her this is part of my cover? That I never enjoyed kissing you in the past, and I promise to never enjoy kissing you in the future?"

Melonie spoke softly. "Jeff, we live in a dirty world and deal with dirty people. Sometimes it's hard not to get a few stains on us. But as far as I can tell, you've been above it all." She straightened her shoulders. "We were all amazed that you managed to gain Troy's trust like that. We said you were lucky and fell into it. I don't claim to understand all of it, but this I do know. If it was me, or Reed, or anyone else instead of you, it wouldn't have worked."

"So now what?"

"Sounds like you'll need to have a long talk with her."

Jeff stared at the ground. "What if she doesn't believe me? Or what if she does believe me and doesn't want anything to do with me?"

"Is she worth the risk?"

Jeff gazed across the bay, not focusing on anything in particular. "Yes. I guess I have to try. As soon as we get back."

"No."

Jeff pulled down one eyebrow. "No?"

"You need to tell her now."

"Are you serious? And jeopardize the whole operation?"

"It sounds crazy, but some people you just have to trust. If you don't tell her, it could make matters worse."

"How could it be worse?"

"Troy finds out you were dating her. If he connects her to Margo and your flying lessons, we're through."

Cold chills rose on Jeff's spine. "That would be worse."

"Think about it. Either way there's a risk, but I think talking to her is the best option."

"Empy would completely freak if he knew I blew my cover with her. Not to mention Gary and the others."

"What they think hasn't seemed to bother you in the past."

"That's when I knew I was right."

"Go to her now. Trust me, I know how she feels."

"The last time you said 'trust me,' my hair ended up looking like a rosebush desecrated by a lawn mower."

"Come on now. Are you gorgeous or what?"

"Yeah, but remember? That's what got me into this mess."

Melonie flashed her generous smile and patted Jeff on the shoulder like a puppy. "You're sweet."

Jeff stood up and marched down the path toward the docks, hoping to find the woman he had grown to love.

It didn't take long. Curled up against a large boulder on the beach, Stephanie stared blankly across the water. Jeff stepped next to the rock. "Mind if I sit down?"

"Yes."

"Look, Stephanie, just let me explain."

"Oh, I think it's all quite clear," she said caustically.

"Remember when I told you that I had something I needed to tell you, but couldn't yet?"

"Yeah, so you're not married. You're just living with her."

"She means nothing to me!"

"Yes, I noticed that."

Jeff rubbed his hand over his face. "Stephanie, will you please just let me try to explain?" Jeff took her silence as a yes. "I'm not what I appear to be."

She snorted in disgust.

"Let me start at the beginning. I am a detective for the City of Idaho Falls. I'm working undercover narcotics. I took flying lessons hoping to find a way to bust Margo."

"I'm not amused by your cutsie little stories—"

"Hear me out!" Jeff lowered his voice and continued. "We busted Margo, and he turned state's evidence. With his help, I worked my way up the ladder and eventually here."

Stephanie closed her eyes and shook her head.

"But I developed this problem. I started to fall for this woman who was teaching the flight lessons. After we busted Margo there was no real reason to see you but personal interest."

"How flattering."

"They made me promise not to break my cover. I wanted to tell you. Really, I did."

"I'm supposed to believe this?"

"It's the truth."

"Let's suppose for a moment that you are some super

spy. You lied to me then, so why should I believe you now?"

"I didn't really lie to you. I just didn't tell you the whole story."

"Oh, you mean the little details like your mistress?"

"She's not my mistress. It's all part of the cover."

Stephanie looked down and started grinding a pebble between her fingers. "Just leave me alone."

"You don't believe me."

"Brilliant deduction, Sherlock. Maybe you actually should be a detective."

"I'll prove it. Ask me any questions about flying."

"Why?"

"I already have my pilot's license. Go ahead, ask me."

"You mean you lied about that too?"

Jeff sensed he had just made a strategic error. "What can I do to convince you?"

"Got any police I.D.?"

"Of course not. I can't carry that when I'm working undercover."

"How convenient."

"Ask Melonie. She'll tell you!"

"Now there's a reliable source. Or maybe I could ask our host. Excuse me, Mr. Tinaco, but are you a drug dealer?"

"If you tell them what I have told you, I will be a dead man."

"Now there's an idea."

"Okay, what about the time you borrowed my car and got pulled over by the cop? The registration said Jeff Foster. That's my real name. He told you it was a mistake and he would fix it. Why do you think he kept the registration? Cops don't do that."

Stephanie hesitated and then looked away. "Look, Jeff Foster, or whatever your name is. Why don't you just leave me alone?"

Jeff sighed loudly. Then, after a moment of silence,

"Stephanie." He looked deep into her eyes and spoke with unwavering gentleness. "There is a way you can know for yourself."

Stephanie looked up and briefly met his gaze in anticipation.

Jeff continued, "I know we share the same values. You can pray about it and ask Heavenly Father if what I'm telling you is the truth."

Staring across the water, Stephanie remained silent.

Jeff stood up to leave. He stooped over and gently kissed the top of her head before trudging back to the gardens. "I'm sorry."

A single tear glided down her cheek, plummeting onto a small smooth rock. Gradually the tear evaporated away, leaving the stone as it was—small and smooth.

Troy stared at the painting of a dark-skinned boy picking grapes. His big toe protruded from his left shoe. A grey torn shirt matched his tattered coveralls. The painting would be considered unremarkable except for the boy's expression. Where other children's images endured dejection and melancholy, the boy's countenance embraced an air of determined aspiration. The title simply read "Ambition."

Tinaco slammed down the phone and whirled around to Troy. "It seems you have a problem."

"What's that?"

"Your *friend* Jeff is an undercover police officer." Tinaco put sarcastic significance on the word *friend*.

"Impossible! How do you know?"

"Sources."

"Are you sure?"

"Yes." The edge in his voice shot quivers of fear through Troy. Tinaco gritted his teeth. "What are you going to do about it?"

Troy's face turned red as the veins in his face bulged. In a controlled monotone, he spat the words, "Kill him."

"You've done enough. I will take care of it."

"No, it's my problem. I can handle it," Troy apologized.

"You bring a cop to my house, and now you say you will handle it?" Tinaco's jaw tightened. He jabbed his finger toward Troy's nose and spoke in a throaty whisper. "You are lucky to be alive!"

Troy stood silent, fumbling for words.

As suddenly as the rage came, it was gone. Tinaco briefly stared at the ceiling and then faced the painting. "Jeff knows enough to cause great problems. He will disappear forever."

"And the girl?"

"She has nothing. We will take her to town and not bring her back. She will no doubt summon help, but it will be too late. They will have nothing to find, and they will be fools."

Tinaco scooped up a handful of nuts. "Richard!" The servant instantly appeared. "Bring Sheila and then invite Ms. Melonie here. Do you understand?"

"Yes sir. I am to bring Sheila and Ms. Melonie."

"You are to bring Sheila first, before you bring the girl."

"Yes sir."

"See that this is done."

Melonie looked up from the water, startled at the man's sudden appearance. She gripped the dock with one hand and kept the other carefully concealed while her legs churned water.

"Ma'am?"

Melonie answered over the edge of the dock. "Hi."

"Mr. Tinaco requests your presence. Could you please come with me?"

Melonie tucked a Ziploc bag containing a shiny object between the boards of the dock. "Sure." She boosted herself onto the dock and followed him.

Sheila, a twenty-year-old blonde, sat in a chair next to

Tinaco while Melonie walked into the house, still dripping.

Tinaco stood up. "Hello, Melonie. Are you enjoying yourself?"

"This place is great!"

"Good. I am happy." Tinaco gazed across the bay. "Melonie, this is Sheila. Would you be so kind as to accompany her to Spokane for a few hours? She would like to go shopping, and I'm afraid none of us are of use to her."

Sheila stared straight ahead with a courteous smile. Tinaco turned to Melonie with his hands clasped behind his back. "Sheila is blind."

"Oh." Melonie fidgeted. "Sure, I'd be happy to."

"Excellent! The plane will be ready in thirty minutes." Tinaco turned and strolled out of the room.

When Melonie returned to the cabin, she found Jeff outside picking at grass absently. "Did you find her?"

"Yeah."

"How'd it go?"

"Not good."

Melonie sat down next to him. "Tinaco wants me to go shopping with some blind woman for a few hours."

"Why doesn't he have someone else do it?"

"Look around. There aren't too many females."

"What did you say?"

"That I'd go. What else could I say?"

Jeff shrugged his shoulders, his mind elsewhere.

Melonie touched the back of his head. "Listen, just give her some time. Play it cool. I should be back for supper."

Jeff followed her into the cabin and plopped down into a chair. "Yeah."

"Well, I guess I'll change into something more appropriate."

Jeff didn't respond.

Melonie stood directly in front of him. "Are you going to be all right?"

Jeff jerked his head up. "Yeah, I'll be fine."

She lifted off a shoulder strap from her bathing suit. "I'm going to change now."

Jeff stared into space. "Yeah, good idea."

"So, like maybe you want to go for a swim or something."

A look of understanding flooded Jeff's face. "Oh, uh, yeah. Well, I think I'll go for a walk or something."

Melonie shook her head thoughtfully.

After she had changed into a yellow tank top and white shorts, Melonie passed by the dock on her way to wait for Sheila. She hesitated at the place where the servant had interrupted her swim and allowed the purse to slip from her fingers. As she bent over to pick it up, she reached over the edge of the dock and casually concealed a shiny object.

As Melonie looked around to see who might be watching, she spotted Stephanie perched by a large boulder a few hundred yards down the beach. Melonie picked up her handbag and hiked to the boulder.

"Hi!"

Stephanie's voice was raspy. "Hello."

"I'm sorry about what happened. He told me who you are."

Tearstained cheeks and red swollen eyes marked Stephanie's mood. "That's okay. It's not your fault."

Melonie sat down beside her. "It's not his fault either."

Stephanie remained silent.

Melonie picked up a flat stone and skipped it across the water. "Funny thing."

Stephanie waited for her to finish the phrase.

Melonie continued, "He's kind of strange. You know what he did?"

Stephanie cocked her head. "What?"

"Back in Idaho Falls, when we set up our cover, he refused to share an apartment with me. Acted like it was against his principles. I mean, the guy is strange. Last night, he refused to sleep in the same bed—and this is supposed to be our cover! So we pretended we had a fight and he slept on the couch. I mean, it's not like I was going to force him to do anything, but he didn't even want to be in the same room. I usually have the opposite problem with guys."

Stephanie glanced at Melonie's low-cut tank top and looked away. Then, clearing her throat, "Why did you, uh . . . ." Stephanie tilted her head forward as if trying to spill the words from her mouth. "Why did you kiss him . . . like that?"

"Credibility." Melonie stopped and thought deeper. Then shrugged her shoulders. "I don't know. Maybe I wouldn't have done it if he was ugly, but under the circumstances, I didn't leave him any options."

"He didn't seem to mind."

"Thanks, but I can tell when a guy's into it. Believe me, he wasn't."

Stephanie shook her head. "I don't know what to believe."

"You don't have any reason to believe me, but I know one thing. If I had a guy like that, I wouldn't let him go." Melonie looked down the beach and recognized Sheila standing by the seaplane.

Melonie reached into her purse and withdrew a 380 pistol. She set it on Stephanie's lap. "I'm going to town for a few hours. I think Jeff might need this more than me. Give it to him."

Stephanie opened her mouth, but Melonie cut her off. "It's ready to fire, so be careful."

Chapter Nineteen

Stephanie stared at the gun as the seaplane tugged, then lifted off the lake's surface. The cold blue metal in her hands sent fissures of anxiety down her spine. She carefully hid the gun under a flat rock and began walking back to the dock along the winding garden paths. Her pink top blended naturally with the mountain flowers.

She stopped. A peculiar sensation crept through her skin, a sense of foreboding. She ran her fingers through her hair, trying to shake the feeling. The sun overhead marked the halfway point between noon and sunset.

The warning returned, casting up waves of anxiety. Obeying the premonition, Stephanie pressed herself into the lilac bushes. She heard voices, men's voices. Sinking further into the foliage, she strained her ears, trying to hear over the pounding in her chest.

Now twenty feet away, she could barely make out the figures of three men marching toward the dock. The lead person had his hands restrained behind his back with handcuffs.

"It's your turn."

The man in the rear protested. "No, I bought last time."

"I'll tell you what. If he makes it a full minute, I'll add dinner to it—double or nothing."

"You're on." Then the second man gave the prisoner a

shove, causing him to tumble face first inches from Stephanie. He managed to land on his chest, driving out a loud grunt.

The rear guard let out a cry of protest. "I want him in good enough shape to swim. Leave him alone or the deal's off."

The second man sneered, "Okay, okay."

Stephanie peered into the prisoner's face. Slicing deep into her heart, the profile of Jeff appeared before her.

With one arm, the burly guard lifted Jeff by his handcuffs up to his feet and snickered, "Be more careful next time."

Jeff endured the treatment in silence.

Stephanie's mind flashed to the gun hidden under the rock on the beach. As soon as they were far enough down the trail, she bolted up and scurried through the brush toward the rock.

Seconds later, she held the gun in her hands. She had fired a revolver before, but never an automatic. Relying on Melonie's statement that the gun was ready to go, Stephanie crept over to the dock.

The burly man cranked the engine of the fifty-foot launch while the other guard waited on the dock, pointing a gun at the back of the head of the figure kneeling before him.

"Okay, let's go," hollered the man in the boat.

The guard grabbed Jeff's arm and brought him to his feet.

Stephanie knew she had to make her move now. While the husky man was out of sight in the cabin portion of the boat, she slid across the dock behind Jeff's guard. Pressing the gun to the back of his head, Stephanie commanded, "Don't move or I'll shoot."

Like lightning, the guard whirled his arm around to knock the gun from her hand. A sharp crack from the .380 rang out and passed harmlessly through the air. Simultaneously, his gun hand followed his first hand with a wider arc, catching Stephanie on the side of the head and sending her sprawling on the dock.

Training the gun on Stephanie's head, the guard prepared to pull the trigger. But almost as soon as Stephanie hit the dock, Jeff bolted to his feet. In a two-step action, he kicked the gun from the executioner's hand and immediately followed up with a sharp kick to his larynx.

The man dropped to his knees, clutching his throat. Jeff spun around as the burly guard jumped out of the boat and onto the dock. With a smile, the man set his gun down and walked toward them. Jeff tried a repeat of his earlier triumph, but this time, his opponent blocked the kick and returned three roundhouse kicks in quick succession to Jeff's head. Jeff toppled over and hit the wooden dock with a resonant *whump*.

Still stunned by the blow to her head, Stephanie gazed up at their conqueror and collapsed.

The connecting walkways above the streets of downtown Spokane make shopping a pleasure for those so inclined. Normally, Melonie would be so inclined, but this wasn't a normal time.

She had just spent two hours leading a blind woman through heavy foot traffic—a blind woman who, as Melonie viewed it, couldn't see what she was wearing anyway.

But now she had a big problem. Her blind friend was lost. Melonie had frantically searched four different stores. Sheila was nowhere to be seen.

Melonie called a cab and dashed out to the airport. As she neared the place where the seaplane should be hangared, she swallowed hard. The plane was gone.

She kicked off her high heels and sprinted to the nearest pay phone. Her fingers punched the numbers in a fury.

"Thanks for using AT&T. How would you like your called billed?" The voice sounded slow and distinct.

"Collect from Melonie," she blurted.

"One moment please."

Melonie counted the seconds. It was Empy who answered the phone. "Melonie?"

"Yes."

"Where are you?"

"Listen carefully. We've got problems. I think Jeff's in trouble."

"Talk."

"I'm at the Spokane Airport. We were staying at a house on Lake Pend Oreille. It's owned by a guy named Tinaco. Security is tight. We ran into Jeff's girlfriend there. He told her about us—"

"What?" Empy yelled in the phone.

Melonie ignored his question. "Tinaco asked me to take this blind woman shopping, so they—"

Empy interrupted, "Stephanie is blind now?"

"No, this other woman. They flew us to Spokane, but Jeff stayed. They searched us and got Jeff's weapon, but they didn't think anything of it. I slipped mine to Stephanie."

"You what?" Empy sounded incredulous. "Jeff I can understand. He's inexperienced. But you!"

"She's clean. I know it."

"How do you know it?"

"I just do."

Empy dropped it for now. "So you think he might be in trouble?"

Melonie swallowed hard. "They left. The blind woman ditched me in a store. I went to the airport to see if she showed up at the plane. It's gone."

"Go to the baggage claim area, and I'll have someone pick you up. As soon as you get there, call me and stay on the line until they arrive."

"Okay."

"Now watch yourself."

"Yeah."

Melonie hung up the phone. She briefly closed her eyes

and massaged her temple. "Be ready, Jeff . . . be ready," she whispered.

Jeff woke to the drone of the boat engines. Forcing his eyes open, the image of Stephanie's head leaning over him gradually came into focus. *Strange,* Jeff thought as he observed her blood-soaked hair matted against her cheek. Then the memory of the encounter on the dock struck him. Raising up quickly, Jeff was paralyzed by the piercing pain attacking his head.

"Shhh." Stephanie tried to soothe him, gently rubbing his head with her hands. Jeff looked closer and saw that her hands were tied together with a nylon cord. He tugged against his own hands and found them tied securely in the front.

Except for the burly driver who had delivered Jeff's headache, the only other person on the boat was a new guard. Jeff grunted in satisfaction that the man he had kicked in the throat was no longer present.

Sharp stabs of pain coursed through Jeff's body as he positioned himself against the side of the boat. "I am so sorry you had to get involved in this."

"Are you kidding? This beats cave exploring any day."

Jeff detected the terror behind her eyes and played along. "Yeah. Not so scary."

Stephanie gazed into his eyes. "I'm just sorry I botched up the rescue." Pausing to collect her courage, she added, "It doesn't look too good, does it?"

"No." Jeff gritted his jaw. "But don't give up on me, Stephanie."

She swallowed hard, her eyes desperate. "They're going to kill us?"

Jeff shrugged. "Oh sure. They can kill us all right. But can they eat us?"

"Huh?"

Jeff shook his head. "Never mind."

The boat neared the halfway point on the lake with the Green Monarchs on one side and Harrison Bay on the other. Burly cut the engine and walked back to where Jeff and Stephanie sat. Initially, he spoke as if he were a tour guide. "This is the deepest part of the lake. Deep enough that a small sub couldn't get to the bottom without being crushed by the pressure."

Jeff stared at him with no expression.

Burly smiled cruelly. "We're going to play a little game. It's called implosion."

Stephanie eyed Jeff nervously.

Burly continued, "The opposite of explosion. By the time you reach the bottom, the pressure will crunch your head to the size of a walnut."

Jeff sat up straighter. "You're crazy. You can't—"

Burly's eyes narrowed as he cut Jeff off. "Look around. There's no one here to save you."

Jeff sank back.

The assassin picked up a piece of rope fifteen feet long with a loop braided into each end. Using a padlock, he attached a twenty-pound iron weight and set it in front of Jeff. "Don't worry. I'm going to make this interesting."

The other guard snorted.

Burly produced another padlock and attached it through the rope, binding Jeff's hands and the braided loop of the other end of the rope. He then grabbed a second rope and repeated the whole process with Stephanie.

"Now here's the rules," he said, jabbing his thumb at Stephanie. "She goes first. If she's got strong legs, she might last a minute or two."

Jeff blurted out, "What do you want from me?"

Burly leered down at Jeff. "Amusement."

"I'll tell you anything you want to know. I'll do anything —just let her go."

Burly shook his head. "It'll be more fun this way."

Jeff started trembling. "Here. Kill me!"

"We will . . . after you watch her play the game."

Then without warning, Burly scooped up Stephanie and tossed her into the lake. Jeff bolted up, but Burly was already prepared. Grasping the weight attached to Stephanie's rope, he held it over the side. "Easy does it, or I drop it."

Jeff froze.

Stephanie managed to tread water exceptionally well, in spite of her hands being tied together.

"Looks like we got us a swimmer." The other guard came around and held his gun to Jeff's head.

Burly turned to face Jeff. "Okay, Mr. Policeman. One wrong move and David here will put a bullet through your head. Now let's see how she does with a little added weight."

Jeff flinched as Burly let the weight fall from his hands.

The weight slid through the clear green water and reached the end of the rope. The sudden tug jerked Stephanie's head under. With a quick scissor kick, she snatched a breath of air. Her legs churned with fury, desperately struggling to stay afloat.

Jeff yelled, "Swim, Steph, swim!" almost willing her out of the water.

As she tired, Stephanie kept her face under the water except to grab a precious mouthful of air. She thrashed with everything she had—her legs, her arms, even her shoulders—straining to survive.

Then her legs quit, no longer able to maintain the strenuous regime. Sinking a few feet in the water, they suddenly came alive again and she struggled up for one last breath. Her neck arched back, and she thrust her lips toward the surface. But she still lacked several needed inches.

Jeff's mind flashed to his childhood. The car crashing into the river. His father's strong arm pulling him from the submerged wreck. How he had stood there on that muddy bank after his father pushed his little sister toward him.

Being paralyzed with fear as his father slid into the depths of the river, too weak from saving his children to save himself. Now he again watched helplessly as the one he loved struggled for air.

With all the energy she had, Stephanie gave it one last supreme effort. But even as she did, her body slid downward, sinking deeper, ever deeper toward the place where water meets earth.

Chapter Twenty

Jeff stared into the watery grave, unwilling to accept it. *Please, Heavenly Father. Give me the strength I need to save Stephanie.*

He felt a surge of hope burn through his veins. With lightning speed, Jeff spun around, knocking the gun away from his head. Instantaneously, he scooped up the weight attached to his rope and threw it where he last saw Stephanie.

Before the rope had a chance to pull, he dove in, racing downward, following the path it led. Diagonal shafts of sunlight spread through the water. At first, everything looked green, a green that turned darker the deeper he went. He kicked with all his might, chasing the weight.

Then he saw it—her dark blonde hair shimmering softly in the rapidly dimming light. The added boost from the weight almost made him speed past her.

He grabbed her rope, looping it around his leg twice, and began thrashing, trying to slow their downward descent. His hands shot down to his belt as he fumbled to get it off. He pulled it from his pants and tugged at the belt's zippered compartment. Ignoring the pressure on his ears, he reached inside and grasped the razor. The thin metal blade between his fingers sawed vigorously through the rope. For a moment, he fumbled and nearly lost hold.

Taking a firmer grip, he continued. After several precious seconds, his hands broke free.

His ears shrieked with pain from the water pressure, so he paused for a brief moment, plugged his nose, and blew. Relief. Now hacking at Stephanie's rope with his dwindling energy, Jeff felt his muscles begin to fail. Uncontrollable craving for air tore at his lungs.

Blackness surrounded him. Suddenly the tug from her rope disappeared, signaling that the weight was now continuing its journey alone. The ear pressure returned, causing pain that no longer seemed relevant.

Suddenly, Stephanie was gone. All alone, Jeff thrashed about wildly, feeling nothing. Forcefully, he calmed himself. Then he touched something. In another instant, he caught her hair. He reeled her in like a fish, grabbed her hands and kicked. *But where is the surface?*

Panic enveloped him again. He turned every direction, searching for some clue of where the surface might lay. He paused briefly and blew out a few small bubbles, hoping to follow their trail to the top. *Too dark to see.* He turned his head and blew again. This time he felt the tickling sensation against his left ear. He turned in that direction and started kicking with all the strength he possessed. Forceful scissor kick after scissor kick propelled them forward. All the while, Jeff steadily sawed at the cords binding Stephanie's hands.

Now her hands were free. But Jeff was numb. He continued, kick after kick, oblivious that the razor blade was gone. Mechanically he persisted, only vaguely aware that the light was returning. The image of his father struggling to push his sister to the surface crowded his mind. The burning in his lungs began to fade. Visions of his sister being pushed toward him, his father's hands slipping under the water's surface . . .

Jeff started pushing air out his lungs involuntarily. The urge overpowered him. Resigning himself to death, he opened his mouth to embrace the lake.

To his surprise, a great breath of air charged his lungs as his head broke the surface, giving him power desperately needed.

He pulled Stephanie beside him and turned her on her back. Pale blue shrouded her face from lack of oxygen. With a prayer in his heart, Jeff sealed his mouth over hers and gave three quick breaths. His legs churned with power he did not possess while holding their faces above the water. Stephanie retched violently and regurgitated a profusion of water. Jeff held her head above the surface as she regained consciousness.

Tears of gratitude formed in Jeff's eyes. "Yes! Thank you."

Jeff's prayer was interrupted by a sharp crack. Spinning his head around, he watched as a fifty-foot cruiser circled toward them.

The gunman holstered his weapon, apparently gloating over the impending collision.

"Get ready to take a deep breath!"

Stephanie, still dazed, nodded her head in understanding.

Jeff yanked his baggy Dockers off as the cruiser bore down on them. "Okay, now!"

Stephanie expanded her chest and ducked her head under the water. Jeff gave her an extra push, forcing her several more feet under the surface. Poised a few feet under, he stretched the pants high over his head and prepared for the attack.

The throaty reverberation from the engine vibrated through the water. The bow came into view, immediately followed by the uncaring propeller.

As the bottom slid across Jeff's hands, he realized that he was too high. Ducking to one side, he fed the pants into the propeller. A piercing stab of pain penetrated his shoulder closest to the prop as the pants were yanked from his grip.

Both Jeff and Stephanie popped up in time to hear the

engine strain against the new obstruction. Then it stopped. The boat sat dead in the water two hundred feet away.

Jeff yelled at Stephanie, "Come on, swim!" while pulling her away from the boat. Jeff kept one eye on the cruiser and thrashed his legs and arms, driving them further from the range of gunfire.

Then the game started. Seeing Burly whip out his pistol, Jeff shoved Stephanie's head under the water and joined her. Stephanie's legs combined with Jeff's to create a team effort. When it seemed impossible to exist in the airless atmosphere any longer, they bolted up, grabbed one quick breath, and plunged immediately back into the less-hostile environment. A high-pitched projectile buzzed by Jeff's ear.

Somehow they continued, repeating this process many times, innumerable times. Finally, they were several hundred yards from the boat. Stephanie mechanically snatched another breath and pulled herself under. Jeff grabbed her arm and panted. "I think . . . we're out . . . of range now."

Stephanie flopped onto her back, sucking in deep breaths.

Jeff held her arm and resumed swimming. "We have to keep moving. Eventually they'll untangle the prop."

Stephanie nodded her head, still huffing for want of air.

The boat lay between them and the other, more populated, shore. Since they were closer to the Green Monarchs, they continued to swim in that direction. Now they were less than a mile from the rocky beach. Jeff scanned for signs of civilization. Nothing—no houses, no boats, no people—just the sheer Monarchs plummeting into Lake Pend Oreille.

Stroke after stroke they persisted. Suddenly Jeff stopped, his face contorted with pain. Immediately, he bent over face down into the water and grabbed his right toe. He straightened his leg and gently massaged his calf.

Stephanie, unaware of his condition, methodically backstroked her way to the shore—up, out, together, up, out, together . . .

Jeff's muscle softened and he changed to a breast-stroke. The boat was now almost a mile away. Between the sheer rock faces in front of them lay a tiny cove at the base of a steep ravine. Having gotten some sense of bearings, he shouted, "Head for the cove."

Stephanie ignored him as the lake water lapped over her ears.

Jeff increased his speed. Finally, he touched her foot. With a start, she whipped around to face him.

Jeff threw his eyes toward the cove. "Over there."

Too exhausted to answer, Stephanie simply altered her course and continued swimming.

Shadows from the mountains on the other side slowly overtook them. Jeff shook uncontrollably as a chill rippled through his body. Then fatigue overwhelmed him. He shifted to a sluggish backstroke.

He watched the lumbering clouds overhead and imagined a shark. Another cloud transformed into a buffalo. His muscles worked by rote. Occasionally water would cover his face, motivating him to increase his efforts. One of the clouds converted into a prehistoric bird threatening to swoop down to scoop up its vulnerable prey. Now the water freely spilled over his eyes. He no longer squinted, but allowed it to flow in and out at will.

The giant bird faded from view. The clouds grew dim, and Jeff drifted to a winter scene. Now snow covered everything. But it was warm. It enveloped him. The softness retreated into a descending darkness, through his eyes, his ears, even through his nostrils. A warm, relaxing slumber. *How odd and yet how wonderful. A snowy substance I can smell.*

Jeff gazed upward. The clouds could barely be detected through the glowing film. Suddenly, Stephanie's face appeared next to the alien bird. She shouted at him. *Strange.* Jeff wondered why she was so upset as he watched tears flow from her eyes.

He reached out to comfort her, but couldn't touch her. Stephanie descended from the clouds. Jeff awoke with panicked lungs. *Air! There's no air!*

Bursting through the airless film, Jeff gagged and sucked in deep breaths. Molecules of oxygen rushed to his heart and on to his brain. Reality swept over him as his consciousness returned.

Stephanie screamed, "Stay with me. We're almost there!"

Drained of energy, Jeff willed his legs to assist. Slow and certain, Stephanie scissored her legs and scooped water with one hand while the other tugged at Jeff.

They were only ten feet from shore, but the bottom of the lake refused to ease their pain. Jeff touched a smooth granite rock jutting out of the water. "Hold on to the rock!" Stephanie placed Jeff's hand on the edge.

Jeff watched curiously as her legs bicycled on the slime-covered granite. She cocked one elbow and tried to lift herself. In apparent frustration, she turned to Jeff. "Okay, Hercules, you want to get us out of this or what?"

With every ounce of stamina left in his clay arms, Jeff mantled the rock and pulled Stephanie from the water. Looking almost choreographed, they collapsed on the rock bench. For several minutes, neither spoke.

Finally Jeff felt strength returning to his body and broke the silence. "Tinaco is gonna be one ticked-off dude."

Stephanie stared at Jeff. A smile crept over her lips. "Yeah, I guess we showed him."

The water lapped at their feet, reminding them of its frustrated desire to bury them in its depths. Stephanie studied the cliffs surrounding them and whispered softly, "You saved my life."

Jeff protested. "You're the one who showed up with the gun."

"Yeah, I did a fine job of it too, didn't I?"

"We're here, aren't we?" Jeff glanced down and realized for the first time that he was pantless. In a flash, he peeled off his shirt and ripped a long strip for a belt. With the remaining material, he formed an Indian-style loincloth.

"What I'd give for a camera."

Jeff curtsied. "You like?"

Stephanie shook her head. "Haven't you heard? Mini-skirts are out."

Jeff folded his arms like Sitting Bull. "Look, Miss Evans, I think you would prefer this to the alternative."

She nodded soberly. "I believe you." She stood up and looked around. "So now what?"

"Wait for a boat to rescue us."

Almost before he finished the sentence, a distant rumble could be heard.

Stephanie held up her hand. "Listen."

Jeff's eyes searched the empty lake. "It's probably a fishing boat trolling the shoreline."

Stephanie stood up on her shoeless feet. "I think it's getting louder!"

Jeff cocked his head and studied the sound. A tight knot formed in his stomach. The sense of foreboding returned. "I got a bad feeling about—"

Jeff was interrupted by Stephanie's shouting as the boat rounded the rocky point, "Hey! Over here!"

She stopped cold and threw her hand over her mouth. The fifty-foot cruiser increased its speed and closed in on the tiny cove.

Jeff swung his head around, glancing at the steep ravine surrounded by cliffs on each side. "Quick, up there." Jeff pushed Stephanie in front of him.

They scampered up the craggy gully, gripping small trees and rocky outcroppings for handholds. Their bare feet cut easily on the sharp rocks. A bullet rang out, but they were still too far away for it to be effective.

Stephanie shot over the top onto a sloping bench

cresting the three hundred–foot cliffs. Jeff followed her lead and stopped to look behind. Burly jumped from the boat and clamored up the ravine.

Jeff jerked his head around furiously and focused on a football-sized rock. He seized it and crept next to the edge of the gully. Motioning toward the south, Jeff whispered, "Keep going. I'll catch up."

"No way. I'm staying with you. We can't outrun him without shoes."

"Might not work. Just go. I'll catch up."

Stephanie reluctantly agreed and disappeared into the underbrush.

Jeff peered through the alder at Burly, now only thirty feet away. In one motion, he leaped from his position of cover. Burly's head snapped up in surprise. He reached for his gun and prepared to shoot, but it was too late. The rock came crashing down on his collar bone, knocking him over. He bounced four times before stopping near the shoreline.

Burly didn't move. The other gunman throttled the engines and thrust the boat away from the shore. In seconds, he was speeding away, leaving his companion, not knowing if he was alive or dead.

Jeff darted through the timber-covered slope. "Steph! It's me. I got him!"

He heard a voice. "Over here!"

Jeff rounded a thicket and found Stephanie sitting on a log, clutching her foot. Blood oozed between her fingers.

Jeff bent down and examined it. A one-inch gash had ripped through her skin. He tore a strip of cloth from his loincloth to use as a bandage.

"Listen, Tarzan. You'd better keep that to cover yourself."

Jeff involuntarily flexed his shoulders.

Her mouth dropped open. "Look at your chest!"

A red slash crossed his pectoral muscle and upper arm but was no longer bleeding.

He continued wrapping her foot. "I think I got it from the prop. I'm pretty sure it didn't cut all the way through the skin."

Stephanie stood, then instantly dropped back to the ground in agony. "Stupid foot!"

Jeff held her arm as tears came to her eyes. "Yeah, I guess we showed them."

Stephanie squared her shoulders, "Yeah. Never mess with Stephanie Evans and Jeff Spene . . . " She choked on the name, remembering his deceit. Her eyes dropped to the ground as she mumbled, "Or whatever your name is."

She sighed and shifted her gaze to the western sky across Lake Pend Oreille. Deep pink with a hint of orange danced through the clouds.

Jeff slid his arm around her. "I'm sorry you had to go through all this. If there was anything I could do to—"

"Shhh." Stephanie pressed her finger against his lips. "Just hold me."

Jeff drew her in close and gently kissed her forehead.

Chapter Twenty-One

Twigs. And diminishing light. Right now these were the enemies as Stephanie and Jeff deliberately picked their way through the mountain forest. Occasional thorns and rocks cropped up, bayoneting their bare feet, but the small sticks pricked tender insteps with almost every step. Intermittent game trails helped, but they rarely extended more than a hundred feet.

Fatigue had been another major foe. Their wounds were superficial, but the struggle through the water had drained them of energy and sent them to near exhaustion.

Jeff dropped to a squat and signaled Stephanie to do likewise. His nostrils flared as he used all his senses to discern the movement ahead.

Without warning, a bull elk raised its mighty head from the thicket ten yards ahead. It too sniffed the air with ears perked. Sensing something unfamiliar, it developed jet propulsion and lunged through the underbrush and bounded down the hill. Now out of sight, all the human intruders could hear was sporadic crashing through the brush. Then silence.

Stephanie whistled through her teeth and let her eyelids sag. "Poor thing was more scared than us."

"I doubt it."

Fatigue began to overcome caution. Jeff paused to examine the evening sky. "Looks like we have less than an hour of light left. We'd better start working our way back to the shoreline."

Following the next descending ravine, less steep than the one they had climbed, they came to a small bluff over-looking the lake.

Stephanie nodded toward the lake. "Do you think they're still looking?"

"No. It's getting too dark. My guess is they're packing up and heading out."

"Then we're safe?"

Jeff stroked his chin. "Looking for us in this wilderness would be like searching for a needle in a haystack. I'll bet Tinaco is already leaving the country."

"And those men?"

Jeff frowned. "He may have left some behind, so we'll still need to be cautious."

"Look!" Stephanie pointed across the opening. A tiny shack made of logs and a cedar shake roof blended into the surrounding trees.

"Wait here. I'll check it out."

Stephanie ignored Jeff's orders and followed him. An overgrown trail connected the shanty to a rocky beach.

Jeff bent over and examined the path. "The game trails are in better shape than this." Stalking up to the cabin, Jeff looked through the window. "Hello, is anybody here?" No answer.

He pushed open the door made of rough-sawed boards and greeted a musty odor. "Hello?"

Wiping a cobweb from the doorway, he stepped inside. "I don't think anyone has been here for a while."

The decor was simple: a tattered mattress in the cor-ner, a dilapidated table propped against the aging wall, and a wooden bench. Less obvious was an old trunk tucked under the table. The only window consisted of two narrow slats next to the door facing the lake. The deep fatigue they felt earlier lightened with new hope.

Stephanie rubbed her hand up her arm, trying to wipe away the goose bumps. "Dingy!"

Jeff nodded and sat on the bench. "It could use a little more light. Kind of stale, huh?"

Stephanie wrinkled her nose. "What *is* that?"

"Smells like an old root cellar."

Stephanie pointed at the floor under the table. "No, I mean that."

Jeff dragged the trunk across the wooden floor and raised the lid. "A lantern! Now if we only had a match and some kerosene."

Digging further, he withdrew an old pair of blue denim overalls—suspender style, work boots, and a couple of well-worn army blankets.

He gave the overalls a hardy shake and climbed in.

Stephanie snickered. "That's definitely you."

He slouched his shoulders and stuck out his jaw. "Da . . . yup. It be me."

Stephanie grabbed her sides and laughed. Then, looking thoughtfully at his ankles, "Expecting a flood?"

Jeff looked down. The overalls barely reached past his knees, but left ample room around the waist. He shrugged. "Beats what I had on."

Stephanie flashed a weary but flirtatious smile. "Oh, I don't know. I kind of liked what you were wearing." As soon as the words passed her lips, she winced. Stumbling backward, she quickly added, "I, uh, don't really care for . . . overalls. I mean, it's okay if you're a farmer or something like that, but I don't . . . I guess"—her voice faded—"like them." Trying unsuccessfully to salvage something, she hastily added, "Not like a suit and tie." Stephanie shuddered and bit down hard on her scarlet cheeks.

Detecting her discomfort, Jeff bore in, "Why, Miss Evans! I don't believe I've ever heard words of this kind from a lady such as yourself."

Tears began to well up in her eyes. Then she shouted, "I didn't mean it!" Both of them stood silent.

Stephanie leaned forward with wide eyes and broke into a smirk. Laughter erupted and lasted longer than it would have had the circumstances been different. They laughed at each other; they laughed at the fear they felt. They laughed at the hate, the doubt, and the pain. They laughed because if they didn't laugh, they would cry.

Finally, Stephanie pulled out the work boots and handed them to Jeff. "Here. See if they fit."

After checking for spiders, he tugged hard and finally coaxed one boot on, then the other. Standing up, he modeled his completed wardrobe. His sockless toe protruded from a sole that flopped open. The worn boots complemented the exposed calves and overalls with straps partially covering his naked shoulders. "It hurts!"

"What hurts?"

Jeff pulled them back off. "These boots. They're too small."

Stephanie glanced down at her bare feet. "At least we have clothes."

Straining his eyes in the rapidly dimming light, Jeff gave the room a once over. "You can sleep here. I'll find something outside."

"No, you can have the bed. I'll sleep outside."

Jeff stopped and folded his arms. "Miss Evans, I am a gentleman."

Stephanie cocked her head. "Okay, at least it looks clean . . . kind of. But what will you sleep on?"

"Needles."

Taking in Stephanie's puzzled look, Jeff gave more information. "Pine boughs, or to be more accurate, fir boughs. I'll probably sleep better than you."

Stephanie led the way out the door. "Come on. I'll help you."

After they picked several loads of two-foot boughs, Jeff began poking their stems into the ground. Before long, it was thicker than a regular mattress. "Try it."

Stephanie lay down on the new bed. "Incredible! It really is comfortable."

"I don't think I'll care."

Stephanie got up and headed for the edge of the bluff. "Let's check one last time for boats."

She stood on the bluff and surveyed the darkened water. Two miles away, on the other side, an occasional light flickered. Distant trees could only be distinguished as a dark mass.

Stephanie tossed a stone toward the lake. The impact was signaled by a distinct plop. "Who are you?"

Startled by the question, Jeff licked the inside of his cheek in thought. "What do you mean?"

"How do I separate the person I knew from the person of the present?"

"Stephanie, I'm the same person."

"What all did you lie about?"

Jeff blushed. "The only thing I exaggerated was my job and my name."

"Exaggerated? Is that what you like to call it?"

Jeff decided he wouldn't be offended. "Sometimes a person has to withhold parts of the truth to accomplish certain objectives."

"So the end justifies the means, huh?"

"No, not usually. I think there are only a very few exceptions when it is justified."

"And you're one of them, right?"

Jeff grew silent.

Stephanie apologized, "I'm sorry if I sound sarcastic, but I really do want to understand how you can justify this with God. Earlier, you said we shared the same value system. Did you go on a mission?"

"Yes. I went to Peru about four years ago."

"How can you defend your dishonesty?" Stephanie acted as if she genuinely wanted to know.

Jeff cleared his throat. "Was Nephi justified in killing

Laban and then pretending to be him? I've done nothing worse than that."

"Why is it that every time someone wants the ends to justify the means, they talk about Nephi and Laban? It's a whole different situation."

"How is it so different?"

"Nephi didn't want to do it. The Lord commanded him to."

"You think I wanted to deceive you?"

"Are you going to tell me that the Spirit constrained you to lie to me about who you were?"

"Stephanie, the whole thing was a lie. "

"That's my point." Stephanie spread her arms for emphasis. "The whole thing was a lie. I remember a scripture in the Doctrine and Covenants that says something about a person feeling justified in lying to deceive because he supposed that someone else lied to deceive."

"I never actually said I didn't have my pilot's license."

"It's not the words. It's the deception. If I were married and didn't tell you, do you think that would be honest?"

"No."

Following up her point, she issued another challenge, "If I was a blood donor and conveniently forgot to tell you I had AIDS, would that be honest?"

"I'm not very good at matching wits with you, but let me ask you this. Do you think it's dishonest to not give all the facts?"

Wary of a trap, Stephanie answered slowly, "I think it's dishonest to withhold information with the purpose to deceive someone."

"What about when Moroni concealed his army to ambush the Lamanites. Was that dishonest? Do you think he should have jumped up from his hiding place and said, 'Yo, guys, I'm over here. I just want to make sure I'm being honest about this whole war thing.'"

"That's totally different. They were the enemy. It was war."

Jeff saw his chance. "So in war, the ends do justify the means? Wake up, Stephanie. There is a war going on out there. Don't you think Tinaco is the enemy? He tried to kill us!"

"Am I your enemy?"

Jeff rolled his eyes impatiently. "Don't be ridiculous."

"Then why did you lie to me? Moroni didn't lie to his own men."

"Stephanie, when I first met you, I didn't know whose side you were on. It's a dirty business, and like any other war, innocent people get hurt."

"And who declared this so-called war?"

"If memory serves me correctly, I think President Bush did in 1986."

"So you think you can lie, use drugs, and fornicate all in the name of serving your country?"

Jeff tried to keep a straight face. "I don't use drugs!"

Stephanie laughed at being caught in her own trap. "Okay, and you don't sleep around either." After a brief pause, she added, "Do you?"

"What do you think?"

Stephanie shook her head. "No. I guess not." Then, remembering the painful experience of seeing Melonie kiss Jeff, "What about Melonie?"

"Melonie!" Jeff remembered her for the first time.

"So you do care about her."

"Yes, I do," said Jeff defiantly. "I care about her because she talked me into trying to explain the truth to you even though it could have jeopardized the whole operation." He felt himself getting angry. "I care about her because she respects me for who I am and doesn't try to impose her values on me. I care about her because she risks her life to do what she believes is right, even if she doesn't measure up to your standard of perfection."

"I'm sorry. You're right. She is probably a wonderful person, and it was childish of me to imply otherwise."

The anger drained from him. "How do you do that?"

"Do what?" Stephanie responded naively.

"It takes an unusually secure person to react like you did after the attack I just launched."

"Melonie doesn't believe as I do. She obviously has different standards. But I believe she is as you say—a sensitive, caring, human being."

Jeff combed his fingers through his hair, "Kind of like another sensitive, caring person I know."

At that, Stephanie seemed to open up a bit and accept Jeff for what she was beginning to see in him. She glowed with a happiness that seemed out of place for their circumstances. Her bandaged foot was forgotten. "Tell me about your mission, your life—everything that's different from what you told me."

"After high school, I worked for a year to earn enough money to go. After returning from Peru, I attended the University of Idaho in Moscow and majored in accounting. At the same time, I got enough hours to fly commercial. I got bored with both and decided to become a cop."

"Is there anything else you told me that isn't true?"

"I really don't think so, Stephanie. You see, it makes more sense to exaggerate as little as possible so you don't have to remember what you said."

"There you go again."

Jeff wrinkled his brow. "What?"

"You always use the word *exaggerate* instead of the word *lie*. You *are* uncomfortable with it, aren't you?"

Jeff stroked his chin, remembering the first time he had used his undercover name and how awkward it had felt. "Maybe you're right. I know the most effective undercover officers can just be themselves. At times, that has made things incredibly difficult. Other times, I think it has helped."

"How did it help?"

"Well, I think Troy basically trusted me because I am a loyal and trustworthy person." Jeff added with a grin, "He just misunderstood what and who I was loyal to."

Stephanie shook her head. "I don't know what to think, but I am convinced you believe you are doing the right thing."

Jeff laughed. "You remind me of a friend in Peru, Brent Marks. He had a way of cutting through all the verbiage. If he didn't agree with something I said, he told me about it."

Stephanie winced. "Am I that bad?"

"No. I mean yes. I mean, even though he was direct, I never took offense. I guess it was the way he said it. You're the same way."

"You like Brent Marks, don't you?"

"He's one of my favorite people. We still write occasionally, but I haven't seen him since my mission. He's still in Peru."

"He's not from Peru originally, is he?"

"No, now he teaches the people how to farm better."

"So he was a farmer?"

"No, he was in the army or something."

"The government sent him to Peru?"

"No. He's doing it on his own."

"Sounds like a nice man."

"It goes deeper than that. I think he's trying to repay some imagined debt to the people of Peru."

Stephanie tossed her hair back. "I always wanted to visit South America."

Jeff nodded. "Someday I would like to go back."

"To visit Brent?"

"More than that. I would like to go back and work with the people in some way."

Jeff stood up and stared into the night sky as if searching for a distant star. Taking a deep breath, he slowly let it out. "Stephanie, I know I've put you through a lot. I didn't mean for it to happen this way. I'll try to put things back to normal as soon as I can."

"It was worth it." Before Jeff could respond, Stephanie pointed to a shooting star. "Look! Did you see that?"

Jeff attached his study to Stephanie's face, intent on memorizing every feature. "Yes. It's beautiful."

Still peering into the heavens, Stephanie pulled down her gaze and met Jeff's eyes. For a moment, neither moved. Jeff leaned forward as Stephanie accepted his lips. The tender kiss lasted several seconds.

Tears formed in Stephanie's eyes. "I love you, Jeff Spen—" They both erupted with laughter.

"Foster," he corrected. "Jeff Foster."

Stephanie tucked her forehead against his chest, her hair tickling his nose. "I love you, Jeff Foster."

"Why?"

Stephanie's smile revealed her dimples. "Because you're so good-looking."

"Is that the only reason?" Jeff teased.

Stephanie grinned as she carefully examined his face. "No, but it helps." She turned her head and looked over the lake. "Actually, it's not even the main reason."

She waited, forcing Jeff to ask.

"I give up. What's the main reason?"

Stephanie turned back to his eyes innocently. "Your ability to swim, of course."

Jeff swept her off her feet and made a swinging motion toward the bank. "I'll show you how to swim."

Stephanie squealed. "Please! I think I've had enough water for one day."

Jeff set her on her feet, still holding her in his arms. Stephanie clung to him as they embraced for a second kiss. Jeff felt his heart accelerate. Desire swelled in his chest and descended through his trunk, urging him forward. He placed one hand on the small of her back and held her tight.

Stephanie seemed to savor the secure grip and wrapped her arms around his neck.

Suddenly, Jeff loosened his hold as he recognized a familiar warning prick his heart. Blood retreated to heart and brain. The more he obeyed the presage, the more apparent the warning became.

Stephanie took a step back. Jeff pretended to look at his nonexistent watch. "I guess we'd better go to bed."

Stephanie raised one eyebrow. "Excuse me?"

Jeff's throat tightened as he stuttered, "To bed. Uh, you in the cabin . . . and me out here."

Stephanie blushed in understanding. "Yes, we need our rest."

Jeff called after Stephanie as she entered the cabin, "If you need anything, just holler."

Stephanie paused in the doorway as if she wanted to say something. Instead she waved. "I'll be fine. See you in the morning."

Jeff wrapped himself in the wool blanket and lay down on the bed of pine boughs. He stared into the sky. The gentle clatter of forest noises invaded his conscious. He focused on the sounds—waves lapping against the rocks below, the scurrying of rodents searching for a nighttime snack, the delicate rustling of leaf against branch, and the distant wind shifting through the trees. The more he listened, the more he could hear. At last peace overtook him and he drifted off to sleep.

Chapter Twenty-Two

Jeff rolled over, bulldozing a cluster of pine boughs against his head. The prickling sensation prodded him into reality. He sat up and rubbed his eyes. The purple tinge lining the eastern skyline betrayed the sun's pending arrival.

Memory of the previous day's events flooded his brain. "Melonie!" Jeff sprang from his forest bed. Gingerly, he barefooted his way up the trail to the shack where Stephanie slept. Not wanting to wake her, he carefully opened the door to retrieve the undersized boots.

Stephanie lay face down on the mattress, her head resting peacefully on her arm. Jeff stole back out and forced the boots on.

Options, Foster. What're your options. Jeff studied the lake. There was no sign of civilization. *They may start looking now that it's light—if they're still in the country.* He studied the broad expanse of water. The thought of swimming back to the other, more populated side felt overwhelming.

He turned his attention to the steep mountain in front of him. *It might be safer, but it will only take me further into the wilderness.* Jeff glanced at the uncomfortable boots on his feet. *And what about Stephanie? How far could she walk with no shoes?* He adjusted the oversized bib overalls. *No, the only option is to go for help.*

He decided to scout around for a few minutes in hopes of finding a trail or road and then discuss the options with Stephanie.

He started by following a rib of the mountain. Hunger gnawed at his stomach. He found some huckleberry bushes and plucked a few berries as he walked. He stuffed several more in his pocket for Stephanie. Motivated by thoughts of Melonie's dangerous position, Jeff pushed his way up the ridge further than he intended to go.

Sensing that he had been gone too long, Jeff stepped out on a crest several hundred feet above the lake. He looked down to the bluff where he'd spent the night. The cabin was hidden in the trees. An occasional cottage dotted the opposite shore. Tiny fishing boats could be seen several miles up the lake.

Jeff looked down toward the cabin. A sharp pang lanced his breast. Anchored below the bluff, he could see a blue and white fifty-foot launch. The ache hammered downward, settling in his stomach.

Jeff dashed back into the trees and ran down the mountain as fast as he dared, his heart pounding. Using a large boulder as a springboard, he leaped into the air, sailing fifteen feet before hitting the steep forest floor. He rolled, jumped to his feet, and continued his rapid descent.

Minutes seemed hours as he crashed through the heavy undergrowth. He ignored the pain caused by the undersized boots. Thick red welts punished his bare shoulders and calves for ignoring the alder bushes.

He hit a spruce tree and bounced to the side. Stunned for a moment, he jumped up and blindly charged ahead.

Jeff stopped short of the cabin. He listened. Nothing. Circling around, he perched by a rotten log on the bluff where he and Stephanie had spoken last night. The boat was gone.

Jeff dashed up to the cabin and flung open the door.

The first thing he noticed was the old table. It lay tipped over with one leg broken off. The mattress lay undisturbed, but empty.

Jeff leaped back out of the cabin. "Stephanie!" he yelled at the top of his lungs. He scrutinized the trail as if he were a dog tracking a scent and followed it to the lake shore. Rows of grooves in the dirt revealed a boat shoe tread. *No blood.*

He ran back up to the top of the bluff. There were no boats in sight. Jeff picked up a large stick and hurled it toward the lake. "No!" The howl echoed off the surrounding cliffs. He flattened his hands over his head and sank to his knees. "Oh, Stephanie!" he whispered to himself. "Stephanie." Jeff clasped his hands together. "Father, I need you. Please help me."

A sense of determination surged through him. Rising to his feet, Jeff looked up and down the shoreline. Nothing but trees. Somehow, he had to get to the other side. To the south, the lake disappeared around a giant bend. To the north, five miles of rugged cliffs guarded the way.

Jeff estimated the distance across the lake to the cottage at about two and a half miles. He had once swum five miles in warmer water. But this was different. He hadn't eaten anything except a few huckleberries for twenty hours. His body rebelled at the thought of more physical work by reminding him of the aches, the cuts, and the bruises that covered him.

"Time," he mumbled to himself. "No other choice." He shoved the handful of smashed huckleberries into his mouth.

Jeff peeled off his overalls and poised over a lump of granite skirting the water. He decided against diving and eased down into the cold water. In two steps the bottom vanished, forcing him to swim.

For the first hundred yards, he swam the crawl with a trudgen adaptation. His mind drifted to his swimming instructor at college. "It's a restful stroke, but not that restful," he had said. Soon he switched to the inverted breast stroke. It allowed him to rest in between kicks and was almost as fast.

He drew an imaginary line through his feet to the cliff to stay on course. Occasionally he turned to look at his destination and corrected his course.

The sun started to warm the water, but it didn't seem to help. *Come on, Foster, endure it.* Each stroke moved him imperceptibly closer to the distant shore.

Halfway across the lake, exhausted, he turned face-down into a survival float. He gently pushed his hands down as he raised his face far enough to snatch a breath of air. His arms slowly returned to the surface as his legs spread for another scissor kick. Breathe out, push and kick, extend . . . He paused to examine the depths of the frosty liquid. From the air, it would look blue. From the surface, it looked clear. But as Jeff let the bubbles slide by his cheek, all he could see was olive green.

A cloud passed over, transforming the olive green into stark blackness. Jeff remembered the burly guard describing the lake as too deep for a small submarine. He wondered what could conceivably live that deep. As his imagination suggested some possibilities, he tried to think about something else and sped up his stroke.

The image of Stephanie's face hovered before him. The kiss . . . *For you, Stephanie. For you.*

His arms ached. Switching from a whip kick to a steady flutter, he let his arms drag loosely at his sides. *Endure it, Foster.* Chills racked his body. His calves followed through on their earlier threats and started to cramp. He went back to the inverted breast stroke.

The water lapped at his ears. Stroke after stroke. The cold left him. No more feeling. Numbness . . .

Hi, Dad. What are you doing here?

Don't quit, son.

But I'm tired. So tired.

I know, Jeff.

Dad, I don't think I can make it.

I understand. But don't stop.

I'm trying, Dad, the best I can.

Yes, son, and I'm proud of you. Keep going.

But—

Son, I'll be here when it's time. Promise me you'll keep going.

I promise.

A wave splashed over Jeff's face, and he jerked up coughing. His legs churned, then slowed.

I'll just wait here. Get real Foster. You're losing it. Don't quit . . . don't stop . . . keep going.

A sledgehammer *whump* sent rivets of pain through his head and neck. Jeff spun around and faced a granite outcropping. He had reached the opposite shore.

Jeff crawled out of the water and gratefully lay on the sun-baked sand. His body shook uncontrollably even though the temperature hovered in the nineties. *At least I'm shaking. Need something to eat . . .*

With his shirt-formed loincloth, Jeff hobbled up to the cottage. An old Ford pickup painted primer grey rested under a ponderosa pine tree. "Anybody here?"

No answer.

Jeff tried the door. It was locked.

There was no sign of phone lines leading to the cottage, so Jeff made his way to the truck.

A chunk of iron protruded from the key hole. It appeared to have been welded to a broken-off ignition key. Jeff jerked open the door and sat down. As he turned the modified key, the truck lurched forward.

Pushing in the clutch, he repeated the process and started the engine. He decided that this was not the best time to meet the owner, so he took off down the dirt road, not knowing where it would take him. Eventually it led to a paved road that in turn led to Highway 95. Following the signs, Jeff turned north toward Sandpoint. He would go directly to town and find the police station.

He urged the battered truck faster. The speedometer indicator pushed eighty-five.

Suddenly a highway patrol car jumped into his rearview mirror with blue lights blazing. Jeff instinctively hit the brakes. Then, realizing that this was exactly what he was looking for, he pulled over and jumped out of the truck to greet the patrolman.

Lieutenant Johnson raced to get out of his car before Jeff met him at the door. "Hold up right there," he said, holding up the palm of his left hand. His right hand lingered near his holster.

Jeff stopped. His teeth still chattered even though he was long since dry. "Officer, I know this looks strange. I'm Detective Foster with the Idaho Falls Police Department. I'm on a special assignment with the DEA."

Lieutenant Johnson stared at him with amusement. "At least you're original."

"I must contact the task force immediately. My partner's life is in danger."

Lieutenant Johnson squinted at Jeff over the top of his reflective sunglasses. "Let's see some ID."

"I don't have any. I'm working undercover."

"It looks like you could use a little more cover."

Jeff tugged at the loincloth. "I know you'll need to check this out, but please hurry. Have your dispatch call Captain Fowler in Idaho Falls. He'll verify it. Tell him to have the task force contact me at your police department."

"Wait in the truck." After Jeff followed his command, the policeman sat back in his car and picked up the microphone.

Ten minutes later, Lieutenant Johnson marched up to the truck. "Okay, let's go."

Jeff hopped into the passenger side. Lieutenant Johnson wasted no time in getting them to the Sandpoint

Police Department. Once there, he escorted Jeff into a room and handed him a blanket. The lieutenant reached for the coffee pot. "Want a cup?"

Jeff was still shivering. "No thanks. Got a candy bar or something?"

"Yeah, sure." The policeman left the room.

Before the lieutenant could return, Special Agent Empy threw open the door with Melonie, Reed, and Barry at his heels. "What happened?"

Melonie ran past Empy's interrogation and threw her arms around Jeff. "You made it!"

Empy folded his arms and tapped his fingers against his elbow, eager to get the niceties over with. Jeff clasped both hands on Melonie's shoulders and whispered hoarsely, "They got Stephanie."

Barry interjected. "You mean Stephanie almost got Jeff."

By Jeff's puzzled expression, Empy decided to supply more detail. "You made a grave mistake, Detective. You created a particularly precarious situation through false trust, which endangered Melonie and almost got yourself killed."

"What!" Jeff demanded.

Reed picked up where Empy left off. "Einstein is saying you screwed up. You didn't keep your cover. You were told not to tell Stephanie. You didn't listen."

Jeff replied angrily, "You don't know what you're talk-ing—"

Barry cut him off. "Oh, doesn't he? The minute you tell Stephanie who you are, she runs to Tinaco." Barry snorted in disgust. "It's not the first time a snotnosed rookie fell for a doper's whore."

Jeff's sanity fled. He bolted across the room in one movement and caught Barry squarely in the jaw with his right fist.

Surprised by the lightning strike, Barry only had time to roll with the punch. Jeff immediately followed with a left hook to Barry's cheek. Reed lunged forward and grabbed Jeff around the middle in a bear hug.

"Stop it!" yelled Melonie.

Lieutenant Johnson burst through the door, spilling a trail of coffee. "What's going on?"

Reed maintained an even voice. "You done, kid?"

Jeff nodded.

Reed released his grip. "It's been kind of an emotional day. He just found out his family was massacred by a group of Anasazi Indians."

Lieutenant Johnson regarded them curiously. "Indians?"

Melonie hung her head. "They didn't stand a chance." Then, looking up tearfully, "Do you have a family, Lieutenant?"

"Uh, yes ma'am. I'm sorry to hear about this. I'll, uh, leave you folks alone." Lieutenant Johnson backed out and quickly shut the door.

Empy rolled his eyes back. "Shall we start at the begin-ning?" He sat down in a chair, signaling for everyone else to do likewise. "Let's start with you, Jeff. Tell us everything that transpired from the time Melonie left."

Jeff expanded his chest and let the air coast through his lips. "First thing I know, these two goons stick a gun in my ribs and handcuff me." Jeff proceeded to tell about Stephanie's attempted rescue and their escape in the lake. "I never should have left her there. I was only going to be gone a minute." He bit hard on his cheek and whispered, "Rookie mistake."

After he finished, Reed cleared his throat. "Sorry, I guess we kind of jumped the gun about Stephanie."

Jeff nodded. "I shouldn't have lost my cool like that."

"Yeah, you shouldn't have." Barry rubbed his jaw.

Empy scooted his chair forward. "Okay, I'll fill you in on what happened on this end. When you first landed in Sandpoint on Friday, we got there first. Before we could get fueled or file any flight plans, you were in the air again.

We did manage to take down the numbers from the seaplane, but it took several hours before we could trace the destination. Once we figured out where you went, we dispatched an observation team. Then we experienced a communication disruption. Apparently, there was—"

Reed interjected. "They got the wrong bay. Until Melonie called from Spokane, our ingenious DEA wonder boys were watching some doctor's mansion on Glengary Bay."

Empy blushed. "Then we had Melonie lead us to Harrison Bay and searched Tinaco's real house—"

Reed chimed in, "As opposed to Tinaco's fake house."

Empy daggered Reed and continued. "It was clean. They had vacated the premises and taken whatever evidence there was with them. We did discover that he had a Cessna Citation hangared at the Spokane airport. We've been watching it, hoping to catch Tinaco leaving the country. It left two hours ago."

"Why didn't you stop it?" Jeff asked.

"Tinaco wasn't on the plane. Two men left with a woman." Empy's eyes dropped to the floor. "We think the woman was Stephanie."

Jeff leaped out of his chair. "And you just let them take her?"

Empy opened his hand and smoothed out the creases in his handkerchief. "We didn't know. We thought she may have been involved. Besides, the plane is scheduled to land in Tucson, Arizona. We have people there to pick up the tail. I'm not sure it would have mattered if we did know. It's our only shot at getting Tinaco."

Jeff gripped the edge of the chair. "No way! You get her as soon as she gets off the plane. I don't want her involved in this anymore. I won't risk losing her again."

Empy prepared to protest, but Barry stopped him. "He's right. It's too risky. I say next time we have a chance, let's grab her."

Empy sighed. "All right, I'll make the necessary

arrangements. Given the allotted time, arrival should take place in one hour and twenty-three minutes."

Empy picked up the phone from a nearby table. He pulled a card out of his wallet and punched in a series of numbers.

Melonie squeezed Jeff's arm. "You look terrible. I'll take you over to the motel and get you something to eat."

"Thanks, I'm running kind of low on fuel."

Empy hung up the phone. "They've been notified of the situation. I'll let you know as soon as they land. Go get some rest."

Once they arrived at the motel, Jeff borrowed a pair of Reed's pants and showered. He wrapped up several inches of the unused denim with a brown skinny belt. Jeff looked in the mirror. The day's growth of whiskers combined with baggy eyes to make him look ten years older. He fell back exhausted on the king-sized bed.

A knock on the door came before he could close his eyes.

Jeff moaned and shuffled to the door. Melonie held two white McDonald's sacks stuffed with french fries and hamburgers. "I hope you don't mind fast food. I was afraid you'd be asleep."

"No, that's fine."

She glanced down at Jeff's pants. "Nice threads."

"It beats a wool blanket."

Melonie sat next to him on the bed and crammed a french fry in his mouth. "Here, you need to eat."

Too tired to resist, he accepted it. Then he ate one of the hamburgers and sat in a stupor.

Melonie reached over and massaged his neck with one hand and set the food down with the other. He gradually leaned against her, his eyes shut. Gently she laid him back on the bed. After removing his shoes, she pulled a blanket over him and kissed his head. Then in a hoarse whisper, "Goodnight, Jeff Foster. Sleep well." A tear rolled down her cheek. "Sleep well . . . "

Chapter Twenty-Three

A knock at the door woke Jeff. He rubbed his eyes and glanced at the clock: 7:15. His mind raced with calculations. *Fourteen hours.* He jumped out of bed, still wearing Reed's pants. "Just a minute."

Jeff opened the door and saw Melonie waiting for him.

"Why did you let me sleep so long?" he blurted out. "Did they get her?"

Melonie pushed her way past Jeff into the motel room. Her customary smile was gone. "Sit down. I brought some clothes for you."

He stood in the doorway. "Well?"

Melonie stopped. "Jeff, the plane didn't land."

He shut the door. "What happened?"

"After the plane didn't show up, they contacted customs. Evidently, it passed Tucson and dropped out of sight."

"What do you mean, dropped out of sight?"

"Empy thinks they went off radar by dropping to tree-top elevation and then headed for the border."

Jeff grabbed Melonie's arm. "So what are we doing?"

"Everything we can. Reed left with Empy and the team last night. They're getting a search warrant on Troy's house."

"Why didn't you come get me?"

Melonie pulled her arm free and tried to calm him. "Jeff, it's too personal for you now. If you would just go back to Idaho Falls and forget about it—"

"Forget about it? They have Stephanie and you want me to forget about it!"

"I know you can't forget it, but just listen to yourself. You can't help her in the condition you're in."

"I'm not going back until I find her."

"Jeff, please let me help you. The best thing you can do is—"

"If you really want to help me, then drive me out to Tinaco's."

"He's gone. The whole place is empty."

"It's a place to start."

"They've already searched it with a fine-toothed comb. You won't find anything. Besides, everyone is gone but Barry."

"I'm going anyway."

"But you can't."

Jeff glared at Melonie. "Watch me."

"Fine! You go on your little rampage, and when you get done, you can fly back to Idaho Falls and be ready in case they need you." Melonie slammed the door and stomped down the hall.

Jeff threw on the clothes she brought and headed out the door. He had to think.

Black clouds rumbled across the churning lake. He left the Edge Water Lodge on foot and followed the beach around to a pier. A sign at the far end of the cement wharf read, "No Swimming, Water Ski Dock." Huge waves threatened to rip the sign from the pole. Jeff zipped up his windbreaker and staggered toward the end. By the time he reached the pole, he was soaked. He wrapped his arms around it while wave after wave crashed into the dock, blasting jets of water.

Doesn't make sense. "How did Tinaco find out?" Jeff

spoke to no one in particular. If he was going to find out where Stephanie was, he would have to get answers.

They were clever enough to lure Melonie away. They only wanted me. But why?

I have something Melonie doesn't have. What? Testimony that could put Troy away?

A massive swell collided with the dock and sent a fire-hose stream of water directly at Jeff's head. He ducked most of it and wiped his face against his already drenched sleeve.

Tinaco must have someone on the inside. Melonie? They didn't try to kill her. Instead, they conveniently dumped her off in Spokane.

Jeff heard a shout behind him. He turned and watched Barry shuffle bowlegged to keep from getting washed over the dock. Barry grabbed the pole and hollered, "Didn't you get enough water yesterday?"

Jeff yelled above the storm, "I guess not. How did you know I was here?"

"Melonie said she saw you walking toward the beach. I looked up and saw some idiot out here. Figured it had to be you."

"And you?"

"We have to talk. It's important."

"Okay, talk."

"I think Tinaco has someone on the inside. Someone who knew you were a cop."

Jeff smacked his fist against the sign. "Exactly! That's the only way it could have gone sour. Any idea who?"

"I'm afraid so."

Jeff eyed Barry in surprise. "Who?"

Barry created a serious expression. "Jeff, I can't just go around making accusations without being able to back them up. I'm going to need your help. This is big."

"Who?" Jeff repeated.

"For now, it's just between you and me. Agreed?"

Jeff nodded.

Barry looked over his shoulder and then put his face in Jeff's ear. "Empy."

"Empy? Are you sure? How do you know?"

"It all makes sense. Think about it. The DEA has been working this case for two years and nothing happens. Then a small town rookie shows up—sorry—and things start popping. The DEA mysteriously does surveillance on the wrong house. Think about it, Jeff. They just don't make those kind of mistakes."

"Could it be someone Empy answers to?"

"No way. When it comes to the top, Empy's it until he files his monthly report with the agency. He's the only one who could pull it off."

"So what do we do?"

"Reed is in Vegas working on the Troy Southwick connection. Help me go back to Tinaco's and find something the DEA missed."

"You mean they're the ones who did the search?"

"Of course. And it was under Empy's personal direction!"

Jeff scratched his head. "What if Tinaco's goons return?"

"That's why I need you. You know the place, and if there's any way of figuring out where they took Stephanie, it's probably there somewhere."

"What about Melonie?"

"She's probably okay, but I don't want to risk it. Do you?"

Jeff shook his head. "Let's go."

Barry squeezed Jeff's shoulder. "It's just you and me, so let's be careful."

"You got it."

Barry pointed his finger at the beach. "I'll pick you up at your motel room in thirty minutes."

Jeff adjusted the metal bulge in the small of his back

and looked in the mirror. Empy was kind enough to see that he had a new weapon. It wasn't a Glock, but for now the five-shot revolver would have to do.

A knock at the door signaled Barry's arrival. Jeff greeted him. "So how are we getting there?"

Barry stuck his thumb over his shoulder at a Chevy Blazer. "Should take about forty-five minutes."

As it turned out, the drive took just over thirty minutes. They drove the last two miles down several steep switchbacks and pulled up in front of the main house.

"Won't Empy have someone watching the house?" Jeff asked.

"I asked him about it last night. He's pulled everyone out. Said their efforts would be better spent following up leads in Vegas."

"So we're the last ones to leave?"

Barry nodded. "Melonie's on the way to the airport by now."

The front door was unlocked. Barry motioned for Jeff to enter first. Jeff walked through the atrium and stopped in the hall. Barry hesitated and followed Jeff inside. "Check this place out. And this is just a summer home!"

Jeff entered a bedroom. "I guess there's a lot of money in coke."

Barry again hesitated before entering the room with Jeff. He pointed forward. "Now, that's a bed!"

A large king-sized bed with a mirrored canopy was in the center of the room.

Jeff whistled softly. "It'd be nice."

"Yeah, I'll bet it beats sleeping on pine needles."

Jeff froze. He turned and looked at Barry. "Pine needles? How did you know about the bed of pine needles?"

Barry laughed nervously. "Don't you remember? When you told us about the night in the forest, you said you slept on a bed of pine needles."

Jeff's neck tightened. He took a step toward Barry. "I never said anything about the pine needles."

Barry stepped back. "Sure you did. How else would I know about it?"

Jeff's fist tightened. "Yes, how would you know about it?"

Barry looked around as if expecting someone. Nonchalantly, he turned sideways, looking toward the window. "Hey, Jeff, it's me. Lighten up!" Suddenly, he jerked his weapon from under his rain jacket and pointed it a Jeff's chest. "Don't even breathe."

Jeff eyed him coolly.

Barry broke the silence. "Now, real slow—take your left hand and pull your gun out by the barrel. If I don't like the way you do it, you're dead meat. Understand?"

Jeff nodded and did as ordered.

"Now drop it on the bed."

Jeff reached out his arm and obeyed. He looked up with sad eyes. "Barry, why did you do it?"

Barry smirked. "Why does anybody do it?" He answered his own question. "Money."

"But why didn't you stop us from coming up if you knew?"

"It happened too fast. When I got back from Vegas, you had already left."

Jeff's shoulders sagged. "How long have you been working for Tinaco?"

"How do you know I'm not working for Troy?"

"If you were working for Troy, you would have stopped me a lot sooner."

Barry nodded. "You're a smart kid. Too bad it has to end this way."

Jeff stalled. "You think you can kill me just like that and get away with it? Don't you think Empy will figure it out?"

"It doesn't matter what Empy thinks. By tomorrow evening, I'll be in Peru." Barry raised his pistol and pointed it at Jeff's head.

Jeff shouted, "Don't do this. Maybe I could work for you! Yes, you know, together we could make a pile of money."

Barry shook his head. "Not a chance. I know you better than that." He began to squeeze the trigger, but whipped around when the door suddenly crashed open. Simultaneously, two black figures dressed in urban camouflage smashed through the bedroom windows. "You move, you die!" yelled the leader.

Barry didn't move. Two AR15 assault rifles and one shotgun followed every breath. "I'm Barry! I work for Mr. Tinaco! That one's Jeff." Barry gingerly pointed at Jeff with his eyebrows.

"Drop the gun," the leader commanded.

"Yeah, sure. No problem. You guys handle it."

After the gun hit the floor, Empy strolled into the room. "You have the right to remain silent. Anything you say can be used against you in a court of law. You have a right to an attorney. If you cannot afford one, one will be appointed for you. You can choose to stop answering questions at any time. Do you understand?"

Barry stood dumbfounded. "But I thought you . . . "

"Were in Vegas?" Empy finished.

Barry hesitated. "Boy, am I ever glad to see you guys. I just found out Jeff was connected to Tinaco! When you busted in, I figured Tinaco's enforcers had—"

Jeff stood up and unbuttoned his shirt. He began to pull athletic tape off his skin. "Ouch!" Jeff smiled as he yanked off a small jet-black box."

"You're wired!" Barry shouted.

"No kidding." Jeff hammered out each syllable.

Barry stared at the urban-camouflaged police with guns still trained on him. His shoulders sagged as he sank to the floor. His arms wrapped around his knees, and he rocked back and forth with his face pressed against his legs.

Jeff's face stiffened. "Where's Stephanie?"

Barry peered up at Jeff and shook his head. He stared ahead with lips pressed together.

"You know the game. What's it going to be?"

Barry closed his eyes and looked up as if in prayer. He shook his head and rubbed his eyes with the heel of his palms.

"Well?" Empy demanded.

Finally Barry spoke. "Even witness relocation won't help. He's got contacts everywhere."

"That's not what I had in mind." Empy motioned for the response team to leave the room. He turned back to Barry.

Barry looked up at Empy with pleading eyes. "You don't understand. Anyway you cut it, I'm dead."

"We have a special program," Empy said. "You aren't going free, but we can change your appearance and—"

Barry cut him off, "You don't get it, do you? I'm dead and there's nothing any of you can do about it." Barry snorted in mockery. "*Nothing* you can do."

Jeff scrutinized Barry carefully and then spoke. "Will you help me get Stephanie back?"

Both Empy and Barry stared at Jeff in disbelief.

"After what he's done, do you think he cares about Stephanie?"

Jeff persisted. "Let me talk to him alone."

Empy nodded and walked out the room.

Jeff asked again. "Will you help me?"

"You got to make me a promise."

"What's that?" Jeff asked.

"You give me an opportunity to do myself in."

"You mean let you commit suicide?"

"Yes. I want it quick and painless."

"Don't you think you're being a little paranoid?" Jeff asked.

"You don't know this guy, Foster."

"Are you going to help me find Stephanie?"

"You going to help me get it done?"

"I can't help you kill yourself."

"A while ago, you were saying you'd do anything to get Stephanie back."

"There's some things I won't do."

Barry breathed in disgust. "Foster, you're so predictable!"

"Well?"

Barry smiled grimly. "It's your lucky day. I'm going to tell you where good old Tinaco is anyway. I'm sure Stephanie will be close by—if she's still alive. The way I look at it, you're dumb enough to go after him. And guess what?"

"What?" Jeff responded with a stony face.

"Based on what I've heard about your little escapades over the last couple days, I think there's a microscopic chance that you'll pull it off. And if you do, you might kill him in the process." Barry laughed. "Maybe I'll win the lottery too."

Jeff waited expectantly.

"Peru, near a small town called Tingo Maria. You won't have any trouble finding the estate. Everyone there knows of him." He shook his head in sad warning. "But you won't get in."

Chapter Twenty-Four

"The answer is no." Captain Fowler sat behind his desk with arms folded. "As of now, I'm pulling you out."

The only other person in the room besides Jeff was Gary, and he wasn't much help. Jeff had arrived at the airport shortly after lunch and had driven straight to the office.

"Look, if I could go down there and just ask around, I've got friends that could help!" Jeff pleaded.

"Forget it. We've tried all that and look what happened. If the DEA can't protect you in our own country, what makes you think you can do it without them in Peru, of all places? The answer is no." Captain Fowler slammed his fist against the desk. "Definitely no."

Gary attempted to strengthen Captains Fowler's position. "Peru is not a friendly place. Sometimes they kill Americans just because they're Americans."

"Look, I spent two years of my life there, remember? I know what it's like."

Captain Fowler shook his head.

Jeff's voice tightened. "And what about Stephanie?"

"The DEA is doing everything they can. They said they definitely don't want you there. It would only make matters worse."

"They said that?" Jeff's voice quivered.

"When Empy briefed me this morning, he warned me that you would want to go to Peru. Said you were too personally involved."

"Personally involved?" Jeff repeated. "They just tried to kill me. Of course I'm personally involved. We're all personally involved!"

"The girl makes it different. Gary warned you not to get involved with her."

"So I'm involved. If anything, that just makes me more motivated."

"That's the problem. You're too motivated."

Gary backed up the captain. "He's right, Jeff. You need to sit this one out. Let the DEA handle it."

Jeff's blood pressure rose further. "You don't understand, do you! They aren't going to get the job done! If anything is going to happen, then it's up to us."

Gary flashed Jeff one of his now-you-did-it looks.

Captain Fowler leaned forward in his chair and growled, "Lower your voice, Foster. You're out of line. I'm trying to be patient because I know what you've been through."

Jeff settled back in his chair, trying to regain his composure. "Too much to quit now."

Captain Fowler became formal. "I think you've made your position quite clear, as I have."

Jeff lowered his voice even further, but with a note of rebellion. "And what if I go anyway?"

Captain Fowler pointed his finger at Jeff. "You go down there and you're through. You understand me? Through! Now, get out of my office."

Jeff stood up to leave. "I'm requesting two weeks' vacation."

"Denied."

"I have it coming—"

"Out!" The walls in the hallway shook with Captain Fowler's final order.

Jeff paused for a full two seconds, staring defiantly at his boss. Then he turned and walked away.

Gary watched Captain Fowler in anticipation. Then, testing the water, "You want me to go talk to him?"

Captain Fowler gave a curt nod, and Gary slid out with speed that indicated more interest in escape than talking to Jeff.

Gary half shuffled and half trotted to keep up with Jeff. "Are you brain dead!"

Jeff strode ahead without comment. He pushed through the double doors and headed up the sidewalk.

Gary ran around and stood in front of him, forcing him to either change directions or stop. "Talk to me, buddy."

Jeff halted. "I'm going after her, Gary. You can help me or get in the way. But make no mistake. I'm going."

"I want to help."

Jeff eyed Gary suspiciously. "In what way?"

"Get Stephanie back. If she was dense enough to try rescuing you like she did, I figure you two are made for each other."

The corner on Jeff's lips turned up. "You mean that?"

"Yes. After the way you handled Fowler, I think you're dumber than a post."

Jeff snorted a laugh and then grew serious. "And what about me going to Peru?"

"I don't think it's a good idea, but it's obvious that you're going." Gary shrugged. "I want to help if I can."

They stopped under a large maple tree in front of the courthouse. Jeff rubbed his palms on his pants. "Get Fowler to give me two weeks' vacation."

"After what just happened? Before your conversation a few minutes ago it would have been easy, but now he knows what you're up to. He'd never go for it."

"You can convince him. Tell him you have a cabin in Island Park and that you talked me into taking a fishing trip. Tell him you'll personally baby-sit me."

Gary looked at Jeff appraisingly. "Lying is coming easier for you, isn't it?"

A sharp sting pricked Jeff's conscience. He pushed it away and protested, "You're the one who said a person was justified in exaggerating the truth when they're undercover."

"Exaggerating the truth! Listen to yourself. You're talking about lying to your own people. You think that's part of it?" Then Gary softened. "Jeff, a lot of cops get ruined when they go UC. They start with pure motives. They just lose track of where the line is."

"What line?" Jeff snapped.

"The line that separates us from them." Gary stopped to let his words settle. "I've seen it happen before. First you lie to the bad guys, then you get comfortable with it. Before you know it, you're lying to the judge about probable cause to help get a search warrant. Where does it stop?"

The words seared Jeff like a hot iron. He knew Gary was right, but pride kept him from accepting it. "Who are you to be telling me what's right and wrong? I'll match my ethics against yours anytime."

Gary shook his head. "You take these high moral stands when it comes to drinking or sharing an apartment with Melonie, but where are your lofty values now, Jeff Foster?"

Jeff ground his teeth with clenched jaw. He was about to launch a verbal attack when he remembered the first time he identified himself to Margo's receptionist as Jeff Spenelie. He remembered how uncomfortable he had felt. He struggled one more time to justify himself. "If someone you care about is in trouble, you're justified in doing whatever it takes . . . " Jeff looked at his feet and shook his head. "Sounds pretty stupid, doesn't it?"

Gary nodded. "Like I said. Sometimes you're dumber than a post."

"You're just saying that to make me feel better."

Gary laughed. "So now what?"

Jeff grew thoughtful. "I go to Peru."

"Just like that?"

"Yes. Just like that."

"And your career?"

"I'll worry about that after Stephanie is safe."

"Well, you're lucky."

"How's that?" Jeff asked.

"Fowler's off tomorrow and Friday. If I dodge him, he may not figure out you're gone until Monday."

"Thanks, but don't do anything that will get you into trouble."

"Just make sure you're back by Monday."

Jeff glanced at his watch. "That gives me plenty of time."

Gary started walking toward his car. "Let's go check your apartment together."

"Empy said they already moved me back into my regular apartment. He said everything checked out."

Gary pursed his lips. "Barry knew where you lived. I wouldn't stay there till this whole thing is over. The only thing standing between Troy and prison is your testimony."

"Okay, let's go get my stuff."

When they arrived at Jeff's apartment, everything looked normal. Jeff picked up the telephone to call the airport and noticed a blinking light on the answering machine. He pushed the playback button. A voice he had never heard floated over the speaker. "Hello, Jeff. I trust you had a safe journey. I just thought you might be interested in hearing this . . . " The voice that followed sent shock waves colliding with the ends of his feet. "Jeff? It's me, Stephanie. I—" The unfamiliar voice returned. "Your silence will guarantee her safety." Click.

Jeff sat back on the bed. "Gary, I think you'd better come in here."

Gary dashed in the room with gun drawn. "What?"

"Listen to this." Jeff pushed the playback button for a second time.

After they listened to the message together, Gary leaned against the wall and holstered his weapon. "Right now the only thing keeping her alive is you. If they find you, they'll kill her."

Jeff stared at the answering machine. "Maybe I should stay here. If I go to Peru and they capture me . . . "

"Give them some time. See what they can come up with."

Jeff nodded and stuffed the rest of his clothes into a duffel bag. Gary followed him out the door to the Camaro. Jeff was about to start the engine when his neighbor, Mrs. Olsen, waved from her steps. "Did they get it fixed?"

Jeff rolled down the window. "Huh?"

She pointed at the Camaro. "Did they fix it—the two men that were working on it?"

"What two men?"

Mrs. Olsen pointed down the road. "They left just before you came out."

Jeff's eyes darted toward the road. He saw two men in a dark blue van parked halfway down the block.

"Get out of the car!"

Both of them threw open their doors simultaneously and jumped. Jeff felt a blast boost him forward as he ducked for the ground. He looked back in time to see a huge fireball engulf the Camaro. "Gary!" Jeff lifted himself and scrambled around the car. Gary lay face down regaining consciousness, otherwise apparently unhurt.

The squealing tires from the van left two patches of rubber as it disappeared around the corner.

Jeff ran after the van, but it was gone when he reached the end of the parking lot. He returned to Gary. "How did you know?"

"What do you mean?" Gary asked.

"When you yelled to get out of the car, how did you know? If you hadn't said anything, I'd be toast."

Gary raised one eyebrow and squinted. "You're the one who yelled to get out of the car."

"I didn't say anything," Jeff insisted.

"Well, someone did."

Jeff wrinkled his brow and looked around. Mrs. Olsen stared out her apartment window at them. A crowd of on-lookers began to gather at a distance.

One of them, a chubby middle-aged man dressed in a business suit, ran up to Gary. "You okay?" He reached out as if to check Gary's pulse.

Instinctively, Jeff drew his weapon and stuck it in the man's face. Without saying a word, the man turned and waddled away. The rest of the crowd backed up.

"Aren't we a bit paranoid?" Gary smiled.

Jeff holstered his gun. "Just because you're paranoid doesn't mean they're not out to get you."

Screeching tires announced the presence of a patrol car as it turned into the parking lot. It was immediately followed by a fire engine.

Someone from the crowd yelled, "He's got a gun!"

Jeff quickly explained what had happened, and the of-ficer posted an APB on the radio for the blue van with Utah plates. Jeff and Gary ignored the paramedic's advice to go to the hospital and drove the Toyota back to the police sta-tion.

Captain Fowler sat bent over his desk, studying some reports. Gary knocked on the open door and cleared his throat.

The Captain glanced up and gave them a quick once over. "Come in." His head jerked back up as his brain reg-istered Gary's singed hair. "What happened to you?" An acrid burnt odor followed Gary's appearance. Captain Fowler sniffed with repugnance and straightened. "What the—"

Gary explained the car explosion and the blue van. When he finished, Captain Fowler leaned back in his chair and laced his fingers behind his head. "Suggestions?"

Jeff started to respond. "Maybe if I could—"

"Not you!" shouted Captain Fowler. "Him!" He stuck his finger at Gary.

Gary stepped forward. "I think we need to tell Empy what happened and ask for protection. Maybe they have a place where Jeff can hide until this thing blows over."

Jeff was about to protest when he saw Captain Fowler's threatening glance and thought better of it.

"He could stay at my house for now," Gary said.

Captain Fowler shook his head. "No, that's one of the first places they'll look."

"Can I say something?" Jeff's tone wasn't insolent, but neither was it timid.

Captain Fowler nodded reluctantly.

"Let's set them up. Let them find me and then we take them. Right now, they're the best shot we have at getting Tinaco." Jeff had been careful not to mention Stephanie.

Captain Fowler shook his head. "For one thing, it's too dangerous. Who's to say we could catch them before something went wrong?" Then he answered his own question. "We wouldn't. And even if we did, Tinaco isn't stupid enough to allow himself to be traced."

Jeff eyed Gary for support. Gary shrugged. "He's right."

Captain Fowler leaned back and studied a blank spot on the wall. "Take my car and go to the Shilo. Rent a room under the name Verl Johnson. Then wait for my call. In the meantime, I'll get hold of Empy."

"Verl?" Jeff wrinkled his nose. "Where did you come up with a name like that?"

"It's my father's name."

"Oh."

Captain Fowler tossed the keys to his new Bonneville on his desk. "Don't wreck it."

Jeff got up and repeated the name under his breath. "Verl Johnson."

He quickly marched to the parking lot. The metallic grey car glistened in the afternoon sun. Jeff drove up the alley and turned west on Broadway. He changed the country western station to Z-103. *I hate rap.* He punched in 100.5 for KRIC. A male voice reached the top end of his potential scale. Jeff turned the radio off and crossed the Broadway bridge.

A sleek new Porsche pulled up next to him at the traffic light. The attractive brunette inside gave him a once over and flashed an interested smile. Jeff returned her smile and checked the traffic light. He looked back at her. She stared at him and wet her lips.

His head immediately swiveled forward and blushed.

He resisted the urge to look back until he noticed her speed in front of him. He casually looked to the side. This time he saw a dark blue van.

Chapter Twenty-Five

Jeff threw himself to the seat as the shotgun blast shattered his front windshield. His car careened to the side as he yanked on the wheel and hit the brakes. The dark blue van flew ahead and spun around for a second try.

With his left foot, Jeff kicked out the remains of the blasted out window on the driver's side. Almost simultaneously, he punched the gas with his right and flew up Lindsay Boulevard. The needle bounced up to 105 as he soared past the city limits.

He glanced at the mirror as the van moved closer. He dived into a corner by a pasture and hit the brakes, spinning the Bonneville to face the van. He jumped out of the car and whipped out his pistol.

At first, the driver of the van tried to slow, but then he accelerated, intent on running his prey down.

Jeff took a deep breath and let it out slowly, trying to calm his quaking hands. He focused his sights on the driver. At exactly fifty feet, he squeezed the trigger and then dropped into a small irrigation ditch.

The van veered toward Jeff, off the shoulder of the road and then up the slope of the ditch bank, sailing over his head. Its engine whined with full throttle as it bounced once and then did a complete roll into the pasture.

Jeff leaped from his hiding place and sprinted to the

wreckage. The driver pulled himself from the van, staggered a few yards, and collapsed. Jeff yanked the unconscious passenger out and pulled him away from the van.

After he decided the van wouldn't explode, Jeff searched both passenger and driver. He took their weapons and ran back to the captain's car radio and called for an ambulance.

He returned as the driver began to stir. The wounded man woke to the barrel of a pistol trained on his face.

"I won't miss this time," Jeff said. "Who are you?"

No answer.

"Who sent you?"

Again, no answer.

Jeff gripped the pistol, preparing to shoot. "Have it your way."

The driver stared at Jeff with steely eyes. When he saw that Jeff wasn't going to shoot, he snorted with disgust.

Jeff grabbed him off the ground by his collar and shouted, "Where's Stephanie?"

The driver spit at him defiantly.

Jeff jerked back and clobbered him with the butt end of the pistol. The driver fell backwards, unconscious again.

With repugnance, Jeff wiped at the saliva on his cheek. He searched the man's pockets and found a motel key and a book of matches with the West Bank logo. "My favorite place," Jeff said as he remembered his first undercover buy with Heather. He executed a quick search of the still-unconscious passenger and van as distant sirens signaled that the police and ambulance were on their way.

Jeff looked at the wreckage. He looked at the approaching patrol car and fingered the matchbook. The muscles in his jaw tightened as he jammed the motel key into his pocket.

The patrolman jumped from his car seconds ahead of the ambulance. "What happened?"

Jeff gave a quick explanation and directed him toward

the captives. "I have a hot lead to check out. I'll call in as soon as I can."

Jeff took off in Captain Fowler's car. Seconds later, he pulled up to the West Bank and hustled directly to room 304.

The key worked. Jeff drew his gun and pushed open the door. The room was empty except for the usual furnishings and a black gym bag next to the dresser.

He unzipped the bag and withdrew its contents. A wide smile grew over his face. Passports, five thousand dollars in cash, and two airline tickets to Cuzco, Peru. Departure time was 6:28 P.M. from Salt Lake City. Jeff glanced at his watch. It was now 2:35. If his Toyota didn't break down, he could make the phone call and get there in time.

Jeff awoke from a fitful sleep as the plane settled onto the Cuzco runway. The morning flight from Lima had left him several hours of daylight. He stretched his arms forward and yawned. By the looks from the woman seated next to him, he needed a bath and a change of clothes. Unfortunately, he had time for neither.

It would only work if he acted fast. Using the hit man's airline ticket was a gamble, but he was able to get it changed to his name. Hopefully they wouldn't already be waiting for him as he left the plane. Either way, the plan was the same.

Jeff exited the 727 onto the tarmac and entered the large room that served as the Cuzco air terminal. So far, so good. With no luggage, he headed directly across the room for the taxi area. He paused to tighten the laces on his running shoes and took a few deep breaths.

Once outside, he walked directly to the first taxi in line. Out of the corner of his eye, he noticed two men moving to intercept him. With a fabricated smile on his face, he acted like he would stop to bargain with the taxi driver.

Instead, he vaulted around the car and sprinted

through the parking lot. The men immediately gave chase. One went after Jeff and the other headed for a car.

Jeff pulled away from his pursuer with ease. The chain-link fence slowed his pace momentarily, but soon he was back at a full sprint. He could hear a car squealing around the corner. He pivoted right and ducked between two houses.

Slowing his pace to three-quarter speed, he made his way down a familiar alley and turned left. The high oxygen-deprived air began to take its toll as Jeff gasped deep breaths. His ears listened for the slowing and accelerating of automobiles. In several minutes, he'd made eight turns and was now only one block from the main road leading to the airport.

Jeff made his final dash into a small dirt-floor restaurant. The odors brought a rush of memories dating back to his mission. He discreetly stepped into the bathroom. Their was no door and only a hole for a window. He crawled out the window feet first, landing on the ground by the alley.

An old Chevy Impala waited ten feet from the window. The trunk was open. Jeff dived in and slammed the lid over him. Immediately, the engine came to life and the car shuddered forward.

Jeff grabbed a few deep breaths. He wriggled backwards and set out to complete phase two of his plan.

Within minutes, the wail of a siren signaled the arrival of the Peruvian police and Jeff's worst fears. There was only one reason they would stop the car. Jeff hoped the plan would work.   ·

The Impala stopped. Two car doors slammed behind him. The muffled sound of a man barking orders were followed by the driver's door opening and then closing.

Jeff felt the grating of a key being pushed into the trunk lock. His chest tightened.

The trunk lid popped open, and he sensed movement of the spare tire and old clothes. Then a commanding voice said, *"No hay nada. Cierra la puerta.* (There is nothing. Close the door.)"

Jeff gave a quick prayer of thanks directed toward the designer of the car's large trunk, especially the part that Brent Marks had altered.

The policeman muttered something about a terrorist and allowed the Impala to proceed. Several turns later, the car accelerated to a steady speed.

Dust mingled with exhaust fumes started to turn Jeff's stomach. Twenty minutes later, the car turned onto a bumpy road and stopped. Jeff waited until the driver opened the trunk and pulled back the false cover before moving.

"Elder Foster!" The seventeen-year-old beamed with excitement. "Less money than taxi, no?"

Jeff bolted out of the trunk and wrapped his arms around his friend. "Jesse! You sound wonderful."

"Yes, my English is much improved."

Jeff held up his hand. "And you are much taller."

"And more handsome, speaks my mother."

Jeff grinned and nodded. "Yes, more handsome too."

The high Peruvian air tasted refreshing compared with the musty trunk but left him queasy.

Jesse slammed the lid and motioned Jeff to the car. "Come, President Marks is waiting."

Jesse still called him "President" even though Brent Marks was released as branch president a year ago. Probably the same reason he referred to Jeff as "Elder."

Ten minutes later, they pulled up to the small village. Jesse directed Jeff to a modest house. Almost before he could get out of the car, Brent Marks was at the door throwing a bear hug around him. "Jeff! I'm so glad you made it." Even as a ranger in special forces ten years ago, Brent Marks looked a little overweight, but it was all muscle. He hadn't changed.

Jeff smiled. "Your plan worked perfectly."

"Uneventful?"

Jeff shook his head. "No, it was close, but thanks to Jesse it worked. I owe you."

Brent put his arm around him and escorted him into the house. "So tell me, is the Church still true in Idaho?"

Jeff grinned. "More than ever."

"Good! Marsha will be glad to hear that. She has a nephew serving a mission in Burley."

Brent had married Marsha after Jeff had baptized him. After they greeted Marsha, Brent directed Jeff into a small but orderly room and shifted the conversation. "I have the things you asked for and a couple other toys you might find useful. Come into my office."

Jeff retold the events of the last week. Brent shook his head, not seeing Marsha enter the room with a plate full of cookies and a cup of *mate* tea for the altitude. "Women! The things we do under their spell."

Marsha raised one eyebrow. "Pardon?"

Brent straightened in his chair. "I said, 'Women! The things they do are a wonder to tell.'"

"That's what I thought you said." Marsha winked at Jeff and walked back into the kitchen.

Brent studied the raisin cemented to his cookie. "Do you have a plan?"

Jeff rubbed his eyebrow. "I thought maybe you'd have some ideas."

Brent smiled. "I was hoping you'd say that. I took the liberty to do a little research after I got your phone call." He reached for a folder and pulled out a hand-drawn map. "I took a small hike and jotted down a few notes."

Jeff examined the map. It showed Tinaco's estate in detail. "Whoa!" He held up his hand in protest. "How did you get all this?"

"You forget my past profession," Brent smiled smugly.

Jeff shook his head. "I can't ask you to do this. These guys play for keeps."

Brent leaned forward in his chair. "Jeff, I don't think you appreciate my position."

Jeff knew when he'd taught him the gospel that he had been in the armed services, but Brent hadn't said much about it. He'd taken early retirement to work with the people of Peru.

Brent continued, "I have some skills that could prove very useful."

Jeff waited expectantly.

"Uncle Sam spent a lot of money training me. The Vietnam War ended right after I joined the service. Most people think there was only Grenada, Panama, Iraq, and Somalia. But they don't realize that since Vietnam, there have been dozens of skirmishes around the world. The politicians like to call them "hot spots." Most of the time, the outside world never finds out."

Brent cleared his throat. "Anyway, we performed a number of missions in Central and South America. One of them got particularly ugly." He looked at the floor. "Many innocent people were killed. And then, well, I decided I was never going to kill again—for any reason."

Jeff nodded his head. "And you joined the people of Anti-Nephi-Lehi."

Brent smiled. "You do understand."

"It's one of my favorite Book of Mormon stories. The converted Lamanites refused to stain their swords with their enemies' blood and allowed themselves to be slaughtered first."

Brent nodded. "But I can use those skills for good now."

Jeff shook his head. "No. It's just like the people of Anti-Nephi-Lehi. You can't allow yourself to go back, and I don't think you have two thousand stripling sons."

Brent laughed. "I have no intention of going back. But I think there's a way to do it without my killing anyone. In fact, given the type of security Tinaco has, I think the only way to do it is without killing."

"I'm listening."

Brent smoothed out the map. "Okay, the first thing we

need to understand is the defense. And he has plenty of defense." Brent outlined the perimeter with his finger. "There's an eight-foot rock wall completely surrounding the property. Two guards patrol the inside with dogs—"

Jeff interrupted, "Dog's name isn't Bruno, is it?"

Brent gave him a puzzled look.

Jeff waved him on. "Never mind."

Brent shrugged. "I counted fourteen different cameras and there may be more concealed. There are two main buildings, probably the servants' quarters and the main house. Then there's a maze of gardens, shrubbery, and rock fences."

"Just like the lake property," Jeff said.

"There are only two gates—one in the front and one leading to his private runway. Both are guarded twenty-four hours a day. The runway is completely closed off with an eight-foot chain-link fence lined with barbed wire. The only road to the runway is through the estate."

Brent paused briefly to let Jeff absorb the information. "The way I see it, there are three main obstacles. Getting in undetected—"

"Couldn't we give the dogs something to eat that will knock them out?"

Brent shook his head. "Any dog worth his salt will only accept food from his master or his own dish. I checked. They feed the dogs inside."

Jeff furrowed his brow. "What're the other two obstacles?"

"Finding her and getting out."

"By the look on your face, I'd say you already have it figured out."

Brent raised both eyebrows. "As far as finding her, that might already be done. One of the windows on the house has bars. None of the others do. My guess is, that's where they're keeping her."

"So how do we get her out?"

"I have some ideas. First, I rig the power cable and backup generator to blow up by remote control. There's a

238

boy named Rosario who drives a gas truck to the estate once a week. He's due tonight at nine o'clock. The sun sets at eight thirty-seven. We'll hide in the equipment panels on the side of the truck. After it drives through the front gate, you count to three and bail out. This should put you right next to a rock fence by some shrubbery. I ride the truck all the way to the runway and bail out by the airplane hangars. I disable all the planes, including his jet, except the Cheyenne II. I assume you can fly a twin."

"Yes, but why the Cheyenne II instead of the Lear?"

"Ever fly a Lear?"

"No."

"That's why." Brent continued, "According to Rosario, the twin is equipped with an extra gas tank that could take you all the way to Miami. Meanwhile, you go in, get her, and meet me at the runway. If there's trouble, and there will be, I'll keep them occupied while you two fly away."

"And Tinaco's men are just going to watch me take Stephanie as we stroll over to the runway?"

Brent grinned. "This is where it gets fun. Ever hear of NVGs?"

"Night vision goggles? Sure, I've heard of them, but I've never used them before. How do they work?"

Brent reached into a duffel bag and retrieved a rigid mask with two-inch tubes protruding from the eyes. "These babies are incredible. When the time is right we cut the lights, and bingo—we see, they don't."

Brent took him into his basement bathroom and showed him how to fit the goggles to his face. "Pull this switch out and turn. The first setting is starlight. It magnifies the existing light. It works better when there is some light, like outside at night. The second setting is I.R."

"Infrared?"

"Yes. It makes its own light that can't be seen with the naked eye. Works great when there's no light, like indoors. Try it." Brent turned off the lights and shut the door.

Jeff flipped on the switch to the starlight setting.

Instantly, the bathroom jumped to life. The fixtures took on a grainy green texture. "Man! This really works."

"Okay, now focus the lens. Left for distance, right for close up. Start by closing your left eye and focusing the right lens on your shoe."

"Got it."

"Now close your right eye and look across the room."

"Okay, I got it."

Brent tossed a towel across the bottom of the door. It blocked the outside light from filtering in. Now Jeff could barely make out Brent's outline, even with the starlight on.

"Now switch it to I.R."

Jeff made the adjustment. Again, the details of Brent's face popped into focus.

Brent held up three fingers. "How many fingers do I have?"

"Three," Jeff said confidently.

"Nope." Brent flashed both hands open. "Ten, if you count my thumbs."

Jeff groaned. "My little sister used to tell that one."

"Remember, you end up with tunnel vision. Things that are close don't show up. Now, turn it off and lift up your mask."

"Whoa! It's black in here. This is incredible."

Brent groped for the mask and made sure the I.R. was turned off. He flipped on the bathroom light. "Never look directly at a light, especially with the I.R. on. It fries the electronics. Any questions?"

"How much do these babies cost?"

"About eight grand."

"Where'd you get them?"

Brent smiled. "Friends."

"Will Tinaco have them?"

"Probably, but they won't have time to get them until it's all over."

They walked back upstairs and into the den. Jeff held up his hand like a dutiful student. "What about the dogs? I noticed that you'll be safely on the other side of the fence inside the airport compound."

Brent chuckled and reached into the same duffel bag. "Toy number two." He withdrew a small gun. "This is a tranquilizer gun. It has a delayed effect. At first, it will make the dog apathetic—basically drunk. After a minute, Fido will lie down and sleep it off."

"Will it work on people?"

"Yes, but that probably won't help you. Not practical. The average gun fight lasts less than seconds. Even with a dog, it takes time to work. If you're charged, it'll be too late. It's best to nail the dog before he sees you. Same for a man, only longer."

"No offense, but do you have anything a little more fast acting, like an S&W 40?"

Brent handed Jeff a Glock similar to the one he lost to Tinaco's men. "I won't use one, but I certainly don't have any problem with you using it." Then he added, "You'll be my two thousand stripling warriors."

Jeff flexed his muscles to imitate the Book of Mormon illustrations. "Yes, Father." Then he grew serious. "Does this Rosario, the gas truck driver, know what you're up to?"

"No, and I think it's best we don't tell him."

Brent again reached into the duffel bag and handed Jeff a gadget resembling a one-eared stethoscope. "And finally, toy number three, an electronic listening device. Hold this up to a wall and you can hear everything in the next room. But you need to hold absolutely still or you'll drown out the conversation with your own body noises."

Brent looked at his watch. "Seven o'clock. We'd better hustle if we're going to get the charges set and make it in time for the gas truck."

Chapter Twenty-Six

Jeff slapped at his face. The incessant buzzing drove him deeper into the foliage. For the most part, the bugs left him alone. He wasn't sure if he should thank the face paint or his body odor.

He checked his watch. *8:20 P.M. Brent should be back by now.*

Jeff scratched at his pant leg. The pant cuffs were tied snug against his ankles, but he was sure that creepy crawlies were finding their way in. He felt a tickle above his right knee. He reached down and ground his thumb into his leg hard enough to leave a bruise. The indestructible tickle moved slowly upward.

In a controlled panic, Jeff grabbed his leg and formed a tourniquet with his hands. He rubbed vigorously. The movement stopped, but like the mythical three-headed snake, two more tickles magically appeared elsewhere.

Jeff tried to think about something else. He checked his watch again. *Only 8:21.*

"Looking for someone?" The deep whisper sent shock waves racing through Jeff's body. He instinctively grabbed for his gun, but a firm arm locked it in place.

Brent's white teeth bounced back and forth in the fading light as he shook his head. "I still got it. Yeah, I still have the touch."

"You got it all right," Jeff whispered. "Scared the tar water out of me." He adjusted his earphone. They both wore tiny microphones and earphones so they could be in constant communication.

Brent whispered, "Come on. Let's get out of here."

Jeff nodded in agreement and then looked back. "Is the power taken care of?"

"The backup generator is by the north wall. It was alarmed, but it's taken care of." Brent reached in his pocket and pulled out a tiny metal carton with a control button. "This will kill all the power. Try to give me some warning."

Jeff shoved the detonator in his pocket. They quickly retreated to Brent's old Chevy and drove to Rosario's gas truck.

Equipment panels ran the length of the bed on each side of the truck. They walked to the passenger side. Jeff held the equipment door open as Brent crawled in. The compartment was arranged like a coffin, with Brent's head near the passenger door.

Suddenly, a door slammed from the old building and Jeff lunged for a clump of bushes. The driver's door opened and closed. A second later, the engine turned over.

"Jeff!" Brent spoke into the microphone.

No answer.

Brent tried again. "Can you hear me?"

"Yeah, I can hear you."

"Are you with me?" Brent asked as the truck rounded the corner.

"More or less."

"What do you mean more or less?"

"We have a slight problem. You'll need to make some extra room."

Brent adjusted his ear piece. "What are you talking about?"

"I'm hanging on the passenger door. As soon as I get the side mirror adjusted so he can't see, I'll join you."

Jeff reached up quickly and shoved the mirror outward. Rosario was busy singing along with earphones plugged into his head.

With his right fingers gripping the door handle and his feet propped against the running board, Jeff flipped up the equipment panel. He grinned at Brent. "Want to help me in?"

Brent tossed a bulky tool box over the side and watched as it rolled a couple times into the ditch. He stretched out and grabbed Jeff's arm. "I gotcha. Give me your leg."

Jeff tried to do the splits.

"Higher!" Brent coaxed.

"That's as high as it goes."

"Jump up with both feet and I'll grab them."

"What if you miss?"

"I won't miss."

"What if I don't jump high enough?"

"Come on!" Brent yelled.

Jeff jumped up sideways and let go of the door handle. He was sucked in by Brent's powerful arms as the lid slammed shut. Nose to nose, they both used Brent's small pack as a pillow.

"Now, that wasn't so bad, was it?" Brent asked.

Jeff rolled his eyes. "And this is supposed to be the easy part?"

Brent acted serious. "Jeff, I want you to promise me one thing."

"What's that?"

"When we finish this, you'll take a bath."

Jeff jabbed him in the ribs. "Believe me, I'd like to."

Brent chuckled, "I can handle it, but once your sweetie takes a whiff, she might decide to go back to Tinaco."

At precisely nine o'clock, the truck rolled up to Tinaco's estate. Jeff felt his stomach churn in anticipation. As the truck started to roll forward again, he counted aloud, "One

thousand one, one thousand two, one thousand three."
Jeff lifted the equipment panel door and pounced onto the
ground. He rolled once and ducked into some bushes. In
another second, he was across the road and against the
wall lined with shrubbery.

"All clear," he whispered into the microphone.

A few minutes later, he received the all-clear message
from Brent. He wasted no time in working his way to the
barred window.

Jeff looked around and spotted a camera pointing at
the direction he had just come from. He hoped Brent was
right—that one person watched several cameras and that
if he hurried he stood a good chance of making it undetected. Jeff unbuttoned one of the leg pockets of his camouflage pants and withdrew the listening device. He in-
serted one end into his ear. As he was about to place the
other end against the window, he heard a strange noise.
Panting? Jeff's stomach churned as he watched a
Doberman pinscher pick up his scent from where he
jumped off the truck.

The dog methodically stalked his prey. Out came the
dart gun. Jeff aimed at the dog, now closing in on his position, and fired. The dart pierced the dog's left hindquarter.
Fido stopped, shook his leg, and pushed on. Jeff's heart
sank. The dog stopped and sat down; then he got up
again, walked a few yards, and collapsed.

Jeff breathed a sigh of relief into the microphone. "One
doggy out of the picture."

"Keep a close eye out for the other one. They usually
stay together."

Jeff gently placed the listening device against the
barred window and watched for the other dog.

Tinaco slammed his fist on the table. "Barry talked."

"Are you sure it wasn't Hunnington?"

"Our attorney friend can talk no more."

Troy understood the implied message and rubbed his hand over his throat nervously. He guessed Hunnington was ignorant about Stephanie's connection to Jeff, but evidently Tinaco didn't care to risk it. "Jeff's probably wandering the streets of Cuzco right now, hoping to stumble onto something."

Tinaco shook his head. "I am a man well known. Once in Tingo Maria, it will not be difficult for him to find me."

"Do you think he'll contact the police?"

"That would solve our problem with ease, but I think it will not be solved with ease. He will come here."

Troy leaned back in his chair. "Better still. Even if your man talked, what could Jeff hope to gain? He couldn't get near this place."

Tinaco shook his head. "This Jeff is a foolish man. He takes many chances. But he is a brave man, and sometimes brave men accomplish difficult tasks."

Troy shrugged. "There's always Stephanie. Evidently he is willing to do anything to get her back."

"That is what I count on. As long as he believes her to be alive, he will seek her."

"Then let's not risk her escape. Just kill her."

"Options." Tinaco let the word hang in the air. "Always preserve your options."

Troy thought of the Idaho Falls attorney but didn't say anything.

An abrupt knock at the door interrupted the conversation.

"Enter."

A pug-faced man opened the room. "Sir, we—"

Tinaco cut him off. "Is the plane ready?"

The man took a remarkable risk and ignored his boss's question. "We have an intruder."

"Where?" snapped Tinaco.

"We have him on camera near the guest window. All routes of escape are sealed. Do you want us to capture him?"

"No."

"Get him while you have the chance!" yelled Troy.

Tinaco shot Troy a withering glance for his outburst. "No, it will be better to let him come inside. There may be others." Tinaco strolled down the hall and entered the surveillance room. Fourteen monitors lined one wall. They were being observed by two men. One studied Jeff's position, and the other searched for more intruders.

"There." The pug-faced man pointed at one of the monitors. Jeff blended into the shrubbery next to the window, but a sharp eye could pick him out.

"What's that?" Troy pointed at the screen.

"A listening device." Tinaco stroked his chin. "Perhaps we need to help Mr. Foster find his way inside." He turned to the pug-faced man. "Is the Cheyenne prepared with the needed papers on board?"

Troy looked puzzled. "I thought we would take the Lear."

Tinaco glanced at his watch. "No, the Cheyenne is the perfect choice for the difficult landing."

Jeff monitored the silence for several minutes before he heard the door open.

"Ms. Stephanie, I trust you are comfortable."

Jeff felt his heart race as Stephanie's voice sounded through the wire. "I would be more comfortable if you let me go."

"That would be quite impossible. Apparently, your boyfriend has come to Peru."

"Jeff?" Her voice sounded hopeful.

"Yes, he was last seen near the airport in Cuzco, but this is unfortunate for you."

Silence.

"Unfortunate, because we no longer need you."

Pause.

"But there might be a way for you to live."

Jeff heard what he thought was the rustling of clothes. "Stop it!"

"You are a beautiful girl. Perhaps you would like to accompany me in my travels."

A loud slap popped over the wire—the sound of palm contacting cheek. "I'd rather die."

This time, the sound of a fist connecting with flesh smacked through the earphone, followed by the soft whimper of a feminine voice.

Jeff flinched. Hostility grated on his tongue like vomit. The icy voice that followed sent chills up his spine. "In ten minutes, we will return. Then you will beg for your life . . . and then you will die."

The door slammed shut. Jeff detected a soft sniffle over the wire. Anger rushed through his veins. *How dare he touch her!*

Wasting no time, he scrambled along the house until he came to an open window. "Lucky break," Jeff breathed quietly, too involved to reject the coincidence.

The darkness was intensified by the thick cloud cover. Jeff slithered through the window. The mystery of why the other dog never came hammered gently at his psyche. A hallway was dimly lit, so he left the goggles hanging around his neck. *All clear.* He crept down the hall and paused every five feet to listen.

A peculiar feeling trickled through his chest, settling at the top of his stomach—the same sensation that had warned him of danger in the past. Jeff forced a deep breath, said a silent prayer, and then continued down the hall until he came to the place where Stephanie's room would be. His hand reached into his pocket and withdrew the listening device.

"You won't need that." The voice shot pockets of adrenalin rushing through his body. Before he could respond, a red-haired man stuck a gun to his head while two others dragged him into a room and propped him into a chair.

A moment later, Troy walked into the room. He greeted Jeff with contempt. "I'm afraid we have some unpleasant business, Jeff Spenelie. Oh yes, it is Foster, isn't it?"

248

Jeff swallowed hard and steadied his voice. "It's nice to see you, Troy. Am I your only guest?"

"Fishing for information, are we? Yes, Stephanie has been good company."

"If you touch her, I'll—"

"You are in no position to make threats. Besides—" he seemed to pause with pleasure—"I am sure Stephanie enjoyed my companionship last night."

Jeff flew into a rage and swung his fist toward Troy's head. Red Hair latched onto it and flung Jeff to the ground. He grabbed Jeff by the hair and smashed his head onto the floor. The toe of a cowboy boot slammed into his ribs. Shades of red and yellow rippled across Jeff's mind as his limbs contorted in pain.

Red Hair sat him back in the chair.

"Emotion. That is your weakness, Mr. Foster."

"I want to see Stephanie."

Tinaco strolled into the room, his voice calm but commanding. "This is no way to treat our honored guest." He stood in front of Jeff with arms folded. "You want to see Stephanie?" He threw a curt nod toward a guard.

Stephanie was thrust into the room, followed by a pug-faced man. A white rag was wrapped around her mouth.

Jeff struggled while the guard held his arms in place. His fingers strained in vain to reach the detonator tucked into his pocket.

Tinaco fingered the NVGs hanging around Jeff's neck. His expression turned to ice as he moved closer to Jeff's face.

Jeff closed his eyes. *Please, Heavenly Father, help us. Please deliver Stephanie from this great evil. Take me instead.*

The ice turned to wet hunger as beads of sweat formed on Tinaco's brow. He carefully watched Jeff's eyes while giving the order. "Take her outside . . . and shoot her."

Chapter Twenty-Seven

The words seared Stephanie's ears like hot branding irons. Her eyelashes settled against her bloated cheeks, squashed upward by the gag. *Please, Father.*

Jeff's mouth dropped open. "Shoot her?"

Tinaco flashed a wicked grin. "Not to worry. You soon will join her." His eyes flamed into angry coals as he grasped Jeff's cheeks with one hand. He forced Jeff's head toward Stephanie. "You will watch her die. You will suffer. You will wish yourself to die. You will suffer again. Then you will die."

Stephanie's head spun. Two more guards stood in the hall carrying assault rifles. Pug Face grabbed her arm and yanked her down the hall. As they stepped outside, Pug Face guided her toward a garden path lined with knee-deep vegetation brightened by several lights.

She jerked her head back toward the building they had just left. Jeff's face was plastered against the window, held there by Red Hair. His features seemed contorted as he frantically mouthed something in her direction.

Pug Face shoved her forward, and Stephanie stumbled over the exposed root of a large tree. She went down on one knee, clutching her ankle. Pug Face reached for her arm.

Stephanie recovered and threw her elbow full force into his big belly. Not waiting to test its effect, she bolted toward a rock fence eighty feet away.

The two other guards accompanying her laughed out loud as Pug Face turned white, gasping for air. By the time he regained composure, Stephanie had covered half the eighty yards to the fence.

She glanced back as Pug Face grabbed his companion's rifle and trained it in her direction. She increased her speed. Her eyes focused on the fence. Blood pounded through her veins.

Her eyes caught the fuzzy image of what looked like a dead branch poking up through the foliage. Pain shot through her leg. An explosion wrapped the air. Stephanie went down hard. Two more quick shots. She lay still.

Jeff stared through the window at the scene before him. He shook his head in disbelief. He felt his throat constrict. His eyes burned. He had asked God to save her. But he hadn't. A forlorn howl escaped his mouth. "No!"

Nothing moved. His abductors stood at arm's length, gawking over the massacre. All eyes centered on the figure half buried in vegetation.

Jeff's muscles tensed. Reason left him. Nothing mattered now. He would have his revenge, and Red Hair would be first.

Jeff pivoted and spun with such speed that even Red Hair didn't have time to react. The blade of his fist caught him directly under the chin. Red Hair went down, clutching his throat. The guard next to him drew his pistol. Jeff kicked the biceps of his arm, rendering that arm useless, and then lunged forward, smashing the man into the wall. The pistol clattered across the floor.

A third guard caught Jeff with a glancing blow to the shoulder. He jerked out a pistol without aiming. Jeff dove to the floor as the guard squeezed the trigger. The bullet narrowly missed, crashing into a chair. Jeff grabbed the pistol on the floor, racked the barrel, and fired three quick rounds. The man dropped, leaving only the acrid scent of burnt gunpowder wafting through the air.

Jeff's eyes searched for Troy and Tinaco. The room was empty. He dashed into the hall. Nothing. He lifted his heels off the floor and sped silently down the hall.

He paused near the entrance to a large room. His nostrils flared. He picked up a magazine laying on a table in the hall and gingerly pushed it around the corner. The blast of a shotgun ripped it from his hand.

Immediately after the discharge, Jeff tumbled into the room. He pointed and shot as Troy squeezed the trigger. The second blast from the shotgun crashed into the wall. Troy stared at Jeff in amazement and sank to his knees. The shotgun slid from his fingers and made a soft thud as it hit the carpeted floor.

Jeff grabbed Troy by the lapels of his white tailored jacket. "Where is he?"

Troy stared at him through unseeing eyes. He was dead.

"Behind you." A metallic click snapped through the air.

Jeff spun around with gun in hand. Tinaco stood by the door with his hands wrapped around a failed pistol. A look of shock covered his face.

Jeff trained his gun on Tinaco's head, now only ten feet away. Tinaco dropped the pistol. He carefully raised his hands high in the air and laughed. "I surrender."

Jeff didn't move.

Tinaco scoffed again. "I am your prisoner. Too bad for you."

Jeff stared at Tinaco in disbelief.

Tinaco stood proud and confident. "Yes. You have captured Ramon Tinaco, Detective Foster. You must take me to jail, here in Peru."

A look of understanding unfolded on Jeff's face.

Tinaco scowled. "You have caused me much inconvenience, Mr. Foster. No matter. You have nothing of the company."

The company. Jeff remembered Troy's reference to the company. As long as the company existed, Tinaco would get out. Whether by corruption, legal maneuvering, or by brute force, he would get out. The realization overwhelmed him. Jeff gripped his pistol. The image of Stephanie hitting the ground flashed through his mind. Bitterness churned inside. He aimed directly at Tinaco's nose and shook his head. "No. We will end the conflict."

The expression on Tinaco's face changed from one of security to unsure anxiety. "I have surrendered. I know you. You cannot do this."

Jeff's face turned to stone. *The system doesn't work. You deserve to die. It's up to me.* He mentally mouthed the words.

Tinaco began to tremble. Jeff let the air drain from his lungs. He gripped the pistol firmly. *For the children on drugs. For the men you killed. For Stephanie.* He started to squeeze the trigger.

No!

The voice was neither loud nor overbearing. It was a still small voice. A voice that penetrated Jeff's heart. At first, he thought it came from someone else, but the room was empty.

Tinaco shook with fear. Apparently only Jeff could hear the voice.

It returned as a small whisper, piercing Jeff to the very center. *Be still.*

The passions Jeff had for revenge surrendered to a peaceful forbearance. He lowered his weapon. "Yes, you are my prisoner."

Tinaco laughed. "Tomorrow you will be dead."

A third voice entered from behind Tinaco. "I don't think so." Before Tinaco could turn around, Brent clubbed him over the neck and he settled to unconsciousness on the floor.

Brent reached down and picked up Tinaco's pistol. He popped the magazine out and frowned. "The hammer's down on one in the chamber."

He ejected the round into the palm of his hand and

examined it. A small dent was punched into the primer. "Didn't go off." He held it up for Jeff to see. "Looks like someone's watching over you, kid."

Brent stared at Tinaco with contempt and nodded soberly at Jeff. "You didn't shoot him."

Jeff studied the defective bullet and shook his head. "Some other time." He leaned back against the wall and tried to sort the events of the past hour.

Suddenly, the memory of Stephanie returned. He slid slowly down the wall and settled on the floor. He gently placed his pistol on the carpet. "Stephanie." He whispered the words so that only he could hear them. "Stephanie, oh, Stephanie."

Jeff looked up with red eyes. Husky emotion filled his voice as he mouthed the words, "They got Stephanie."

"I have her. She's safe."

He clutched Brent's arm. Hope mingled with disbelief converged on his face as he forced out, "But I saw—"

"You saw her fall as you heard a shot. But she started to fall first."

"Then you—"

Several voices sounded in the courtyard. "No time to explain. You still got the detonator?"

Jeff felt in his pocket and nodded his head. "Where is she?"

"She's back in the same room they kept her in." Brent glanced at Jeff's puzzled expression. "I knew they wouldn't look for her there."

"Twisted logic."

Brent smiled. "It works for me." He grabbed his night vision and slid it onto his forehead. "Same plan as before."

"What about Tinaco?"

"Leave him. There's no other option."

Jeff hesitated. He slid the goggles above his eyes. Brent motioned for the hall. "Don't detonate until you get ready to leave the building. That'll give you more time."

"What about you?"

"Don't worry about me. I still have lots of surprises lined up." Brent disappeared into the adjoining room.

Jeff glided into the darkened hallway and slid the night vision over his eyes. He quickly made his way down the hall using the starlight setting.

"You won't need that." The voice cut through the darkness, shooting pockets of adrenalin through Jeff's body. He spun around in time to see a shotgun muzzle pointed at his head. Immediately after, he was blinded by lights.

"NVGs don't work with the lights on, do they?" The voice laughed as Jeff sensed two others join him. He was about to raise the goggles off his head, but stopped. Instead, he jammed his hand into his pocket.

"Hands up!"

Jeff knew he wouldn't get another warning. His thumb reached desperately for the switch Brent had given him to kill the power. "But I can't see . . . " Suddenly, everything went dark. Simultaneously, Jeff dropped to the floor. He could now clearly see three men in front of him with weapons pointed in his direction.

A shotgun blasted over his head. He lunged forward and twisted the gun from the man's hands. With lightning speed, Jeff gripped the shotgun barrel in both hands, dropping a sightless attacker with each stroke. A second later, all three men lay unconscious on the floor.

Jeff's ear's perked at the sound of footsteps approaching the hall. With no time to retreat, he charged down the hall and met a guard at the corner. Jeff drew his gun and pointed it at the guard's face. "Don't move!"

There wasn't enough light for the guard to see the gun or the intruder. Jeff watched him reach for a flashlight.

It blinked on long enough for the guard to focus. Before the guard could evaluate the information fed to his brain, Jeff's foot sprang out and kicked him in the stomach. He followed up with a blow to the neck. The fourth blind victim toppled to the floor.

As a result of the tunnel vision dictated by the goggles,

Jeff wildly swung his head as if he were an owl searching for its prey. He ran back to Stephanie's door and smashed it open.

His attention centered on the figure sitting on the edge of a bed, straining to see through the darkness. He flipped the switch from starlight to infrared. Stephanie's image jumped into the scope. Her face was marked more by bewilderment than fear.

"Steph. It's me."

"Jeff?"

"Come on!" Jeff led her down the hallway outside. Now in a full run, hand in hand, they bolted toward the gate leading to the runway.

He wondered why the gate was wide open until he saw a guard sleeping peacefully with a dart firmly implanted in his rear end, evidence of Brent's handiwork.

An explosion on the opposite side of the house marked the first of Brent's diversions planned to aid in their escape. They sprinted past the hangars to the end of the runway, where Brent had Tinaco's Cheyenne twin-engine airplane warming up. Jeff noticed another man, apparently unconscious, on the ground.

Brent stepped from behind a pile of crates. He still wore the night vision goggles. "You okay?"

"Yes. Is the plane all set?"

Brent pointed at the man on the ground. "He already had it running."

Jeff scanned the runway. "You going to be okay?" He turned back to look at Brent, but he had vanished.

Jeff jumped into the pilot's seat. "Get in."

Stephanie numbly obeyed.

Jeff grabbed a mini-mag flashlight from his pocket and tossed it at Stephanie as he taxied to face the confusion of the compound. "We're going up dark. You watch the instruments, I'll watch the runway."

"But it's pitch black! The runway—"

"Trust me." Jeff tapped his goggles. "These babies work. Just watch the instruments." Already Jeff had accelerated to 25 mph.

Stephanie watched the blackness slide by and pulled her head down to the instruments. 35 . . . 40 . . . 50 miles per hour.

Several flashlights bounced up and down toward them at the end of the runway. Suddenly, a large spotlight lit up the entire runway, blinding Jeff.

"Take over, I can't see!"

Stephanie immediately took hold of the controls while Jeff ripped off the night vision goggles. Another explosion extinguished the spotlight and sent the flashlights scurrying for cover.

"Speed!" Jeff yelled.

"Seventy-five!"

Jeff fumbled with the goggles and jammed one eyepiece over his left eye. Bullets flew through the air.

"Ninety!" yelled Stephanie.

Jeff made one last correction and pulled the control handle back. The Cheyenne lifted off the ground amid a shower of gunfire. Jeff glanced over his shoulder and watched the flashing muzzles, amazed they were airborne.

Then it occurred to him that they were probably also shooting at Brent. For a moment, he thought about returning, but he knew Brent would make it.

At one thousand feet, he turned on the running lights and set the night vision equipment in his lap. Another switch retracted the landing gear. The fuel gauge registered full. Jeff leaned back and exhaled through his teeth. "Was that a ride or what?"

Stephanie looked into his eyes, ignoring his attempt at humor. She shook her head. "How?" Her eyes began to fill with tears. She buried her head against his shoulder and sobbed.

"Shhh, it's okay," Jeff whispered. "It's okay."

Chapter Twenty-Eight

The eastern sky turned dark pink in preparation for the rising sun. Jeff lay bunched up in the backseat of the Cheyenne, struggling for sleep. A briefcase he found on the floor had become a pillow. He shifted it, wrestling for comfort. Comprehension began seeping into his brain. He readjusted. Memories of the night flashed through his mind. He bolted upright.

"Where are we?"

"Good morning, Sleeping Beauty!" Stephanie munched on a sandwich left for the intended occupants while she guided the twin-engine aircraft from the copilot's seat. "We rounded the edge of Cuba about fifteen minutes ago. Should be almost to Florida."

Jeff twisted his head, trying to work the kink out of his neck. He shoved the briefcase to one side in disgust. He hesitated. It felt heavy. "Turn on the cabin light."

Stephanie reached for the switch. "Too tired to sleep?"

"No, I just want to check this out."

The briefcase resembled the one his father had carried to church, with the addition of a combination lock. Jeff fumbled around and found a small bag with hand tools. He jammed a flathead screwdriver in the lock and popped it open.

His brow furrowed. A small laptop computer and a few

disks. He punched the switch, giving it life. Letters blinked across the screen.

"PASSWORD?"

"Got any ideas for a password?"

Stephanie shrugged. "Most people pick something easy to remember. How about *cocaine.*"

Jeff tried it. "No luck."

"Careful," she warned. "You might only get three chances. That's how the one at my office works."

Jeff typed the word *money.*

Nothing.

He rubbed his nose. "Looks like I've got one left."

"Picture yourself as Tinaco."

Jeff's mind flashed to the picture hanging on the wall of Tinaco's estate on Lake Pend Oreille. The small boy amid poverty—his determined look. Jeff massaged his fingers against his temple and whispered. "What was the name . . . "

It flashed through his mind. *Ambition.*

He punched in the letters. The machine buzzed and whirled. New letters flickered across the top of the screen.

"MAIN MENU"

"We're in!"

Stephanie turned around in her seat. "What's it say?"

Jeff's fingers glided across the keys. He paused and whistled softly. More key strokes. His eyes sparkled as the corners of his mouth turned up. "Yes." he whispered. Then louder, "Yes!"

"What is it?"

"It's his financial records—names, amounts, places, quantities—he's got everything here."

"Do you think he'll want it back?"

Jeff snorted. "Yeah, I think he'll want it back." The full meaning of Stephanie's question emerged before him. "Yes, I imagine he'll do anything to get it back."

"It's hard to imagine him getting any worse."

Jeff mentally reviewed the attempts on his life in the past two days. He shoved a disk into the computer and began copying files.

Stephanie's voice changed. "I think we've got a problem."

"No bigger than before," Jeff said.

"No, I mean I think we really have a problem. Look!" Stephanie pointed at the fuel gauge.

Jeff's eyes bulged. He hurtled into the pilot's seat and flicked the gauge with his finger. It registered empty.

Jeff snatched up maps and began studying. "This baby was well fed before we left. You didn't take a side trip to Jamaica while I was sawing logs, did you?"

Stephanie wrinkled her nose. "Why is it that every time we face a crisis, you start making jokes?"

Jeff shrugged. "Sorry. I guess that's the way I deal with it." He studied the map closer. "We have got problems. If that gauge is accurate, we'll never make it to Miami."

Stephanie raised one eyebrow. "You didn't miscalculate our fuel consumption, did you?"

"No way. Besides, I had a great teacher, remember?" He inspected the wings. "One of those bullets must have punctured the tank or something."

"Where's the closest landing?" Stephanie asked.

"Cuba."

She took the map. "Besides Cuba. I'm not up to spending the next twenty years in a Cuban prison."

Jeff took the controls while she studied the map. Stephanie tilted her head. "I guess it would be the Bahamas, but they're not much closer than Miami."

Jeff frowned. "That leaves two choices."

"What's that?"

He jerked his head back toward his side window. "We could probably make Cuba . . . "

"And the other choice?"

Jeff smiled grimly. "Did you pack your swimming suit?"

Stephanie quivered. "Do you think you can land this thing on the ocean?"

"Probably not very well. But we do have retractable landing gear. Landing with our wheels sticking out would have been a treat."

Stephanie adjusted the fresh-air vent. "At least you'll get a chance to bathe."

"Ouch! Now look who's joking in the face of danger."

"Who's joking?" She smiled. "Are you going to deny that you're the source of these marvelous fragrances?"

Jeff sniffed the air. "Miss Evans. What odors could you possibly be referring to?"

"The ones resembling a goat."

Both of them forced nervous laughter. Stephanie wiped her hands over her arms. "It's not working."

"What's not working?"

"Attempt at humor. I'm still terrified."

Jeff placed his hand over hers. "We'll make it."

Stephanie reached over the seat and kissed his cheek. "I want you to know that—"

Suddenly, one engine coughed twice and sputtered to a stop. "Looks like Cuba is out," Jeff said as he gripped the controls harder. Seconds later, the other engine followed. "It's not supposed to work this way. Two engines, seconds apart . . . " His voice trailed off.

Stephanie pushed the rudder forward to prevent a stall. "We're going down."

Jeff motioned to the back. "Look for life jackets or anything that might help." He grabbed the radio microphone, "Mayday, Mayday, Mayday, forty miles south of Miami, engine failure."

Stephanie released her seat belt and climbed into the back. "Survival pack, some rations, and a raft—the kind that blows up by itself. There's some coats and other stuff too."

Jeff watched the altimeter needle slowly roll backwards. "Just bundle it together and strap yourself in."

"I'm coming up. You'll need my help."

"No, you'll stand a better chance back there. You might have to pull us out of this thing."

"Okay, but how are you going to do this?"

Jeff held up one finger. "We can't do a regular landing. After a couple of skips, it'll play submarine."

"So what do you have in mind?"

"We'll stall."

"You can only stall so long. We're going down."

"No, I mean stall the plane, like a bird landing on the water. Problem is, it won't work that way. We'll still have too much forward speed, and if we stall too early, we'll be completely out of control."

"So either way you look at it, we're going to crash."

"Well . . . kind of. But it might be a survivable crash."

Stephanie tried to smile. "No fuel, no fire. That means no explosion. I'm beginning to like this plan."

"Now you're getting the hang of it."

She finished getting the supplies ready and strapped herself in. Jeff watched as the needle continued to spin backwards. "It's going to sink fast. We've got to bail out as soon as we can—but then, we've experienced deep water before."

Stephanie gave a visible shudder.

Jeff stuck his thumb toward the backseat. "Tie yourself to the raft and hold it in your lap."

She fastened a cord around her foot and another around Jeff's waist. "We're in this together."

"Just remember to wait till it's outside the plane before you pull the cord."

Stephanie's expression was sober.

As they neared the ocean, he adjusted the flaps. "Air speed eighty-five miles per hour."

Stephanie shook her head. "Too fast."

His voice soothed the plane, "Not yet, easy, not yet."

Stephanie pulled her jaw in and squinted her eyes as the plane skimmed over the surface of the ocean.

"Now." Jeff spoke with controlled precision. Immediately, he tugged on the steering control. The Cheyenne strained upward like a clumsy chicken trying to clear a fence. For a moment, they hovered eighty feet above the water, coasting forward at half their prior speed. Then the plane plunged to the water.

The tail hit first, skipping across the first ocean swell. For a while, it plowed through the water as if it were a seaplane making a normal landing. But then the nose caught, sucking the craft to a rapid stop. Jeff smashed through the seat belt against the instrument panel. The plane abruptly tipped forward, following the weight of the engine. Water began pouring in.

"Jeff!" Stephanie yelled as she shoved him through the door. She snatched a final gulp of vanishing air, pushing his limp body in front of her.

Still clutching the raft in her left arm, Stephanie yanked on the cord. The CO_2 cartridge did its job. In seconds, the small package expanded into a raft.

Stephanie shoved Jeff against the edge of the raft. His head rose a few inches above the water and rocked back. "Come on, Jeff, help me!" Tears joined the salty water as she tried again. This time, his head fell forward.

Stephanie grabbed the rope attached to the raft and made three quick wraps around his wrist. She planted both of his hands high on the raft's edge and pulled herself up, then pushed. Her face rubbed the floor as she slid over the edge. Immediately, she swung around and clutched the black hair of Jeff's head floating near the front. Lifting his head from the water, she reached around his armpits and hauled him into the raft.

Blood oozed from a cut across his left cheek. No other visible injuries. But also no visible sign of life, except for a weak pulse. Stephanie laid him across the rubber floor, kneeled at his side, and planted her mouth across his. Two quick breaths. Nothing. Again a deep breath. She placed her fingertips across his neck. The uniform cadence still showed life. Again another breath.

Jeff retched once, then vomited salty water.

Stephanie shoved him on his side. His throat trumpeted as he exchanged seawater for air.

Jeff's abdominal muscles tightened as he tried to sit up. A sharp pain shot through his arm. He dropped back, withering in pain.

Stephanie ran her hand across his forehead. "Lie back, Jeff. You've been hurt."

Her image blurred with the memory of the crash. Jeff focused on a string of hair plastered to her cheek. He bit back the pain and showed his teeth. "See, that wasn't so bad."

Stephanie stuck her hands in her lap and leaned forward on straightened arms. Tears streamed down her cheeks. She opened her mouth, but nothing came out.

He reached out to wipe her tears. His arm recoiled in agony, and he clenched his teeth with determination. "So, what's the prognosis, doctor?"

"I think your arm might be broken and you have a nasty gash across your cheek. It looks like you've lost some blood."

Jeff glanced at his arm and looked away. "So other than that, I'm in pretty good shape."

"At least you don't smell quite so bad."

"Great, then things are getting better."

Stephanie shook her head soberly. "We're in the middle of the ocean with no land in sight, no water, no food; you've lost half your blood, and there's a psychopath trying to kill us." She paused and wiped seawater from her face. "Yeah, I guess things are better than yesterday."

Jeff searched Stephanie's face. "Did they do anything . . . " He couldn't bear to finish the question, but she understood.

"No." Tears started to well up in her eyes again. She buried her head in Jeff's chest. "Why can't they just leave us alone?"

He soothed her hair with his good hand and said nothing.

The raft rose up and down to the gentle swell of the ocean waves. Water on Jeff's face melted away and sweat formed in its place.

Jeff looked up at the sun. "How long was I out?"

"Only a few minutes." Stephanie raised her head from his chest and gazed into his eyes. "Jeff, you weren't breathing. I had to . . . " She let the words fade away.

Jeff winked at her. "Just can't keep your lips off me, can you?"

They both erupted in laughter.

"Ouch!" Jeff grabbed at his arm.

"Don't move." Stephanie placed her hand over his chest.

"Good idea."

Stephanie had ripped the legging from Jeff's torn Levi's and used the material to bandage his wounds.

Jeff twisted his neck, searching the raft. "Anything besides us in here?"

"You mean like a jug of ice water?"

"Something like that."

"Sorry. I didn't have time for anything else."

"At least you got the important things out."

"Yeah. Us."

Jeff's mind flashed back to the laptop computer. "We had it." He swallowed in disappointment. "Right in our hands, and now it's gone."

"The disk?"

Jeff nodded with down-turned eyes. "It had his records, everything. We could have exposed his whole organization."

A smile crept over Stephanie's lips. "You mean this?" She pulled a Ziploc bag from her pants pocket containing a disk and a smashed peanut butter sandwich.

"The disk?" Jeff stared in unbelief. "I thought you didn't have time."

"After the crash. I didn't have time *after* the crash. While I was getting the raft ready, I stuck it in with the sandwich. I forgot about it until now."

Jeff pressed his hand against his cheek as the full implications settled into his brain. "He's ours," he mumbled. Then louder, "He's ours!"

Jeff leaned his head on the side of the raft, a broad smile pasted on his face. "Things *are* looking up."

Stephanie studied the water in all directions. No land and no ships. She looked at Jeff and raised her eyebrows.

He laughed at her unspoken question. "Don't worry. Florida can't be too far away. There's bound to be a ship."

Stephanie closed her eyes. "There's bound to be a ship."

Chapter Twenty-Nine

"Stephanie! Watch out!"

Stephanie smoothed the wet rag over Jeff's forehead and paused to caress his sun-parched lips. "Shhh, it's okay. I'm here."

She held his shivering body in her sweat-stained arms. The ocean lapped a steady rhythm against the small raft.

Jeff squinted his eyes and shook his head. "How long was I out this time?"

Stephanie gave him her everything-is-fine voice. "About an hour."

Drops of sweat trickled down his neck, replacing the chills that seemed to come more often. "I'm not doing too well, am I?"

Stephanie fought back the tears and forced a smile. Her voice quivered, "You've been better."

Jeff winked at her. His voice grew raspy from lack of water. "Don't bury me yet."

"Bury you? I've got big plans for you, Jeff Foster."

His eyes sparkled. "Do tell, Miss Evans."

Stephanie soothed her fingers across his forehead. "Well, we'll start with flying lessons—like how to land on the water without demolishing the airplane."

Jeff hacked out a short laugh. "And then?"

"And then, maybe we can learn to scuba dive since we spend so much time under the water anyway."

"And then?" Jeff persisted.

"And then, maybe we could, uh . . . ," Stephanie's face flushed. "What plans do *you* have, Mr Foster?"

"After my flying lessons?"

"Yes."

"Treat my flying instructor to a lime sherbet at Baskin-Robbins."

"And then?"

His eyes widened with innocence. "Take scuba lessons, Miss Evans."

"And then, Mr. Foster?"

"And then, Miss Evans, I think . . . well, I think it's about time we talked about a name change."

"How so?"

"Evans isn't bad, but I think Foster sounds much better."

Stephanie's eyes widened. "As in Stephanie Foster?"

"Unless you have other plans."

Stephanie threw her arms around his head, scraping his torn cheek.

"Ouch!"

"Sorry." Stephanie shifted her weight and pressed against his broken arm.

"Ahhg!" He screamed in terror at the pressure on his arm.

She jumped back in horror. "Oh, Jeff, I'm so sorry."

Jeff tried to wave it off with his good arm. "We better make this a short engagement. I'm not sure I can survive the affection."

A wicked smile grew over her face. "Don't worry; before I get too physical, I'll wait until the life insurance policy is signed."

"Might be kind of tough. They probably wouldn't consider me a good risk right now."

"You weren't a good risk before we crashed."

"Yeah, I seem to have caught a bad case of Tinaco-itis."

Stephanie's smile faded. "Is there a cure?"

Jeff stared across the water. "With the disk and our court testimony, I think we can put him away for a long time."

"But even if he's in jail, would we be safe?"

Jeff wet his lips, tasting the saltwater. "Nothing is for sure, but with Empy's help, we can probably go someplace safe."

"Who's Empy?"

"DEA. I'd trust him with my life."

"And mine?"

Jeff swallowed. "Stephanie, there's no going back. If only I had never met you. Then you'd be safe."

"If you had it to do all over again, you'd still go after them, wouldn't you?"

Jeff nodded his head. "These guys are bad news. Somebody has to stand up to them."

"And that somebody has to be you." It wasn't a question.

"Like I said, I'm sorry I got you involved."

Stephanie threw her hair back and straightened her shoulders. "Well, I'm not sorry. I wouldn't have missed this for anything."

"Right."

"Okay, so I could do without the water sports, but finding you was definitely worth it."

Jeff clenched his teeth involuntarily, contorting his smile to a grimace.

Stephanie soaked up the sweat from his brow with the rag. "I wish I could do something for the pain."

"Don't worry about . . . " Jeff slipped back to the dreamy world where pain had no authority.

Back and forth. Up and down. The sweltering air enveloped the tiny raft as it rose and fell with each swell. Stephanie lay curled up to Jeff, her arm partially shielding their blistered faces from the incessant rays of the sun. Her stomach pitched with each surge.

The hum of an insect droned through her head. She swatted at her ear, but the drone continued. She turned her head and licked her parched lips. The salty tang she had learned to loathe flooded her mouth.

The droning returned. Now it resonated through both ears.

Stephanie bolted upright. "A plane!"

Jeff didn't move.

Stephanie searched the horizon. She spotted a black dot flying overhead. She stood up and started waving her arms. "Hey, down here!"

Her head reeled, forcing her to her knees. She collapsed next to Jeff and stared upward. She had no energy to do or say anything—only watch.

The dot grew larger and circled downward. Stephanie stared numbly. The image of the plane transformed into a fly landing on her mother's fresh-baked pie. Stephanie shooed the fly away and headed for the kitchen door. Her mother's voice echoed through her psyche. *"Don't forget your coat, honey."* "But, Mom, it's too hot," she answered blankly. *"I don't want you catching a cold."* "Yes, Mother." She stepped outside the back-porch door and waved at her father mowing the lawn. The sound of the mower grew louder as he came closer.

The image of the plane flashed in front of her as she returned to the present. It tipped its wings and roared by, two hundred feet above the water's surface.

Stephanie lifted one arm and waved.

As the plane disappeared, she drifted back to another time and another place.

Chapter Thirty

Stephanie hung up the phone and strolled down the sterile hallway. The odor of antiseptic permeated the air. To her it smelled of death, and she hated it.

A husky woman wearing a white uniform strutted down the hall and entered room 307.

Stephanie paused by the door. The corners of her mouth turned up as she watched the scene inside.

"I can do it myself."

"Look, honey, the doctor didn't say bathtub." The nurse jabbed her finger at the chart. "It says"—she mouthed the words with authority—"sponge bath."

"Why can't I just use the bathtub?"

"The doctor said—"

"I don't care what the doctor said. You're not giving me a bath."

The nurse rolled up her sleeves, revealing eighteen-inch biceps, and ignored Jeff's protest.

"Can I help?"

The nurse barely glanced up at Stephanie.

Jeff called out in mock terror, "Stephanie, help! She's stolen my blood and now she's come back to finish me off."

The nurse rolled her eyes and looked to Stephanie for relief. "You know this blockhead?"

Jeff butted in. "Claire, this is Stephanie, my future

son's mother. Stephanie, this is Claire. She works part-time as a nurse, but at night she collects debts for a loan shark."

Claire shook her head. "Must be the medications."

"No, he's like this all the time."

"Listen, honey. You want to visit him, then you can visit him. I'm off shift in fifteen minutes. With any luck, he'll be gone when I come back tomorrow." Without good-byes, Claire marched out of the room.

Stephanie bent over the bed and kissed Jeff on the forehead. "How are you doing?"

Jeff glanced at his left arm. The cast included his wrist and elbow. He flexed his hand. "Could be worse." He studied Stephanie's sunburned face. "How are you?"

Stephanie arched her back and stretched. "I could use some sleep, but I'm fine."

"Did you get hold of him?"

"Yes. After getting transferred all over the world, I ended up talking to him right here."

"In Miami?"

Stephanie nodded. "Here in Miami. He said he'd be right over."

"I wonder what they're doing here."

A burly man pushed through the half-open door. "Baby-sitting a lost narc."

"Reed!" Jeff adjusted the tilt on his bed upward. "Stephanie, I'd like you to meet Reed Denning, Las Vegas Narcotics. Reed, this is Stephanie."

Reed studied her carefully and nodded his head. "Now I understand."

"She's mine, you big ape." Jeff's eyes shifted to the door. "Where's Empy?"

"His Highness took the stairs. Doesn't trust elevators. Melonie and Gary are with him. Probably worried that he'd stroke out."

"Hardly." A small man wearing wire-rimmed glasses and a dark blue suit paraded in, followed by Melonie and

Gary. Melonie raced to Jeff and threw her arms around him. "You're safe."

Gary grabbed Jeff's good hand and started pumping it. Empy set a brown briefcase on Jeff's bed. He took off his glasses to emphasize his newly formed scowl. "I don't approve of the risk you took, but it's difficult to argue with success."

Jeff grinned. "It's good to see you too."

"Stephanie requested me by name. I presume someone told her of my involvement."

Jeff scrutinized Empy for disapproval but found none. Instead he opened the briefcase and pulled out some notes. "We maintained surveillance on Tinaco until he arrived at Miami."

"Tinaco's here?"

"We facilitated the arrest as soon as he landed."

Stephanie's countenance brightened. "He's in jail?"

Empy rocked back on his heels and grew sober. "We initiated the capture with the hope that further discovery of evidence may indeed be established. Unfortunately, the evidence hoped for failed to materialize."

Reed sighed. "Wonderbrains is trying to say that we busted him with almost no probable cause. We hoped to catch him dirty but came up dry."

"Now we have personal testimony," Gary said, looking at Stephanie. "Problem is, the organization is still intact."

Jeff grinned. "You didn't think we'd come back empty-handed, did you?"

Reed eyed Jeff suspiciously. "What do you have?"

Jeff nodded at Stephanie. She reached into her pockets and retrieved a disk from a sandwich bag and held it up. It had a small amount of peanut butter smeared on the side.

"The password is *ambition*." Jeff settled back in the bed with his one good arm tucked behind his head. "It has everything—names, amounts, dates, locations—everything."

Empy took the disk from Stephanie with both hands

273

and held it carefully. His cheeks wrinkled. A smile pushed through to his teeth. "If what you say is true . . . " He giggled like a schoolboy. Then he immediately regained composure. He wrapped the disk in a clean handkerchief and placed it into his briefcase.

"All right!" Reed gave Gary a high five. Melonie flashed a relieved smile.

Jeff swallowed as he remembered Captain Fowler's order to stay away from Peru. "Has anyone talked to Captain Fowler?"

"I don't believe he's aware of your current status. In fact, we were unaware of your present situation until Stephanie's call."

Gary jabbed Empy in the ribs with a hint. "Didn't the agency request an urgent meeting with Jeff in Miami?"

Empy squinted his eyes, not understanding. "No, in fact I believe Captain Fowler gave him specific instructions to—"

Reed picked up on Gary's plan to protect Jeff and faked a cough. "That was my fault. I must have forgot to tell you that I called Jeff and told him to get his tail down here."

The wrinkles disappeared above Empy's nose as his eyes widened with understanding. He studied Jeff without passing judgment.

Jeff shook his head. "No. I appreciate what you're doing, but I'd rather face the consequences."

Gary's expression changed to one of concern. "You know this could mean your job."

"Whatever it takes. I started to cross the line once. It's not going to happen again."

"Meaning?" Reed asked.

"I'm not going to lie to him. Sometimes the only thing that separates us from them is our integrity."

Gary mumbled thoughtfully. "The line."

Jeff nodded. "The line."

About the Author

Steve Roos, sergeant over detectives for the Idaho Falls Police Department, has had firsthand experience working undercover. A number of the situations in *Deep Cover*, his first novel, are based on real events.

The author wrote a regular column for the local newspaper, the *Post Register*, for two years. He and his wife, Rebecca Robinson Roos, are the parents of seven children. The family lives in Idaho Falls.